GREAT SCIEN
BRILLIAN

That's right...the stories in this latest Armchair Fiction Science Fiction Gems collection are a pretty brilliant group—a real nice batch for you to cozy up to. If you're searching for the perfect woman, try "Accept No Substitutes," but you may find out that too much perfection is not always a good thing. If you love innocent little kids, you may learn that innocence and evil are not that far apart in "Zero Hour." "The Thing in the Truck" should satisfy your cravings for potatoes, only make sure they're well cooked. Like a good murder mystery? Try out "Earth Transit" for a nifty whodunit in outer space. "The Man With X-Ray Eyes" shows you how blind ambition can make you see a whole lot more than just the simple facts. And "Someday" will give you a bird's eye view of the entire phenomenon of self-awareness. All in all, there are some grand futuristic thrills waiting for you in the pages of this new collection. So be bold...and step into the future.

TABLE OF CONTENTS

ACCEPT NO SUBSTITUTES   5
By Robert Sheckley

THE THING IN THE TRUCK   18
By Milton Lesser

IN THE SCARLET STAR   31
By Jack Williamson

ZERO HOUR   57
By Ray Bradbury

GLOW WORM   69
By Harlan Ellison

THE MAN WITH X-RAY EYES   80
By Edmond Hamilton

SECRET OF THE ROBOT   95
By Chester S. Geier

EARTH TRANSIT   117
By Charles L. Fontenay

SOMEDAY   133
By Isaac Asimov

THIS STAR SHALL BE FREE   144
By Murray Leinster

PHANTOM HANDS   165
By Berkeley Livingston

ONE-WAY TUNNEL   176
By David H. Keller

THE TIMELESS MAN   212
By Frank Belknap Long

SCIENCE FICTION GEMS

Volume 15

MILTON LESSER
and others

Compiled and Edited by
Gregory Luce

ARMCHAIR FICTION
PO Box 4369, Medford, Oregon 97504

The original text of these stories first appeared in
Imagination, Amazing Stories, Infinity, Super Science Fiction, *and* Planet Stories

Armchair Edition, copyright 2018 by Gregory J. Luce
All Rights Reserved

Cover painting by Ed Emshwiller

For more information about Armchair Books and products, visit our website at…

www.armchairfiction.com

Or email us at…

armchairfiction@yahoo.com

Accept No Substitutes

BY ROBERT SHECKLEY

The Sexual Morality Act was fierce to buck, but the Algolian sex surrogate was...er...even fiercer!

Ralph Garvey's private space yacht was in the sling at Boston Spaceport, ready for takeoff. He was on yellow stand-by, waiting for the green, when his radio crackled.

"Tower to G43221," the radio buzzed. "Please await customs inspection."

"Righto," said Garvey, with a calmness he did not feel. Within him, something rolled over and died.

Customs inspection! Of all the black, accursed, triple-distilled bad luck! There was no regular inspection of small private yachts. The Department had its hands full with the big interstellar liners from Cassiopeia, Algol, Deneb, and a thousand other places. Private ships just weren't worth the time and money. But to keep them in line, Customs held occasional spot checks. No one knew when the mobile customs team would descend upon any particular spaceport. But chances of being inspected at any one time were less than fifty to one.

Garvey had been counting on that factor. And he had paid eight hundred dollars to know for certain that the East coast team was in Georgia. Otherwise, he would never have risked a twenty-year jail sentence for violation of the Sexual Morality Act.

There was a loud rap on his port. "Open for inspection, please."

"Righto," Garvey called out. He locked the door to the after cabin. If the inspector wanted to look there, he was sunk. There was no place in the ship where he could successfully conceal a packing case ten feet high, and no way he could dispose of its illegal contents.

"I'm coming," Garvey shouted. Beads of perspiration stood out on his high, pale forehead. He thought wildly of blasting off anyhow, making a run for it, to Mars, Venus... But the patrol ships

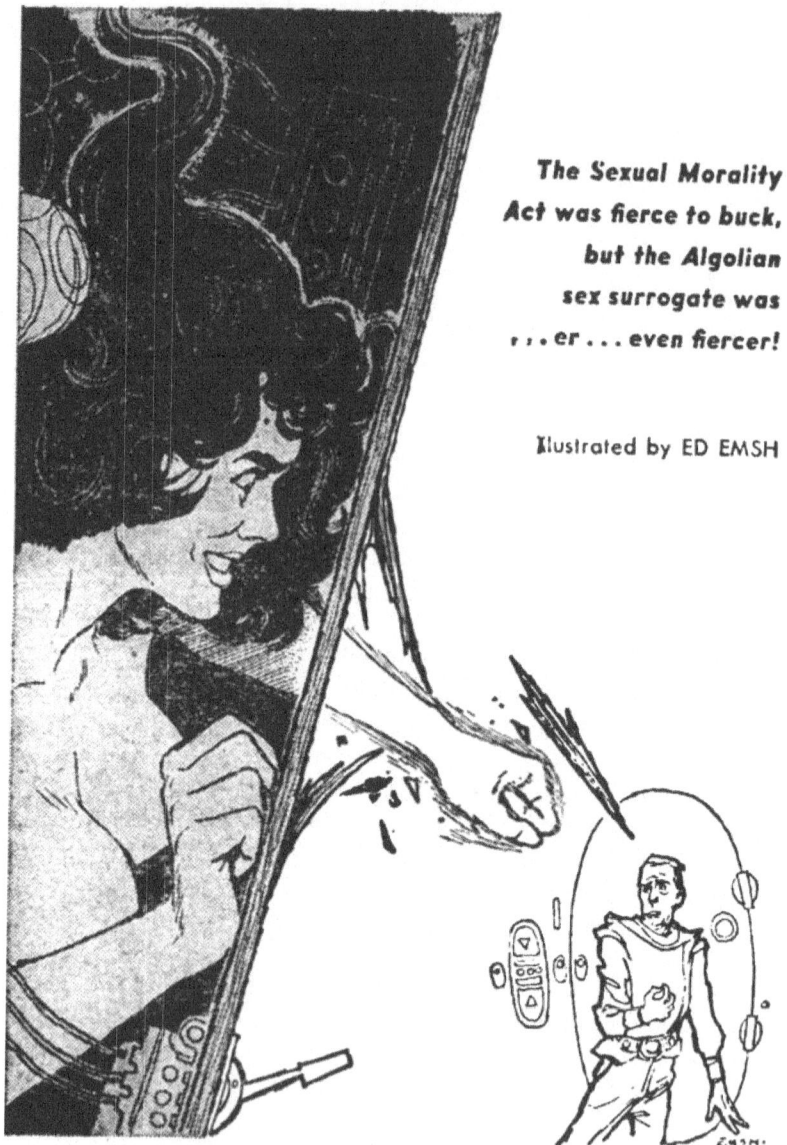

would get him before he had covered a million miles. There was nothing he could do but try to bluff it.

He touched a button. The hatch slid back and a tall, thin uniformed man entered.

"Thought you'd get away with it, eh, Garvey?" the inspector barked. "You rich guys never learn!"

Somehow, they had found out! Garvey thought of the packing crate in the after cabin, and its human-shaped, not-yet-living contents. Damning, absolutely damning. What a fool he'd been!

HE TURNED back to the control panel. Hanging from a corner of it, in a cracked leather holster, was his revolver. Rather than face twenty years breaking pumice on Lunar, he would shoot, then try—

"The Sexual Morality Act isn't a blue law, Garvey," the inspector continued, in a voice like steel against flint. "Violations can have a catastrophic effect upon the individual, to say nothing of the race. That's why we're going to make an example of you, Garvey. Now let's see the evidence."

"I don't know what in hell you're talking about," Garvey said. Surreptitiously his hand began to creep toward the revolver.

"Wake up, boy!" said the inspector. "You mean you *still* don't recognize me?"

Garvey stared at the inspector's tanned, humorous face. He said, "Eddie Starbuck?"

"About time! How long's it been, Ralph? Ten years?"

"At least ten," Garvey said. His knees were beginning to shake from sheer relief. "Sit down, sit down, Eddie! You still drink bourbon?"

"I'll say." Starbuck sat down on one of Garvey's acceleration couches. He looked around, and nodded.

"Nice. Very nice. You must be rich indeed, old buddy."

"I get by," Garvey said. He handed Starbuck a drink, and poured one for himself. They talked for a while about old times at Michigan State.

"And now you're a Customs inspector," Garvey said.

"Yeah," said Starbuck, stretching his long legs. "Always had a yen for the law. But it doesn't pay like transistors, eh?"

Garvey smiled modestly. "But what's all this about the Sexual Morality Act? A gag?"

"Not at all. Didn't you hear the news this morning? The FBI found an underground sex factory. They hadn't been in business long, so it was possible to recover all the surrogates. All except one."

"Oh?" said Garvey, draining his drink.

"Yeah. That's when they called us in. We're covering all spaceports, on the chance the receiver will try to take the damned thing off Earth."

Garvey poured another drink and said, very casually, "So you figured I was the boy, eh?"

Starbuck stared at him a moment, then exploded into laughter. "You, Ralph? Hell, no! Saw your name on the spaceport out list. I just dropped in for a drink, boy, for old time's sake. Listen, Ralph, I *remember* you. Hell-on-the-girls-Garvey. Biggest menace to virginity in the history of Michigan State. What would a guy like you want a substitute for?"

"My girls wouldn't stand for it," Garvey said, and Starbuck laughed again, and stood up.

"Look, I gotta run. Call me when you get back?"

"I sure will!" A little light-headed, he said, "Sure you don't want to inspect anyhow, as long as you're here?"

Starbuck stopped and considered. "I suppose I should, for the record. But to hell with it, I won't hold you up." He walked to the port, then turned. "You know, I feel sorry for the guy who's got that surrogate."

"Eh? Why?"

"Man, those things are poison! You know that, Ralph! Anything's possible—insanity, deformation… And this guy may have even more of a problem."

"Why?"

"Can't tell you, boy," Starbuck said. "Really can't. It's special information. The FBI isn't certain yet. Besides, they're waiting for the right moment to spring it."

With an easy wave, Starbuck left. Garvey stared after him, thinking hard. He didn't like the way things were going. What had started out as an illicit little vacation was turning into a full-scale criminal affair. Why hadn't he thought of this earlier? He had been apprehensive in the sexual substitute factory, with its lowlights, its furtive, white-aproned men, its reek of raw flesh and plastic. Why hadn't he given up the idea then? The surrogates couldn't be as good as people said...

"Tower to G43221," the radio crackled. "Are you ready?"

Garvey hesitated, wishing he knew what Starbuck had been hinting at. Maybe he should stop now, while there was still time.

Then he thought of the giant crate in the after cabin, and its contents, waiting for activation, waiting for him. His pulse began to race. He knew that he was going through with it, no matter what the risk.

He signaled to the tower, and strapped himself into the control chair.

An hour later he was in space.

TWELVE HOURS later, Garvey cut his jets. He was a long way from Earth, but nowhere near Luna. His detectors, pushed to their utmost limit, showed nothing in his vicinity. No liners were going by, no freighters, no police ships, no yachts. He was alone. Nothing and no one was going to disturb him.

He went into the after cabin. The packing case was just as he had left it, securely fastened to the deck. Even the sight of it was vaguely exciting. Garvey pressed the activating stud on the outside of the case, and sat down to wait for the contents to awaken and come to life.

THE SURROGATES had been developed earlier in the century. They had come about from sheer necessity. At that time, mankind was beginning to push out into the galaxy. Bases had been established on Venus, Mars, and Titan, and the first interstellar ships were arriving at Algol and Stagoe II. Man was leaving Earth.

Man—but not woman.

The first settlements were barely toeholds in alien environments. The work was harsh and demanding, and life expectancy was short. Whole settlements were sometimes wiped out before the ships were fully unloaded. The early pioneers were like soldiers on the line of battle, and exposed to risks no soldier had ever encountered.

Later there would be a place for women. Later—but not now.

So here and there, light years from Earth, were little worlds without women—and not happy about it.

The men grew sullen, quarrelsome, violent. They grew careless, and carelessness on an alien planet was usually fatal.

They wanted women.

Since real women could not go to them, scientists on Earth developed substitutes. Android females were developed, the surrogates, and shipped to the colonies. It was a violation of Earth's morals; but there were worse violations on the way if these weren't accepted.

For a while, everything seemed to be fine. It would probably have gone on that way, had everyone left well enough alone.

But the companies on Earth had the usual desire to improve their product. They called in sculptors and artists to dress up the appearance of the package. Engineers tinkered with the surrogates, rewired them, built in subtler stimulus response mechanisms, did strange things with conditioned reflexes. And the men of the settlements were very happy with the results.

So happy, in fact, that they refused to return to human women, even when they had the opportunity.

They came back to Earth after their tours of duty, these pioneers, and they brought their surrogates with them. Loud and long they praised the substitute women, and pointed out their obvious superiority to neurotic, nervous, frigid human women.

Naturally, other men wanted to try out the surrogates. And when they did, they were pleasantly surprised. And spread the word. And—

The government stepped in, quickly and firmly. For one thing, over fifty percent of the votes were at stake. But more important, social scientists predicted a violent drop in the birth rate if this went on. So the government destroyed the surrogates, outlawed the factories, and told everyone to return to normal.

And reluctantly, everyone did. But there were always some men who remembered, and told other men. And there were always some men who weren't satisfied with second best. So...

GARVEY heard movements within the crate. He smiled to himself, remembering stories he had heard of the surrogates piquant habits. Suddenly there was a high-pitched clanging. It was the standby alarm from the control room. He hurried forward.

It was an emergency broadcast, on all frequencies, directed to Earth and all ships at space. Garvey tuned it in.

"This is Edward Danzer," the radio announced crisply. "I am Chief of the Washington branch of the Federal Bureau of Investigation. You have all heard, on your local newscasts, of the detection and closure of an illegal sexual substitute factory. And you know that all except one of the surrogates have been found. This message is for the man who has that last surrogate, wherever he may be."

Garvey licked his lips nervously and hunched close to the radio. Within the after cabin, the surrogate was still making waking up noises.

"That man is in danger!" Danzer said. "Serious danger! Our investigation of the molds and forms used in the factory showed us that something strange was going on. Just this morning, one of the factory technicians finally confessed.

"The missing surrogate is not an Earth model!

"I repeat," Danzer barked, "the missing surrogate is *not an Earth model!* The factory operators had been filling orders for the planet Algol IV. When they ran short of Earth models for humans, they substituted an Algolian model. Since the sale of a surrogate is illegal anyhow, they figured the customer would have no kickback."

Garvey sighed with relief. He had been afraid he had a small dinosaur in the packing case, at the very least.

"Perhaps," Danzer continued, "the holder of the Algolian surrogate does not appreciate his danger yet. It is true, of course, that the Algolians are of the species *homo sapiens*. It has been established that the two races share a common ancestry in the primeval past. But Algol is different from our Earth.

"The planet Algol IV is considerably heavier than Earth, and has a richer oxygen atmosphere. The Algolians, raised in this physical environment, have a markedly superior musculature to that of the typical Earthman. Colloquially, they are strong as rhinos.

"But the surrogate, of course, does not know this. She has a powerful and indiscriminate mating drive. *That's where the danger lies!* So I say to the customer—give yourself up now, while there's still time. And remember: crime does not pay."

The radio-crackled static, then hummed steadily. Garvey turned it off. He had been taken, but good! He really should have inspected his merchandise before accepting it. But the crate had been sealed.

He was out a very nice chunk of money.

But, he reminded himself, he had lots of money. It was fortunate he had discovered the error in time. Now he would jettison the crate in space, and return to Earth. Perhaps real girls were best, after all...

He heard the sound of heavy blows coming from the crate in the after cabin.

"I guess I'd better take care of you, honey," Garvey said, and walked quickly to the cabin.

A fusillade of blows rocked the crate. Garvey frowned and reached for the deactivating switch. As he did so, one side of the heavy crate splintered. Through the opening shot a long golden arm. The arm flailed wildly, and Garvey moved out of its way.

The situation wasn't humorous anymore, he decided. The case rocked and trembled under the impact of powerful blows. Garvey estimated the force behind those blows, and shuddered. This had to be stopped at once. He ran toward the crate.

Long, tapered fingers caught his sleeve, ripping it off. Garvey managed to depress the deactivating stud and throw himself out of range.

There was a moment of silence. Then the surrogate delivered two blows with the impact of a pile driver. An entire side of the packing case splintered.

It was too late for deactivation.

GARVEY backed away. He was beginning to grow alarmed. The Algolian sexual substitute was preposterously strong; that seemed to be how they liked them on Algol. What passed for a tender love embrace on Algol would probably fracture the ribs of an Earthman. Not a nice outlook.

But wasn't it likely that the surrogate, had some sort of discriminatory sense built in? Surely she must be able to differentiate between an Earthman and an Algolian. Surely...

The packing case fell apart, and the surrogate emerged.

She was almost seven feet tall, and gloriously, deliciously constructed. Her skin was a light golden red, and her shoulder length hair was lustrous black. Standing motionless, she looked to Garvey like a heroic statue of ideal femininity.

The surrogate was unbelievably beautiful—

And more dangerous than a cobra, Garvey reminded himself reluctantly.

"Well there," Garvey said, gazing up at her, "as you can see, a mistake has been made."

The surrogate stared at him with eyes of deepest gray.

"Yes ma'am," Garvey said, with a nervous little laugh, "it's really a ridiculous error. You, my dear, are an Algolian. I am an Earthman. We have nothing in common. Understand?"

Her red mouth began to quiver.

"Let me explain," Garvey went on. "You and I are from different races. That's not to say I consider you ugly. Quite the contrary! But unfortunately, there can never be anything between us, miss."

She looked at him uncomprehendingly.

"Never," Garvey repeated. He looked at the shattered packing case. "You don't know your own strength. You'd probably kill me inadvertently. And we wouldn't want that, would we?"

The surrogate murmured something deep in her beautiful throat.

"So that's the way it is," Garvey said briskly. "You stay right here, old girl. I'm going to the control room. We'll land on Earth in a few hours. Then I'll arrange to have you shipped to Algol. The boys'll really go for you on Algol! Sounds good, huh?"

The surrogate gave no sign of understanding. Garvey moved away. The surrogate pushed back her long hair and began to move toward him. Her intentions were unmistakable.

Garvey backed away, step by step. He noticed that the surrogate was beginning to breathe heavily. Panic overtook him then, and he sprinted through the cabin door, slamming it behind him. The surrogate smashed against the door, calling to him in a clear, wordless voice. Garvey went to the instrument panel and began to evacuate the air from the after cabin.

Dial hands began to swing. Garvey heaved a sigh of relief and collapsed into a chair. It had been a close thing. He didn't like to think what would have happened if the Algolian sexual substitute had managed to seize him. Probably he would not have lived through the experience. He felt sorry at the necessity of killing so magnificent a creature, but it was the only safe thing to do.

He lighted a cigarette. As soon as she was dead, he would jettison her, crate and all, into space. Then he would get good and drunk. And at last, he would return to Earth a sadder and wiser man. No more substitutes for him! Plain old-fashioned girls were good enough. Yes sir, Garvey told himself, if women were all right for my father, they're all right for me. And when I have a son, I'm going to say to him, son, stick with women. They're all right. Accept no substitutes. Insist up on the genuine article…

He was getting giddy, Garvey noticed. And his cigarette had gone out. He resisted a tremendous desire to giggle, and looked at his gauges. The air was leaving the after cabin, all right. But it was also leaving the control room.

Garvey sprang to his feet and inspected the cabin door. He swore angrily. That damned surrogate had managed to spring the hinges. The door was no longer airtight.

He turned quickly to the control board and stopped the evacuation of air. Why, he asked himself, did everything have to happen to him?

The surrogate renewed her battering tactics. She had picked up a metal chair and was hammering at the hinges.

But she couldn't break through a tempered steel door, Garvey told himself. Oh, no. Not a chance. Never.

The door began to bulge ominously.

Garvey stood in the center of the control room, sweat rolling down his face, trying desperately to think. He could put on a spacesuit, then evacuate all the air from the ship…

But the spacesuits, together with the rest of his equipment, were in the after cabin.

What else? This is serious, Garvey told himself. This is very serious. His mind seemed paralyzed. What could he do? Raise the temperature? Lower it?

He didn't know what the surrogate could stand. But he had a suspicion it was more than he could take.

One hinge shattered. The door bent, revealing the surrogate behind it, pounding relentlessly, her satiny skin glistening with perspiration.

Then Garvey remembered his revolver. He snatched it out of its holster and flipped off the safeties, just as the last hinge cracked and the door flew open.

"Stay in there," Garvey said, pointing the revolver.

The Algolian substitute moaned, and held out her arms to him. She smiled dazzlingly, seductively, and advanced upon him.

"Not another step!" Garvey shrieked, torn between fear and desire. He took aim, wondering if a bullet would stop her...

And what would happen if it didn't.

The surrogate, her eyes blazing with passion, leaped for him. Garvey gripped the revolver in both shaking hands and began shooting. The noise was deafening. He fired three times, and the surrogate kept on coming.

"Stop!" Garvey screamed. "Please stop!"

Slower now, the surrogate advanced.

Garvey fired his fourth shot. Limping now, the surrogate came on, her desire unchecked.

Garvey backed to the wall. All he wanted now was to live long enough to get his hands on the factory operator. The surrogate gathered herself and pounced.

At pointblank range, Garvey fired his last shot.

THREE DAYS later, Garvey's ship received clearance and came down at Boston Spaceport. The landing was not made with Garvey's usual skill. On the final approach he scored a ten-foot hole in the reinforced concrete landing pit, but finally came to rest.

Eddie Starbuck hurried out to the ship and banged on the port. "Ralph! Ralph!"

Slowly the port swung open.

"Ralph! What in hell happened to you?" Starbuck cried.

Garvey looked as though he had been wrestling with a meat grinder and come out second best. His face was bruised, and his hair had been badly scorched. He walked out of the ship with a pronounced limp.

"A power line overloaded," Garvey said. "Had quite a tussle before I could put everything out."

"Wow!" Starbuck said. "Look, Ralph, I'm sorry to put you through this now, but—well—"

"What's up?"

"Well, that damned surrogate still hasn't been found. The FBI has ordered inspection of all ships, private and commercial. I'm sorry to ask it now, after all you've been through—"

"Go right ahead," Garvey said.

The inspection was brief but thorough. Starbuck came out and checked his list.

"Thanks, Ralph. Sorry to bother you. That power line sure kicked up a mess, huh?"

"It did," Garvey said. "But I was able to jettison the furniture before it smoked me out. Now you'll have to excuse me, Eddie. I've got some unfinished business."

He started to walk away. Starbuck followed him.

"Look, boy, you'd better see a doctor. You aren't looking so good."

"I'm fine," Garvey said, his face set in an expression of implacable resolve.

Starbuck scratched his head and walked slowly to the control tower.

GARVEY caught a heli outside the spaceport. His head was beginning to ache again, and his legs were shaky.

The surrogate's strength and tenacity had been unbelievable. If she had been operating at her full capacity, he would never have survived. But that last shot at pointblank range had done it. No organism was constructed to take punishment like that. Not for very long.

ACCEPT NO SUBSTITUTES

He reached his destination in the center of Boston and paid off the heli. He was still very weak, but resolutely he marched across the street and entered a plain gray stone building. His legs wobbled under him, and he thought again how fortunate he was to have gotten the surrogate.

Of course, the surrogate, with her amazing vitality, had also gotten him.

It had been brief—

But unforgettable.

He had been damned lucky to live through it. But it was his own fault for using substitutes.

A clerk hurried up to him. "Sorry to keep you waiting, sir. Can I help?"

"You can. I want passage to Algol, on the first ship leaving."

"Yes, sir. Round trip, sir?"

Garvey thought of the tall, glorious, black-haired, golden-skinned women he would find on Algol. Not substitutes this time, the real thing, with the all-important sense of judgment.

"One way," said Ralph Garvey, with a little smile of anticipation.

THE END

The Thing in the Truck

BY MILTON LESSER

There's nothing peculiar about a load of potatoes going to market—but we knew something was wrong when the spuds suddenly come to life!

IT STARTED with a load of potatoes.

Joe Loftus and I were driving the big semi-trailer back from Montauk that night after delivering a load of fishing gear to one of the big resorts out there and wondering if we'd be able to pick up a truckload of anything on the way back to increase the take when Joe spotted this sign.

It was one of those standard hand-painted *Return Load* signs, so we pulled in and I climbed down from the cab while Joe remained behind the wheel, ready to roll if they had nothing for us.

The sun was going down in a bank of heavy black clouds. I figured it might rain before the trip was over. I went over to the door of the farmhouse and knocked. Pretty soon I heard footsteps inside and a man chewing a mouthful of his supper opened the door for me. He needed a shave and he had tired, defeated eyes.

"What's the load, friend," I said. "I saw the sign."

THE THING IN THE TRUCK

"Potatoes." He named a price.

"Well," I said in surprise. "That's cheap."

"Tell you the truth, bub. They got blasted."

"Blasted? What do you mean?"

"Well, now, it's hard to say. Something fell and hit the storage barn."

"Fell?"

"Fell, bub. A bitty explosion. But nothing much. Maybe seventy percent of the load is good. The bad ones will be in sacks in the middle. Won't even know it. What do you say?"

That season potatoes were going good in the wholesale markets around the city. I figured Joe Loftus and I could clear a neat profit even if thirty percent of the load was waste. So I agreed to the deal and for the next hour or so used the muscles of my back along with Joe, the farmer, and the farmer's two grown boys to load the sacks of potatoes into the empty van of our big semi-trailer. When he had finished I paid off the farmer and his wife gave us each a cup of coffee. Then Joe and I climbed into the cab and we rolled.

"Hear something?" Joe asked about half an hour later.

It was dark by then and traffic on the Montauk Highway was light. "Potato sacks shifting around," I said. "We didn't pack 'em too good, I guess."

The noise came again. Maybe it didn't really sound like sacks shifting around in the van, I don't know. I was in a hurry to get home. It had been a long day.

I was driving. Joe squirmed around and peered through the rear window of the cab but could see nothing. "Stop the truck," he said.

"What for?"

" 'Cause I don't like that noise. Something's going on back there."

"Sure," I said, grinning, "our farmer's a shrewdie. His boys are back there and they're eating up all the potatoes."

"Very funny. Just stop the damn truck."

I turned my head and looked at Joe's face. He was scared. Maybe he had one of those premonitions you read about. I shrugged and found a widened stretch of road shoulder and pulled the big semi up. Joe hopped out of the cab and went around back.

After a while I heard the rear doors swing open. Then they closed again and Joe came back. I hadn't heard him stomping around inside the van or anything.

"Sacks shifting around like I said?" I asked.

Joe's face was white in the dash light. He shook his head.

"Harry," he said. That's my name. Harry. "Harry, we was tricked."

"What do you mean, tricked?" I was getting a little annoyed with Joe. He stood half in and half out of the cab. I wanted to get moving.

"Ain't no potatoes," Joe said.

"No potatoes? What the hell are you talking about? We loaded those spuds ourselves."

"Ain't no potatoes," Joe repeated in a funny voice. "Harry, listen. Let's just leave the load and truck and everything and get the hell out of here."

I LOOKED at him and snorted, then swung out of the cab on my side and went around back. I undid the chain and the door-bar and pulled the tongue down so I could open the rear doors. Then I swung up into the van in the darkness.

There was a smell in there. Not a potato smell. To this day I still can't say what it was. But it was a funny smell and it made the short hairs on the back of my neck feel all cold and prickly-like.

I lit a match and swore. Joe was right. There just weren't any potatoes, I don't care *who* loaded them.

But there *was* something back there.

Call it jelly, if you want. I saw it and I can't do better. Say, two or three tons of quivering jelly filling up the center of the floor of the van.

Joe called: "Well?"

I was carrying a lighted match into the van with me. It burned my fingers. I lit another one and slowly approached the jelly. It didn't seem to have any color, so it took on the orange glowing color of the flaming match. It pulsed. I went near it, then stopped. There were still a few potatoes on the floor of the van, after all. I stood by while the jelly rolled sluggishly toward them. The potatoes were enveloped. In a minute there weren't any potatoes.

Then the jelly-thing stopped quivering. I came close and touched it gingerly with one finger. It burned. I withdrew my hand.

"Harry?" Joe called.

Just then I heard the sound of glass breaking. A section of the jelly had blubbered over against the van's small front window, smashing it. I didn't think a soft jelly would have the strength.

"Harry!" Joe shouted. It was like a shout of animal fear. I heard the sound of more glass breaking. The rear window of the cab, I thought. I hopped over the rear tongue of the van and sped around to the cab.

Joe was sitting there, smoking a cigarette.

"What's the matter?" I asked him. "What happened?"

"Nothing's the matter," he said. "You want to drive or want me to drive?"

"You just now yelled."

"Me? You sure I yelled, Harry?"

A car sped by, following its headlight beams. "Window's broke," I said.

"Is it?" Joe Loftus asked me in mild surprise. "Is it now? That's what you get for trying to shift those potatoes around in the middle of the trip."

"Potatoes!" I yelled.

"Hell, yeah. Potatoes. Hey, what's the matter with you, anyhow?"

"Potatoes," I said. "All right, so go take a look."

Joe scowled but went. In a little while I heard the tongue and doors slamming and the chain being dragged across. Joe came back and gave me a long funny look. "Yeah, potatoes," he said.

I didn't push it. We'd been on the road a long time today. Sometimes the road can get to you like that. Maybe you read something about highway hypnotism. If you're driving too long on a good road like the Montauk Highway or one of the throughways, after awhile you get to see things which aren't there or don't see things which are there. It can be plenty trouble but it wasn't going to hurt me tonight if I imagined a return load of Long Island potatoes was a big glob of jelly.

I scratched my head. "Highway's got you, huh?" Joe said. He knew the symptoms. "Tell you what, Harry? Why don't you sleep it off? I feel pretty good. I can take her in."

I thanked Joe and climbed upon the slab bunk in the rear of the cab. The window was broken back there, all right. You couldn't argue about that. But it was too dark to see into the van, except that I could see the van window was likewise shattered. I drifted off sleepily, not thinking about it much. Joe was a good driver, one of the best. Maybe when I opened my eyes we'd be in the city, heading for one of the big wholesale produce markets..."

IT WAS RAINING when I awoke. Thunder rolled and rumbled and then split like a pine board overhead. Lightning was stabbing at the sky.

"Joe?" I said, sleepily.

He grunted a wordless answer.

"We near the city yet?"

"You only slept maybe half an hour, chum. Why don't you catch another forty?"

I said: "That's real white of you, pal."

Joe grunted again.

The truck lurched around a turn. The rain beat down. I opened my eyes and looked down past Joe's head. Just then a flash of lightning lit up the night. I caught a glimpse of a narrow two-lane asphalt road and stunted scrub pine growing in what looked like sandy ground.

"Hey!" I shouted. "This isn't the Montauk Highway. This isn't the way back. What's going on?"

"Just get some sleep, will you?" Joe said. "Detour back there."

"Wasn't any detour when we came out."

"Well, there's a detour now."

I was wide-awake. I didn't like the way Joe sounded. "Listen," I said. "The road's fine. There wasn't anything wrong with the road. So why the detour?"

"Flash flood, I guess."

"It's raining. But it hasn't been raining that long and it isn't raining that hard."

"So I'm not the highway commission," Joe said. "Now get some sleep, will you?"

It was this on top of what I'd thought had happened to the potatoes. Something was up, I didn't know what. Funny how sometimes a thing like that doesn't get to you at first. What had the farmer said? Something fell on his load of potatoes. Fell? I thought now. From where? And hadn't he said something about a little explosion? Ten hours on the road, I thought. Ten hours on the road or we'd have asked him sure.

"Hey, Joe," I called down from the bunk. "When do we cut back West?"

"Soon as there's a road."

But soon a crossroad flashed by, dimly seen by the glow of distant lightning. Joe's face was set. He didn't look at me.

"Joe," I said. "Stop the truck."

"What's the matter now?"

"I want to check the potatoes," I said. "You know the lock bar isn't what it should be. Don't want to lose the load, do you?"

"I thought you said it wasn't a load of potatoes?"

"Highway hypnotism," I said. "I'll take your word for it. Hell, I loaded them, didn't I?"

"You loaded them," Joe said, slowing the truck. I didn't really know what I wanted to do. I'd look inside the van, sure. If it had been highway hypnotism, I'd know it now. Because the illusion wouldn't last. They never do. But after that? After that I hadn't figured yet. Joe was acting funny. Real funny.

The truck stopped. I went around back in the hard, driving rain. It was an unfamiliar road, but the kind you find all up and down the East Coast near the ocean, with scrubby growths of pine on either side in sandy soil and no sign of civilization except the marching files of telephone poles. I pulled out the lock bar and swung down the tongue and opened the backdoors.

Just then the truck growled to life. The rear tires spun and whined and threw pebbles at me. The truck lurched forward. I lunged after it, grabbing the swinging lock-chain and pulling myself up on the tongue. My right foot scraped along the ground and for a minute I thought I was going to lose my hold and fall off. But slowly I pulled myself up while the rain beat down on me. I tried to keep it quiet. As far as I knew, Joe thought he left me back there. That crazy Joe, I told myself, climbing into the van. The rear doors swung in the wind, banging against the frame. Joe must have known I had opened them. He didn't seem to care. He was like a crazy man up there. We didn't work for any trucking company. This truck was ours. With what we made on it we hoped to buy another before long and start a fleet. Joe and Harry, trucking. But Joe was up there in the cab, acting like a crazy man, and I was back here in the van—with what?

I LISTENED. Nothing but the sound of the motor and the rain outside. I sniffed. That odd smell was gone. I fumbled for my matches and scratched one against the flint. It made a faint sodden sound and I thought I wasn't going to have any luck. But just then the match spluttered and flared and caught.

There were no potatoes. There wasn't any glob of jelly.

"Come on in away from the rain. Come over to me, Harry, honey," she said.

I dropped the match and it went out. It was a woman. There was a lovely blonde-haired woman in the van there. She had been dressed up like for a party, at least in the little I saw of her I thought that was the way she was dressed. And she was absolutely dry, as if she hadn't somehow come in out of the rain or anything.

"Come on, Harry," she called in a seductive voice. "I'm waiting, Harry."

I walked stiffly into the van. Well, I'm human, aren't I?

I was fumbling again with the matches. I had to see her once more. If this was highway hypnotism, I was all for it. In the light of the first match she'd been beautiful. I struck the second match but the head crumbled wetly. I tossed it away irritably and was about to strike a third when her hand touched me. "Harry," she said. "Harry."

I never did get her name. What the hell, it didn't matter. She was only there for one purpose. Probably she didn't even have a name. She didn't need one. There was no before and no after for her. Only the all-containing now and a guy named Harry Miller.

"Do you like me, Harry?" she asked.

THE THING IN THE TRUCK

She came against me, softly firm and straining. She had a strong, musky perfume on her. Her hair touched my face and her voice whispered in my ear.

"Desire me," she said. "Do you desire me?"

Damn fool question, I thought without pushing it. Hell, yes, I desired her. Who the hell wouldn't?

Outside, the rain drummed down. In the cab, Joe gunned the motor. I kissed the girl in the van and she returned my kiss hotly, avidly. "Harry," she said. I folded her in my arms and sat down on the floor of the van. The truck lurched and something rolled against my leg. I reached down with one hand. The woman sensed this. Her warm fingers touched my arm as she tried to draw my hand back. But I found what had rolled against my leg anyway. It was a potato. It was what should have been back there in the van in the first place, no lump of glob and no beautiful dame, just a return load of Long Island potatoes for market. I pushed the woman away from me and stood up, holding the potato like it was a talisman.

"Harry?" she cried, hurt in her voice. "What is it? What's the matter?"

I didn't answer her. I walked to the rear of the van and looked out. It was dark out there. The rain came down in a heavy, faintly silver curtain. After a while lightning lit the sky and I saw the road was running parallel to the ocean now. I figured we were somewhere not too far from Riverhead. Probably south and a little west of Riverhead, down by the water. But why? Why?

TEN MINUTES later, the big truck rolled to a stop. I jumped down from the van and sped around to the cab; slipping on wet sand. There was a salt spray with the wind-driven rain in the air, and I smelled the sea. I thought I could make out the gleam of the breakers through the darkness, but it might have been my imagination. I did hear the pounding roar of the surf, though.

I saw Joe's dark bulk getting down from the cab just as I reached it. "Are you gonna be any trouble, boy?" Joe asked me.

"Trouble?" I repeated his word. "What are you doing? What did you drive here for, Joe?"

He didn't answer. He went around to the van and helped the woman down. She said something and it almost sounded like she was crying. "Take it easy, baby," he told her. "It won't be long now."

The rain poured down, drenching all of us. The surf roared and hissed and boomed across the beach.

"Hey, where are you going!" I shouted. They were heading down across the sand.

They didn't answer. I could stay with the truck. I could pull the truck out of there. Or I could follow them and see what the hell was going on.

But just then Joe came back from the beach. I couldn't see his face, but his voice sounded odd. "You better come down with us, Harry," he said. "She figures you know too much. I figure she's right."

We stood very close. In the dimness I could barely make out the big monkey wrench in Joe's hand. If I said no, he'd bop me one with the wrench. If I said yes and went down there with him, would he use the wrench on me later? It didn't look as if I had much choice. I went down across the sand with Joe.

The woman was waiting for us at the water's edge. The breakers were faintly phosphorescent with glowing plankton and I could see the outline of the woman's figure against them. Then Joe's bulky silhouette came between us. I stood there and stared out across the black sea.

Neither of them paid any attention to me. The breakers broke and foamed and rolled themselves out on the sand. The tide was coming in. The wind blew spray.

"You're waiting for something, aren't you?" I asked. It was a dumb question. They weren't down here for their health.

"Something coming in from the water?" I guessed, "submarine, maybe?"

Joe said; "We're not waiting for something coming in from the water."

The woman said: "Don't tell him, Joe."

Joe said: "Funny, you calling me Joe. Still calling me Joe."

The woman: "You're Joe. You're Joe until we leave."

Joe: "Yeah, but it's funny."

THE THING IN THE TRUCK

The woman: "I hear something, Joe."
Joe: "No. It's the wind."
The woman: "Will it be soon?"
Joe: "Yeah, soon. What we gonna do with him? With Harry?"
"He knows too much," the woman said, "but does it really matter?"

They were talking about me as if I wasn't there. Or like two grown people will talk about a little child in his presence, or maybe even like two people will talk about a dog, right in front of the dog, feeding the dog a juicy bone, maybe—the day before they take it down to the pound.

They stopped talking. They stood there, waiting. After another twenty minutes or so, I began to hear something. Maybe they were listening too hard. Anyhow, I heard it first. A distant hissing sound. Before I knew it the sky had begun to grow brighter.

"Joe!" the woman cried happily. "Listen!"

"Yeah, and look at it," Joe said.

They ran by me, not down toward the water but back up the beach toward the truck. "Wait a minute, baby," Joe called. "You can't go near it till the changeover. The heat..."

I whirled and followed them. I saw it as soon as I turned, but I couldn't believe my eyes. It was why they had come down to the water's edge. It was why Joe had picked out the untraveled road. I gawked.

The big truck was glowing.

Not burning, not on fire—but glowing. As if it had suddenly gone phosphorescent—say, a million times more so than the plankton-glowing surf. It stood out as clear as day.

Joe and the woman stood between the glowing truck and me, standing hand in hand, watching it, waiting.

The truck changed.

IT WASN'T highway hypnotism.

Too much had happened. Too much still would happen. The square lines of the truck were flowing, shifting, coalescing, like a slow fade on the TV, as one-scene shifts slowly into another. The glowing truck flowed and altered and—wasn't a truck any longer.

"Take him with us!" Joe said suddenly.

The woman grabbed my arm. I pulled loose from her and she started to yell. She came after me, throwing herself on my back. I was plenty scared by what I had seen, and I wasn't having any, not if I could help it. I threw the woman off my back and she fell away yelling into the rain, but Joe came after me with the wrench. I stumbled and fell just as Joe swung the big wrench. It thudded in the sand half a foot from my face and I got up and started running.

Joe threw the heavy wrench this time and it hit the small of my back, driving me down to my knees. Joe came after me, kneeing my face as I swung around and tried to get up. I flipped over but grabbed his foot as he tried to stamp it down on me. He didn't know what he wanted, that boy. I guess if he couldn't take me with him, he was going to try and kill me. I twisted his leg and he yowled and fell down on top of me and we rolled over and over in the sand, clawing for each other's throat.

The woman was yelling something but I didn't hear what it was and I'm sure Joe didn't either. We were both breathing raggedly and swinging without much force at each other now. Call it almost a draw—except I was fighting for my life and I knew Joe had an ally in the woman. I climbed to my feet slowly, unsteadily, and found the monkey wrench on the ground. I wielded it, shaking it in Joe's face.

I said: "You can do what you want. I won't stop you. But just leave me the hell out of it."

All of a sudden something struck my back. It was the woman, trying to knock me over from behind. I whirled and she backed out of my reach, but then Joe was on his feet again and when I turned to face him she clawed at my back. "Kill him, Joe!" she cried. "Kill him now! "

Joe came for me. He didn't pay any attention to the monkey wrench in my hand. He lunged at me and I took a swat in his direction with the wrench. We both missed but Joe was still half out on his feet. He stumbled past me and I turned and shoved him. He struck the woman and they both went down.

"Joe," the woman said. "Joe! It's starting."

She meant the truck. Or what had been the truck. It was a gleaming silver globe now, and something was hissing at the bottom of it. I didn't know what it was, but they knew. I didn't know it then, but I had won. I'd delayed them past the point where they could take me with them by force or kill me. They had to hurry.

I wasn't going to stop them. I stood there, hurting all over, and watched them run for the thing which had been the truck. It was still glowing, but the glow was fading. A hole seemed to open in its side for them, but then suddenly the glow became so bright that I couldn't see anything but the dazzling light.

Which—slowly but with increasing speed—rose into the rain and the night.

On a pillar of flame.

I blinked. I smelled ozone. The sphere was gone, but there was an afterglow in the sky.

Numbly I walked over to where the truck—then the sphere—had been.

I found Joe. Or what was left of Joe. It was a dry husk of a body, hardly recognizable, as if some great power had taken Joe and twisted him while an enormous heat had dried all the moisture from his body without burning the skin.

I never found the woman. Instead, there were a few hundred dry husky things near Joe. I didn't recognize them at first, and when I did I suddenly got hysterical and ran. I couldn't figure it out then, and I still can't although I've tried to.

The husky things were burned potatoes. Next to Joe. Where the woman had been. But the way I figure it, they went up there. Both of them..."

THE POLICE gave me a rough time but eventually let me go. What happened to Joe could have been the result of lightning. Lightning, they said, can do funny things. Nobody ever found the truck. I could have told them that. It had gone—up there.

Home?

I did some investigating. There'd been a meteor fall two days before we picked up the load of potatoes. I saw the farmer and asked him about the meteors. But he merely insisted—vague as before—that something had fallen into his barn, through the roof, from the sky.

Figure it got among the potatoes. A sentience of some kind. Figure it was sleeping. Figure the motion of the truck stirred it to life. Figure it could—well, takeover things. Like the potatoes. It became the girl, to keep me busy. Like Joe. It took over Joe so it could drive off on the deserted beach. Like the truck. It took over—and changed the truck into a, well, something—so it could get back where it started from. Me? I must have been immune.

Or am I? Because a few minutes ago something crashed through the roof of my new truck, into the van. I don't know what, but I'm afraid to go look...

THE END

In the Scarlet Star

BY JACK WILLIAMSON

This story, by one who is justly called a favorite author, describes life in the Stone Age, when man was in the most primitive state of advance. It tells of the discovery of fire and of the combats of the herculean ancestors of our present race.

ON a hot afternoon in June, 1930, I was standing in front of a newsstand in El Paso, Texas, examining the latest copy of a magazine of science fiction.

"Like 'em?" a pleasant voice inquired at my elbow.

"Yes," I said. "Merritt and Wells and—"

I caught myself, looked up swiftly to see who had accosted me. A young man stood beside me. Tall and well built he was, in shirtsleeves. His black trousers and cheap shoes had seen better days. But his eyes were blue and brilliant with strange enthusiasm.

He stood still, smiling a little, while I measured him. "Beg your pardon," he said. "I read 'em myself. It struck me we were kindred spirits."

"Glad you spoke. I haven't anything to do. And I like to talk science fiction. If you like, we can go somewhere to lunch."

There was something about his face that suggested my words; and a quick gleam in his brilliant eyes replied to them. But he flushed a little, spoke quickly,

"No. Thanks. I've just eaten."

"I was going. We can talk as we eat—"

He weakened visibly, collapsed.

"All right. I'll come. A fifteen cent feed at that Coney Island joint—anyhow—"

We found a promising place, dark and cool, with electric fans whining overhead. My new acquaintance did his best to conceal impatience, while we waited for two full orders. I discovered that he thought Wells and Verne a bit old-fashioned and dry, that he had vastly enjoyed Merritt's story, "The Moon Pool."

The Jimmy Miles, who had vanished through the crystal one minute before, had been clad in conventional civilized clothing, if a bit shabby. Now a half-naked savage stood on the glistening surface of the crystal.

When the soup and roast beef came, with coffee and pie and whatnot along with it all, conversation lagged. He ate with the gusto of one who has been for sometime practicing economy in his diet. At last he pushed back his cleaned plate, rose, flushing a little again.

"You know, this is darned good of you, Mr.—"

"Stewart, John Stewart. And it's quite all right. Glad I met you."

"My name's Jimmy Miles," he said as we strolled back out into the baking street. "Sort of roving electrical engineer. No college. But I've worked in powerhouses—nineteen of 'em, to be exact.

"And if you're interested, I've got something to show you—pay you for—"

"Don't worry about the dinner!" I said, "I write a little, and am interested in characters."

"Business proposition, eh?" He laughed. "Well, this might give you a plot. Strange enough!"

"Of course I want to hear it. What is it?"

"Well, to begin at the first, I came here a couple of months ago. Failed to land any job down at the light-plant. Should have been drifting on—I had enough to carry me on till I found something. But one day I got to looking in a pawnshop window—" He paused.

"Yes, they fascinate me," he went on. "Every bright, useless article under the sun. Diamonds and watches and jewelry. Pistols and knives. Kodaks and phonographs. Probably a thrilling story for every one of them!

"I FOUND a strange thing in that window. Sort of a crystal. Looked like red glass, or ruby. Star-shaped. A big thing, heavy, nearly three feet across. I'd never seen anything like it—from what I know of chemistry, there isn't any known substance that crystallizes in five-pointed stars.

"I went in to examine it. The proprietor said that a Mexican had brought it in two or three weeks before. Seems he'd smuggled it across the river from Juarez, said it came from the ruins of an old fallen building in the desert, way down in Chihuahua."

"I know the sort of thing," I said. "Big mounds of dirt, crumbled mud walls with broken pottery and stone axes and whatnot mixed in. I've just been down on the Casas Grandes River—uncle has a ranch down there. Saw lots of the mounds—

the Mexicans call 'em *montezumas*. They have been digging them up, treasure hunting—some of them have pieces of *matte* in them, copper alloyed with silver and gold, just as if it had came out of a prehistoric furnace. Nobody knows when those fellows lived there. To judge from the ruins, the whole valley must have been farmed."

"Well anyhow, this peon had brought the crystal across the river, claiming he had dug it up in an old ruin. Seemed to think it was a diamond, fabulously huge. The pawnbroker knew it wasn't any diamond, of course. But he let the fellow have something for it.

"The thing aroused my curiosity immensely. The pawnbroker wanted two hundred dollars for it. That was more than I had in the world. After three days, I drove him down to a hundred and seventeen. That left me with sixty-one dollars. I've lived six weeks on that, and spent twenty of it for apparatus to test the crystal with.

"Dingy little room I have, hot as a furnace. It looks out on a ventilator shaft. Three dollars a week. Living on dry bread, and raisins and a slab of cheese, in my room. When I want to celebrate, a little cheap fruit, or a glass of milk and a slab of pie at that Coney Island joint." He grinned.

"But what about the crystal? What is it?"

"I don't know what it is. But I do know that it's worth every cent I paid for it. I've been starving along, struggling with it, hoping to learn the secret of it, before I had to turn it over to some museum or college professor for a song. And I've done it!

"That crystal is the greatest thing since Columbus!"

"How?" I pressed him.

"You read those stories about worlds in the Fourth Dimension, worlds in the atom, worlds in the infrared spectrum, worlds—"

"Read 'em and laugh, mostly. I can admit people on other planets, but as for the Fourth Dimension stuff—"

"I used to be that way. But Stewart, you know that crystal is a connecting link with another world! I've never gone through, myself. But I tied my watch on a string, and let it through."

HE laughed, ruefully. "And something happened to it. I'd been planning to pawn it. It came back all right; but it wasn't worth pawning any more. Crystal broken, figures faded off the face, case worn and works corroded and ruined. Looked like it had been lying out in the weather a century or so."

I looked keenly at the man, to see if he were paying for a good dinner with a good lie. A smile of enthusiasm was on his thin face, his blue eyes were very bright. He seemed quite grave and serious, and for the life of me I could not doubt his sincerity.

"Come around to my room, if you like, and I'll show it to you."

"I'm coming!

What he said had appealed indeed to my love of the marvelous and the fantastic.

We had been strolling down the sultry street. Now he quickened our pace, led the way toward the river, where there were many mysterious doors, where there were little fruit stands and dirty street peddlers, where there were signs in Spanish and Chinese, and an alien note to the voice of the crowd.

"Not the best neighborhood in town," Jimmy Miles observed. "But one cannot be a chooser on three dollars a week."

He slipped between a swarthy Mexican and a strapping colored woman, and led me into a dingy lobby, a dark and stale smelling lobby, where a crippled man and a white-haired patriarch were playing a languishing game with dirty cards, and a thin dyspeptic fellow was wearily rattling a newspaper.

He led me quickly across the room, up a narrow steep stairs, and down a long dark hall, that was hot and unpleasant with a faint, sickly odor. He stopped before a blank door, and turned a key in the lock. I followed him.

A mere cell it was, with a narrow bed, a tall-scarred bureau with cracked mirror, a broken rocking chair, and a tottering stand. The one little window opened on a hot, black roof, with a blank wall eight feet away. The room was stifling in the sultry midsummer afternoon.

"See!"

Jimmy Miles pointed to the strangest piece of apparatus that I had ever seen. It stood in the corner of the little room, back of the door, filling most of the available floor space.

Set on a low bench, apparently made mostly of packing boxes, was a wonderful, blazing gem. A five-pointed star, nearly three feet across, perfectly formed of scintillate crystal, scarlet, ruby red, sparkling. It was like a five-pointed star sawed out of an inch-thick sheet of flawless blood-ruby.

Beside the crystal, on the bench, was a little stack of dry cells, a Ford coil, and a small brass switch, connected with wires that ran under the bench. I saw a radio "B" battery, an electron tube and rheostat, and some more wiring that I did not understand.

"There she is," he said.

"Quite interesting. I hardly see what it's all about."

"Well, I found out something interesting about the crystal. It isn't a natural formation. It's artificial—"

"Artificial!"

"Made by man—or at least by some intelligent being—without a doubt! There are two little platinum studs on the lower side of it, that I have the coil connected to. And it's got metal parts inside it. The crystal stuff may just be cast over it to protect it."

"BUT those Indians, whose ruins are the *moctezumas*, didn't know anything about the use of metals, even if they did smelt them a little."

"No use to argue that. They may have found the thing in the ruins of an older civilization. It's hard as diamond; it must be nearly indestructible. Just another puzzling relic of a lost civilization, like the Great Pyramid. More than likely the people that made it went inside it—went through it to that other world. You say you write stories. There's drama for you. A doomed continent sinks into the sea and the scientists toil to make the star to let them into another world.

"And of course there is the interesting possibility that it was made by a race of that other world, who wanted a window into our space."

"How does it work?" I demanded.

He looked around the bare, little room, evidently in search of something, then fumbled in one of the bureau drawers, where there was half a loaf of bread and some grocer's sacks. He produced an empty sardine tin, which he laid on the scarlet, star-shaped crystal.

"I send the discharge of the coil through it," he said. "It glows, phosphoresces like the diamond does under cathode rays. But the emanation from it has a queer effect."

He closed the little switch. The Ford coil buzzed angrily, and purple sparks played about its points. And a soft crimson fire shone from the crystal, it seemed to melt into a rosy fog. Pale weird lights of green and purple and blue played about the edges of the red flame.

Bathed in soft, red fire, the tin can sank through the crystal. Gleaming crimson mist flowed over it—the crystal seemed to have become a mere nebulous scarlet haze. The tin vanished as if it had been dropped into a basin of blood. And quickly though the man still held down the key, the coruscating mist faded, and the star was real again, sharply distinct.

"It isn't on the other side of the crystal," Jimmy said. "Not on the bottom, I mean. It has somehow gone through it to another world. It may come back when I break the circuit; that somehow reverses he process. My watch came back—rather the worse for the experience."

He raised his finger from the key. And the shimmering red mist rose about the scarlet star again, until the crystal itself seemed to dissolve in a fog of dancing red molecules. And the sardine tin popped up through the ruby fog.

BUT it was a sadly altered can, battered and rusty as though it had been lying out of doors for months, "Gone to the bad, like the watch," he said.

"Mostly, things come back when I break the circuit. That somehow seems to reverse the process. There is an analogy in electricity. When you have a secondary coil wound about a primary, a current is induced, for a moment, when you send a current through the primary coil. When the primary current reaches its full value, the secondary drops to zero. But when you break the primary circuit, the induced current again flows through the secondary circuit, this time in the opposite direction. This phenomenon must be of the same order."

"But where is it that the can went?"

"Frankly, I don't know, not positively. But I think it went through the space that mathematicians call the Fourth Dimension, until it entered another plane alongside our world, parallel to it. Let us say that this crystal is just a sort of boundary, or meeting place, between that other world, and this, in the Fourth Dimension.

"When we send the current through the coil, a sort of magnetic effect carries the body through the opening, as it were, into this other space; and when the circuit is broken the magnetic effect is reversed, drawing the body back."

"I've read stories of the Fourth Dimension."

"So have I—written mostly by men who considered it a sort of weird fairyland, without any conception of the scientific factors involved. But the Fourth Dimensional hypothesis seems to fit all the elements here better than anything else I can think of."

The man turned toward me suddenly, with fierce determination glowing in his blue eyes. "I'm going through tonight," he said. "I wish you would operate the switch for me."

"Going into that! Without knowing!"

"That's the way to find out. The watch and the can came back. I ought to manage it."

"Well, I can stand by, of course. But I'd wait—"

"I need a condenser, and another coil and more batteries, to increase the power to man size capacity. If—I wonder if—if you could let me have a few dollars—"

"Of course. Whatever you need."

"The crystal and apparatus will be security."

"That's all right, You don't realize that you're giving me a real adventure."

I handed the man a twenty-dollar bill, which he blushing'ly accepted.

"If you need more—"

"This is ample. And you might come back—say, at eight o'clock. This hole will be cooler then. I'll try to have everything ready."

I followed him down the dark hall, and out into the street. I went to a show, and then tried to read in my room at the hotel. But my mind kept running back to the marvelous crystal that seemed to carry objects to another world—and to the amazing young man who was eager to undertake a voyage of discovery more marvelous than that of Columbus.

Ordinarily, I should have suspected chicanery, and a plot to separate me from some money. But I had not the slightest doubt of Jimmy Miles' sincerity.

My imagination, following his suggestion, persisted in building up rather a fantastic story out of it. I pictured a mighty civilization grown up on the Earth, and suddenly faced with a cataclysmic doom—a submergence of continents, or an age of ice, or collision with a comet—the struggle to build the crystal, the escape, through it to a new world in the Fourth Dimension—and the crystal, by some freak of fate, the sole memento of that vanished race upon the Earth—though what an empire they might have in the new world!

IMPATIENTLY I awaited the appointed hour; and when it came I hurried down to the shabby little hotel, so wrought up that I hardly noticed the bright windows and the gay, half-alien throngs that ordinarily I studied so intently. I found my way up to Jimmy's room, and knocked on the door.

When he let me in I saw that he had new apparatus attached to the crystal, to bring a more powerful and more accurately regulated current through it I found that he had not eaten, so I insisted that we go down and get supper before the trial. He came rather reluctantly, but ate heartily enough.

By nine o'clock we were back in the little room. Jimmy gave me detailed instructions for operating the rheostat and switches—I was to hold the key down for exactly one minute. He handed me a long legal envelope. I opened it, and found this document:

To Whom it May Concern:
This is to certify that I, James R. Miles, do this night of June 3, 1930, enter upon a most perilous adventure, in full knowledge of the peril to my own life and person thereby incurred, Mr. Stewart, or no other person, is to be held responsible in the event of my injury or complete disappearance.
(Signed) James R. Miles

Below was the signature and seal of a notary public who had acknowledged the document.

"In case something happens," he said, you might find that useful. Not likely to be any inquiries, though. I haven't a relation in the world."

With these words, he stepped lightly upon the flat, polished surface of the scarlet crystal star, and stood waiting, slender, erect, eager, his blue eyes burning intensely.

"Shoot!" he said.

Suddenly I felt a lump in my throat. For no very good reason, I felt tears springing into my eyes. I tried to say something, but at the moment I could not speak. I realized there would be no dissuading the young man from his adventure.

With an eye on the second hand of my watch, I pressed the little button that completed the circuit. The coils buzzed, wasp-like. A soft red mist rose about the crystal—it seemed oddly as if the gleaming thing vanished, ceased to exist in our space at all, leaving a sort of door that was screened with the dancing rosy mist.

And Jimmy Miles fell through the scarlet star.

Quickly, as if some strong magnetic attraction were drawing him, he dropped into the three-foot blur of crimson fog. He waved his hand briefly, as I pressed the button. And he opened his lips, to breathe a sound that might have been "Goodbye" if he had stayed to finish it.

It was over in a split second. The red mists had faded, and the gleaming star had recovered its appearance of brilliantly polished ruby.

I SAT on the broken chair, in the stuffy little room. My watch was on my knee, and I held the key down with a finger. The coil was buzzing merrily, with purple fire flashing from its contact points. My eye traveled restlessly between the crawling second hand of the watch and the rude apparatus that had sent a man on an amazing voyage of exploration. I moved a little, sat straighter, in my tense nervous strain. In my pocket I heard the rattle of the document which was to absolve me from prosecution for murder, if Jimmy did not come back.

It was all beginning to seem very wild and fantastic, when the end of the minute came. And I felt an icy chill of fear. What if that vaguely guessed at reversed magnetic power of the crystal failed to function? What if it failed to draw Jimmy Miles back into our world?

I was near crying out with the strain when the end of the minute came, I raised the key. The hum of the coil ceased abruptly. And the glistening surface of the scarlet star seemed to melt into a dancing mist of ruby-particles.

And an amazing apparition plunged up through that bloody fog.

The Jimmy Miles, who had vanished through the crystal one minute before, had been clad in conventional civilized clothing, if a bit shabby. Now a half-naked savage stood on the glistening surface of the crystal. He had a good deal of beard, and unkempt hair fell to his naked bronzed shoulders. There was a livid scar across his great bare breast. His only garment was a tawny skin, dressed with the hair on, crudely fastened about his middle. In one mighty hand he grasped a coil of rawhide rope.

And this amazing stranger raised a bronzed arm, cried out in astonishment evidently as great as my own. Then he grinned at me in astounded recognition, and I realized that he was indeed Jimmy Miles, but changed immensely. Instead of a slight boy, or little more, he was now a powerful man, tremendously muscled—and extremely unkempt.

It seemed as if he had aged years in a single minute of our time.

"Still here, Stewart?"

He spoke hesitantly, in a voice rusty, it seemed, from disuse.

"Yes. Yes, of course. But what has happened to you."

"Of course? And still in this same little room? And you don't look—why you look as I might have left you yesterday!"

"Yesterday? I held the key down just one minute—"

"One minute! Man you're foolish! It's years! I've been roaming a strange world for years. A moment ago I was stalking a wild horse with Harr Garr, without a thought in the world of the old life. And to be snatched up like this!

"You don't believe it? Look at this hair, this beard! Look at these!" He touched the great scar on his chest, a livid white spot on his forehead. Evidently wounds, long healed. "Does a man collect such things in a minute? You're crazy!"

"No. No. But a strange world, you say?"

YES, I can tell you about it. Plenty of time. But this! Still 1930? I had figured it ought to be '35, at least. How in the Sam Hill—"

"I have it!" I interjected. "The watch and the tin can! They showed the effects of months of time. *Time passes faster in that other world!*"

The giant bowed his shaggy head, considered.

"Yes, it could be. Relativity and so on. And it must really be in the Fourth Dimension. The crystal is just a door between two worlds. The magnetic attraction draws one way when the current is turned on, and jerks the object back with the reversed field when the circuit is broken."

"Logical enough, as such things go."

"I'd given up all hope of coming back. I was making the best of things there. The Lord knows I had thrills enough!"

"Tell me!" I demanded.

"Give me time!" The naked, bronzed giant stepped down from the little crystal, flexing mighty limbs.

"You need some clothing."

"Presently. Before I go out, of course. But I'm pretty well used to going as I am." He looked down at the spotted, tawny hide about him. "Skin of a leopard I killed myself," he commented.

"Shoot! Spill it!" I demanded.

He stepped over to the bed, a splendid bronzed giant, and deliberately seated himself upon a none-too-clean sheet, fixing his brilliant eyes upon me.

"To begin with," he said, "it seems to me that it about five years since I saw you last. I was not able to measure time very exactly, however, for on the planet where I found myself, seasonal changes were not perceptible. And the sky was uniformly cloudy, so that only occasionally was I able to see sun or stars. I did get enough glimpse of the sky there, however, to assure myself that, by day and by night, it looks somewhat as the sky of Earth, though the sun seems rather larger and bluer, and the constellations of the stars are strange.

"That world, too, seems much younger than the Earth—say, about like what the Earth probably was when man first appeared upon it. There was no winter while I was there, no frost, and the climate was uniformly warm and wet. It is a world of luxuriant jungle.

"But I suppose I should begin with the sensations of the change. When I stood upon the crystal, and you depressed the switch, I felt as if I were floating on immense waves of *power*. Then the room grew black, about me, and vanished. I reeled, had a dizzy feeling of falling. That is all.

"Then I was standing in that new world.

"Literally new, I suppose. I found myself in a rank, luxuriant jungle. Above me towered a larger tree than I have ever seen on Earth. It must have been nearly a thousand feet high; sometimes its top was actually hidden in the low gray clouds. For it was always cloudy in that world, and warm, rain drizzled almost endlessly down upon the rank, fern-like undergrowth that rose in the gray light.

"I was standing there, in a primeval jungle, rather amazed, and a little terrified. I was expecting to be brought back to this world in a minute, of course. I even tried to count the seconds, after I got over the first amazement and began to be worried. I had expected to find the crystal still visible in that other world.

I COUNTED to many times sixty—and nothing happened. I felt a chill of horror. I knew that I was not going back.

"For a few hours I could do nothing but wander about beneath that mighty tree, staring up at the unbroken ceiling of cloud, lost in wonder. There was no doubt that I had found another world, but what I was to do with it seemed a highly uncertain matter.

"Presently it began to rain harder, so copiously that even the foliage of the giant tree was scant protection. While it was raining, night fell, a sudden pall, that blotted out all the gray light of the sky. I wandered about in the darkness, now very keenly sensible of the fact that I was utterly cut off from the world I had left, with no apparent means of getting back.

"Suddenly, I heard the beat of great wings in the darkness. And something screamed with a hoarse, raucous voice that wrecked my nerves. I felt something *swoosh* past me in the air, heard the click of snapping jaws.

"I know now that it was a most foolish thing to do. But I turned and ran off through that black jungle, through utter darkness and rain and mud, blundering into trees, caught and tripped by vines, splashing into pools and streams. Two or three times something started up near me, only increasing my terror.

"Then I was suddenly embraced in great muscular arms. I think I screamed with fear. I struggled my best to get away. But a baby might as well have struggled in a giant's grasp. Hairy arms enfolded me. And presently seeing that my struggles availed me nothing, and that my unseen captor offered me no. Immediate harm, I relaxed my frenzied efforts.

"I was carried up into a tree. Using a free arm to feel of my captor, I was soon satisfied that he was something on the order of an ape or a hairy man; and his low gutturals had something of the human voice in them.

"That was the beginning of my acquaintance with Harr Garr, the savage man of this new world. The meeting was to prove a most fortunate one for me. He was the rudest of savages, ignorant of metal, even of fire, and armed only with such sticks and rocks as he might pick up. Yet he was better prepared for existence in that world than I was. We seldom think of how poorly the civilized man is equipped to care for himself unaided. Our work in this world depends so much upon machines—upon machines that we must have other machines to build. And we are all so highly specialized—no man knows how to do all the tasks required for his daily comfort.

"I should probably have starved to death, if it had not been for Harr Garr—or more likely, should have been eaten before I had time to starve. The fellow kept me in the tree until morning—he seemed oddly disposed to share my company, and laid mighty hands on me, whenever I attempted to move.

"For some reason, he seemed rather kindly disposed toward me—it turned out that he was separated from his tribe, and his gregarious instinct made even my companionship desirable. He seemed much interested in sniffing me and feeling of me at first. Presently he released me, but showed an inclination to lay hold of me again when I moved. And in the darkness and on our unfamiliar perch, I did not dare to make any violent attempt to leave him.

"It was not long before daylight came—the day on that other world is only about six hours long."

"THE Earth had a shorter day during the early ages, before the tidal drag from the moon slowed it down," I commented.

"When the light came, he descended to the ground, a vague hairy shape in the half-light. He waited below, and when I missed my footing on a branch, and thrashed about in the foliage, holding by my hands, he laughed at my misadventure in a wholly human, if rather inconsiderate manner.

"He seemed inclined to be vaguely friendly, and I realized that his good will might be worth a great deal, since I had not the slightest idea of how I was to get back to El Paso. He began looking for his breakfast at once, and I knew no better way of satisfying my own hunger than by imitating his methods.

"The berries and fruits that he ate I could stomach well enough. But when he took to overturning stones and eating the little grubs and hard-shelled things he found under them, it was too much for me, though he gave a guttural grunt that I interpreted as an invitation to join him. While he was thus engaged, I contrived to stalk a clumsy, bird-like thing, and to kill it with a luckily directed stone. I tore the skin off it, and divided my gory prize with Harr Garr, thereby, I think, proving my friendship. I was not yet extremely hungry, but I thought that since I should probably be reduced to such fare in the end, I might as well begin at once and conserve my strength.

"When our meal was over, my companion wiped his great bloody hands on hairy thighs, and made off through the jungle, grunting as if to ask me to come on, if I wished. I thought I could do no better than to go with him. A strange creature he was, loping along before me, a gray, hairy shape, hunched and shambling, with great arms hanging almost to the ground and shaggy head thrust forward. But he was much more human than animal.

"We wandered together for two months or so. I made a great effort to learn his language. He was amiable about it, and willing enough to help, though he tired very easily. His language seemed to consist only of a few hundred grunts and clicks, sufficient to express only the most simple and concrete ideas, and them most crudely.

"As I have said, the name of my odd companion was Harr Garr. Though he did his best with the jabbering grunts, he could give me but the vaguest idea of his past history. It seemed that he had always lived among 'The-People-of-the-Mountain' and that the 'Old-Man-of-the-Winged-Stone' had driven him out, not to return until he brought a 'she.'

"That 'she' seemed to be the object of Harr Garr's present rather aimless quest. I had been with him two or three months before we got on the trail of another rambling tribe, and then it was another month before the paleolithic* love affair came to a climax.

"The method of courtship seemed to be to steal along in the wake of the other tribe, avoiding the males, who would be only too eager to kill and eat us. But, as I was a little surprised to note, the lucky lady was not to be seized by force. For, in that event, as Harr Garr dramatically expressed it, she would be likely to smash his head with a rock while he was asleep, and run off.

"HE did his best to persuade me to accompany him on these surreptitious, amatory expeditions, evidently under the impression that I was in need of a

*An early period in human origin, characterized by weapons made of stone. It is assigned to the second place of the stone ages or is sometimes used to include four divisions or the whole of them.

female of my own. But while he was absent on these trips, I usually spent the time up a tree, grasping a sharp rock—a sort of triangular 'fist-hatchet' which was the best weapon I had come across.

"In the first few days I had been filled with great ideas of rubbing sticks to make fire, and then smelting metal, and doing other marvelous stunts. But pretty soon I found that Harr Garr was just about my equal in civilization, until I got a little more practical knowledge of this young planet. Everything I knew how to do depended upon tools to work with.

"I remember very well the day when Harr Garr's courtship came to a climax. He brought the grinning bride to my hiding place. She was a much better specimen of humanity than I had anticipated. Her body was erect, almost hairless, and certainly lithe and graceful. She was clothed to the knees in a wealth of curly brown hair. Her face was not unlovely, and the eyes were clear and bright, glowing with a love for the gigantic Harr Garr.

"I was a little amused at the intensity of their affection, and sometimes almost brought to tears by the pathos of it. They were bound up in each other, usually oblivious to my presence. They would sit together for long periods, holding hands, gazing into each other's eyes. And when we hunted food, each shared the choicest morsels that he found.

"During the first few days, however, there was little time for lovemaking. It seemed that the male relations of Tol-ga, as the girl was called, were immovably opposed to the match. We traveled night and day, frequently crossing streams and doubling on our track. Once a solitary hairy man caught up with us. Harr Garr joined furious combat with the hulking, shaggy beast, first with hurled stones, then with tooth and claw. What the issue of the fight would have been, I do not know, for Tol-ga, at considerable risk to herself, ran in and smashed the other creature's head with a rock; her mate rose victorious.

"We hurried on, and presently threw off the pursuit. Then life was easier; and Harr Garr and Tol-ga had time for lovemaking. The weather was always warm; there was plenty of fruit and a good many little animals that might be killed with stones. We lived well enough.

"There were a few adventures with wild animals. It seemed that the deeper morasses were inhabited by a huge, winged reptilian monster, something like the old *pterodactyl;* and there were huge tiger-like beasts that roamed the forest at night. But Tol-ga and

Harr Garr knew their habits, and were able to keep us from harm—though we had escapes that seemed perilously narrow to me.

"At last we arrived at the settlement of Harr Garr's tribe, 'The-People-of-the-Mountain.' A narrow trailed up the face of a cliff to a broad shelf of rock, five hundred feet above the jungle in the canyon. A huge dead tree—it was something like a pine—grew upon this shelf, which was of some acres extent, and there was a scattering of other vegetation.

"BEHIND the tree was a narrow cave mouth, opening out into a vast cavern in the mountain. We had been met by a sentry on the path, and a horde of naked cave people came pouring out of the gloomy opening as we came upon the broad ledge. All were naked and somewhat hairy, of about the same type as Harr Garr.

"There were seven or eight young men, all somewhat older than my companion, and perhaps three times that many women—mostly scrawny, horrible hags, though one or two were nearly as good looking as Tol-ga. There were so many naked, squalling babies that I made no attempt to count them. The autocrat of the tribe seemed to be a huge, gorilla-like creature, rather old and hideously scarred. Younger men, females, and dirty children seemed equally in awe of him, and he appeared to enjoy cuffing all that happened within his reach. He was called Kog, or sometimes 'The-Old-Man-of-the-Winged-Stone.'

"The savage creatures seemed amazed at my comparatively white, hairless skin. They crowded around, feeling of me. They were not exactly fragrant, and at my objection, Harr Garr sprang to my aid and herded them off. They seemed willing enough to admit me to the tribe on equal terms, though Kog made it plain that he would like nothing better than to knock me about, as he did the others, if I gave him any excuse.

"I saw nothing more desirable than to make my home with them—for all I know they were the most highly civilized race in that world. I hoped presently to get my scanty scientific knowledge reduced to a state practical enough to bring these people some of the gifts of civilization, fire and metal at least.

"But fire was brought to the tribe before my clumsy experiments were successful.

"I had been with the tribe two months, I suppose, had learned the names of most of the adults, was a lodger in the cavern on equal terms with any except old Kog, and had been on a few hunting trips with Harr Garr.

"There was a dense thicket below the cliff, with the trail leading up from it to the shelf. This thicket, I early discovered, was inhabited by a savage creature, comparable to the saber-toothed tiger, that was the terror of prehistoric man on Earth. The savages seemed to worship him almost as a god, offering him a part of every kill, in the belief that his spirit hunted with them. The offerings were left on a great stone before the cave, at night. Fortunately the entrance was too narrow to admit the monster. His presence perhaps really had some practical benefit, in keeping away other and less dangerous enemies.

"Soon I learned of the human sacrifice to the tiger. One of the hunters had been bitten by a poisonous snake. Shrieking, contorted with pain, his body already turning black and swelling, he was carried to the cave. But instead of taking him inside, the men at the order of Kog, lifted one side of the great boulder on which the offerings to the tiger were left, and set it down on the feet of the howling, bloated cave man.

"The swift darkness fell; we heard the padded foot falls of the great beast outside. Then a fresh outburst of screaming, that was mercifully clipped off…

"TOL-GA seemed rather more attractive than any other woman of the tribe—most of them were aged hags. I suppose she came from a tribe a little more highly advanced. Almost from the first I had noticed Kog, the brutish, hulking chief, casting greedy eyes upon her as she sat in the cave with Harr Garr, slender and graceful and clad in flowing brown hair, laughing at her lover with her eyes.

"I think Tol-ga and Harr Garr realized the danger, too. They talked to me of leaving and establishing a new tribe. But they knew of no other cave like this one, and the great beasts of the jungle were too frequent to permit a tribe or family to exist without some such impregnable shelter.

"One day, Kog ventured to assault Tol-ga, when Harr Garr was outside. Her screams brought her mate into the cavern on the run. As he came scrambling through the narrow entrance, Kog flung aside the girl, reached for his sharp edged hurling stone.

"Harr Garr did not hesitate an instant, though he had no weapon, and knew that Kog was much more powerful, and cunning with the experience of a thousand bloody battles.

"He charged across the cave.

"Kog hurled his stone. It missed, was splintered on the rocks, Harr Garr, struck him, bore him to the cavern floor.

"They rolled about furiously, biting, gouging, kicking, and clawing, each seeking to get his hands on the other's neck, so as to sink fangs in his throat.

"Tol-ga sprang to the aid of her lover as she had done once before. But the old hags that belonged to Kog seemed to have enough affection for their brutish master to pull the girl off, in spite of her furious struggles. In fact, it was all I could do to keep one of them from braining Harr Garr on her own account.

"Harr Garr fought furiously, but the other creature was far heavier, and experienced in combat. Once my friend got a hold upon him that made him howl with agony. But he broke away, and in a moment was on top, driving Harr Garr's head against the cavern floor.

"With a shriek, Tol-ga, struggling like a Fury, broke loose from the withered creature that was holding her, and flung herself upon Kog. I succeeded in tripping up the female that had been attempting to smash Harr Garr's head, and ran to aid the girl.

"Between us, we managed to pull the monster off her mate. The young cave man was stunned, unconscious. But his marvelously thick skull had saved his life—for the time being.

"Kog insisted that, as was the rule with the wounded, aged, or disabled, the boy should be given to 'The-Watcher-Who-Cries-in-the-Night.' In spite of Tol-ga's frantic screams, and my own vain objections, Harr Garr was carried out in front of the cavern. The great rock was tilted up by four straining men, and the injured

man's feet crushed beneath it, so that the vast strength of the tiger alone would suffice to draw them forth.
"The quick night fell."

"HARR GARR was still apparently unconscious. Tol-ga stayed with him, crying out in agony, and holding his bleeding head in her arms. The terror of the coming night drove the cave men into the cavern. Even then she would not have left her mate, I think, but Kog seized her and dragged her inside, holding her struggling form in huge hairy arms, while he breathed amatory mouthing's into her face.

"Outside, in the darkness, a thunderstorm was sweeping down the canyon. Through the narrow horizontal slit of the cavern door, I saw the blue glare of lightning flickering against sheets of falling rain. Thunder crashed and rolled in booming echoes in the canyon, while the men in the cave crouched in cowering terror.

"And out in the stormy night, two or three times, I heard the blood-chilling scream of the tiger, first far below, then so near that I knew he must be in the broad ledge before the cave.

"By the brief flashes of lightning that illuminated the gloomy cavern, I saw that Tol-ga had relaxed in the foul embrace of Kog, silent and inert, as if resigned to fate. But suddenly I heard the sound of a sharp scuffle, and the fall of a heavy body.

"When the next dazzling flash of lightning came, I saw that Tol-ga had somehow tripped Kog, who now lay sprawled on the floor. She had escaped his grasp, was running, already was half way across the cave. In the momentary illumination she seemed motionless, like a statue of a splendid figure in action.

"By the time the next flash came, she was leaving the narrow mouth of the cave. Kog had recovered his feet. But coward that he was, he could not have been tempted out into the stormy night, where the tiger waited, for a whole harem of jungle beauties.

"There was another screaming roar as Tol-ga ran out, as if the tiger were surprised and angry. Quickly I scrambled past the huddled, terrified cave men, to a point where I could watch from the narrow mouth of the cavern, though I lacked courage actually to leave it.

"As I reached my point of vantage, a flickering series of purple flashes lit the scene before me. Harr Garr still lay with feet beneath the rock. He was conscious now, half sitting up, and staring in a paralysis of horror at the huge, tawny beast that crouched a dozen yards away, giving vent to a frightful scream.

"As I looked, Tol-ga, a slender, trim, wild thing, mantled in rippling hair, ran across before me, stood between her lover and the tiger. Another flash came, and showed her poised there, noble and erect, while the tiger seemed in the very act of springing.

"Then there was a crashing detonation. The air was thick with purple sparks—I felt a powerful shock even as I stood in the cave's mouth. A blinding glare of light showed fragments of wood raining down before the cave. Lightning had struck the old pine before the entrance—splintered it.

"For the moment, the tiger was driven away by the explosive crash. Tol-ga flung herself upon her mate, tried vainly to drag him from under the stone. Her efforts resulted only in a cry of agony from him. She collapsed on his breast, weeping.

IN a few minutes I heard the tiger screaming again, an approaching. There seemed to be something querulous, hesitant, in his tones. In a moment I saw the reason. The lightning had fired the dry, resinous trunk of the old pine. Flickering red flames were dancing merrily up the splintered bole.

"I heard Harr Garr madly entreating Tol-ga to run back to the cavern to save herself. She did not stir. Then for a long time they were still—the girl there on the ground, holding up the bleeding head and shoulders of the mighty man whose feet were crushed beneath the stone. I suppose they were listening for the footfalls of the beast.

"At last Tol-ga looked up and saw the tiger. The fire was fifty yards away from them, the tiger was slinking uneasily up and down, from time to time raising a low, impatient growl. The lurid, uncertain light of the burning tree shone in his eyes.

"With her quick mind, Tol-ga must have understood at once that the fire was what kept him away. With a low, soft word to Harr Garr she rose, and stood staring at the flames. I would give a good deal to know just what she thought. It is possible, of course, that she had seen fire before; but that is not likely, for the cave men seemed to know nothing of it.

"She stood looking at it thoughtfully, for perhaps an hour. If it was something new to her, she must have been reasoning pretty clearly, for what happened afterwards showed that she understood it pretty well, showed that she knew it was supported by dry wood, and that the wood was consumed in the process.

"At first the roaring blaze had swept up in a lurid volcano, lighting the whole shelf before the cavern. Slowly it died down. And as it died down the restless tiger came nearer and nearer, and began to repeat his dreadful screams—he was evidently getting into a bad humor. Above the crackle of the dying flames, I could hear his light, quick footfalls; his impatient course was traced by the red coals that seemed to gleam in his eyes.

When the flickering, smoky blaze had fallen so that the tiger seemed about to come up past it, the girl ran to the lire and seized a blazing branch. She dragged it up close by the man under the rock.

"The first one went out, through too rough handling. She burned her hand painfully on the next, and cried out; but she was too plucky to give up. Soon she had a little heap of blazing sticks in front of Harr Garr. Then she made the great discovery that the phenomenon could be transmitted to a new piece of dry wood.

"At once she set about gathering up the scattered fragments of pine scattered about the shelf. By this time the tiger seemed extremely impatient about his delayed dinner—even the storm had frayed his nerves, before this weird business of fire. He persisted in coming nearer, leaping restlessly about the fire, champing his teeth and squalling.

"Twice, the girl very narrowly escaped him, while she was gathering wood. Then she hit on the idea of carrying a blazing brand with her. Soon the sticks near the cavern mouth were exhausted, and she had to go farther afield. While she was gone, the tiger crept upon Harr Garr, determined to get at him in spite of the flames.

COURAGEOUSLY, the girl ran at the huge, tawny beast, flourishing her flaming pine-knot. The tiger snarled savagely, refused to retreat. The girl came on, drove the blazing stick into his face. He sprang back with a howl of pain.

"And Tol-ga went after him.

"She passed out of my sight. She was driving the tiger toward the narrow end of the shelf, toward the sheer precipice behind it, I heard savage growls, squalls of pain. And then the crashing rattle of stones, as a heavy body plunged down the mountain side.

"She had driven the tiger over the cliff.

"In a moment she was back to Harr Garr. She took his body up in her arms again. But she did not forget the fire, but presently rose to gather sticks for it again.

"And then she came into the cave with a flaming pine-knot in either hand. The cave men cowered back from her, shivering and mouthing in terror. With dauntless courage, she flourished her torches and shot jabbering clicks and grunts at the men, until she got three or four of the younger savages to hurl themselves upon Kog.

"The young bucks fought with a good heart—they hated the old bully cordially enough—and she helped with her firebrands. In a few minutes he was driven out of the cavern, broken and terrified.

"Then Tol-ga, with the authority the blazing pine-knots gave her, superintended the efforts of a half dozen cave men who lifted the boulder from Harr Garr's feet. No bones had been broken; and with the amazing vitality of his race, he seemed as well as ever in a day or two.

"Kog had been driven from the cavern, but he was back in a short time, with his females gathered around him, at his old bullying habits once more. He seemed to have learned a lesson, at first, and left Tol-ga and Harr Garr severely alone. But his brutish mind soon forgot.

"Tol-ga and Harr Garr kept the fire burning before the cave. The tribe soon realized the value of it as protection from wild animals, and for warmth on stormy nights. The art of cooking—or at least of broiling meat—was soon discovered. And an attempt to cook something in a woven basket waterproofed with a lining of clay resulted in a rude pottery vessel—the beginning of the ceramic art. When Tol-ga mastered fire on that night before the cave, she made the first step of her race on the long road to civilization.

"As keepers and masters of the fire, the young couple soon enjoyed a prominence quite unprecedented for those of their age. Kog grew insanely jealous of Harr Garr. A few months later he made a desperate and treacherous assault upon Tol-ga, armed with a jagged stone.

"Harr Garr had just started on a hunting trip.

"With her mental quickness, the girl escaped old Kog, provoked him to throw his stone, and dodged it. She got past him to the fire, and with a blazing stick kept him at bay until her calls had brought Harr Garr back on the run—Kog had not had self-control to wait until the young hunter was beyond hearing distance.

"THERE, on the wide ledge before the cavern, the two of them fought the final battle for mastery of the tribe. Kog, having flung his stone, was armed only with fang and claw. Harr Garr carried a wooden spear, the end shaped and sharply pointed. As they closed, he caught Kog in the abdomen with that crude weapon. Though the old bully carried the young hunter to the ground, he died of the wound before his superior strength could be turned to account.

"Thus Harr Garr and Tol-ga became rulers of "The-People-of-the-Mountain' and brought them the blessings of fire—in very much the same way that fire must have come to our world. When I last saw Tol-ga she was nursing a pink little infant.

"It must have been three or four years, as time goes in that other world, that I lived in the great cave. Twice, in those long years, I was wounded, once in an encounter with a pterodactyl, another time in a battle with a tiger. On both occasions Harr Garr saved me at the risk of his own life, I came to feel a real friendship for him, savage that he is.

It is only a few minutes ago that Harr Garr and I were hunting in the forest, stalking a shaggy little prehistoric horse that we were trying to capture. I was standing there in a little glade in the lush green jungle, silent and tense with the excitement of the hunt. Then a dizzy sensation of reeling, falling. And the next moment I was standing on the red crystal, looking at you. Do you wonder that I was amazed?"

And the bronzed giant straightened in his seat on the bed, fingering the tawny striped tiger skin about his waist. Blue eyes gleamed restlessly above an unkempt beard as he said.

"And you know, Stewart, I'm going back to that world in the star!"

THE END

Zero Hour

BY RAY BRADBURY

When this nifty short story was published by Planet Stories magazine in 1947, they referred to it as "one of the best science-fiction stories we have ever seen..."

OH, IT WAS TO BE SO JOLLY! What a game! Such excitement they hadn't known in years. The children catapulted this way and that across the green lawns, shouting at each other, holding hands, flying in circles, climbing trees, laughing...Overhead, the rockets flew and beetle-cars whispered by on the streets, but the children played on. Such fun, such tremulous joy, such tumbling and hearty screaming.

Mink ran into the house, all dirt and sweat. For her seven years she was loud and strong and definite. Her mother, Mrs. Morris, hardly saw her as she yanked out drawers and rattled pans and tools into a large sack.

"Heavens, Mink, what's going on?"

"The most exciting game ever!" gasped Mink, pink-faced.

"Stop and get your breath," said the mother.

"No, I'm all right," gasped Mink. "Okay I take these things, Mom?"

"But don't dent them," said Mrs. Morris.

"Thank you, thank you!" cried Mink and boom! She was gone, like a rocket.

Mrs. Morris surveyed the fleeing tot. "What's the name of the game?"

"Invasion!" said Mink. The door slammed.

In every yard on the street children brought out knives and forks and pokers and old stovepipes and can-openers.

It was an interesting fact that this fury and bustle occurred only among the younger children. The older ones, those ten years and more disdained the affair and marched scornfully off on hikes or played a more dignified version of hide-and-seek on their own.

ZERO HOUR
By RAY BRADBURY

Meanwhile, parents came and went in chromium beetles. Repairmen came to repair the vacuum elevators in houses, to fix fluttering television sets or hammer upon stubborn food-delivery tubes. The adult civilization passed and repassed the busy youngsters, jealous of the fierce energy of the wild tots, tolerantly amused at their flourishing, longing to join in themselves.

"This and this and *this,*" said Mink, instructing the others with their assorted spoons and wrenches. "Do *that,* and bring that over here. No! *Here,* ninnie! Right. Now, get back while I fix this—" Tongue in teeth, face wrinkled in thought. "Like that. See?"

"Yayyyy!" shouted the kids.

Twelve-year-old Joseph Connors ran up.

"Go away," said Mink straight at him.

"I wanna play," said Joseph.

"Can't!" said Mink.

"Why not?"

"You'd just make fun of us."

"Honest, I wouldn't."

"No. We know you. Go away or we'll kick you."

Another twelve-year-old boy whirred by on little motor-skates. "Aye, Joe! Come on! Let them sissies play!"

Joseph showed reluctance and a certain wistfulness. "I *want* to play," he said.

"You're old," said Mink, firmly.

"Not *that* old," said Joe sensibly.

"You'd only laugh and spoil the Invasion."

The boy on the motor-skates made a rude lip noise. "Come on, Joe! Them and their fairies! Nuts!"

Joseph walked off slowly. He kept looking back, all down the block.

Mink was already busy again. She made a kind of apparatus with her gathered equipment. She had appointed another little girl with a pad and pencil to take down notes in painful slow scribbles. Their voices rose and fell in the warm sunlight.

All around them the city hummed. The streets were lined with good green and peaceful trees. Only the wind made a conflict across the city, across the country, across the continent. In a thousand other cities there were trees and children and avenues, businessmen in their quiet offices taping their voices, or watching tele-visors. Rockets hovered like darning needles in the blue sky. There was the universal, quiet conceit and easiness of men accustomed to peace, quite certain there would never be trouble again. Arm in arm, men all over earth were a united front. The perfect weapons were held in equal trust by all nations. A situation of incredibly beautiful balance had been brought about. There were no traitors among men, no unhappy ones, no disgruntled ones; therefore the world was based upon a stable ground. Sunlight illumined half the world and the trees drowsed in a tide of warm air.

Mink's mother, from her upstairs window, gazed down.

The children.

She looked upon them and shook her head. Well, they'd eat well, sleep well, and be in school on Monday. Bless their vigorous little bodies. She listened.

Mink talked earnestly to someone near the rose-bush—though there was no one there.

These odd children. And the little girl, what was her name? Anna? Anna took notes on a pad. First, Mink asked the rose-bush a question, then called the answer to Anna.

"Triangle," said Mink.

"What's a tri," said Anna with difficulty, "angle?"

"Never mind," said Mink.

"How you spell it?" asked Anna.

"T-R-I—" spelled Mink, slowly, then snapped, "Oh, spell it yourself!" She went on to other words. "Beam," she said.

"I haven't got tri," said Anna, "angle down yet!"

"Well, hurry, hurry!" cried Mink.

Mink's mother leaned out the upstairs window. "A-N-G-L-E," she spelled down at Anna.

"Oh, thanks, Mrs. Morris," said Anna.

"Certainly," said Mink's mother and withdrew, laughing, to dust the hall with an electro-duster-magnet.

The voices wavered on the shimmery air. "Beam," said Anna. Fading.

"Four-nine-seven-A-and-B-and-X," said Mink, far away, seriously. "And a fork and a string and a—hex-hex-agony...*hexagonal!*"

AT LUNCH, Mink gulped milk at one toss and was at the door. Her mother slapped the table.

"You sit right back down," commanded Mrs. Morris. "Hot soup in a minute." She poked a red button on the kitchen butler and ten seconds later something landed with a bump in the rubber receiver. Mrs. Morris opened it, took out a can with a pair of aluminum holders, unsealed it with a flick and poured hot soup into a bowl.

During all this, Mink fidgeted. "Hurry, Mom! This is a matter of life and death! Aw—!"

"I was the same way at your age. Always life and death. I know."

Mink banged away at the soup.

"Slow down," said Mom.

"Can't," said Mink. "Drill's waiting for me."

"Who's Drill? What a peculiar name," said Mom.

"You don't know him," said Mink.

"A new boy in the neighborhood?" asked Mom.

"He's new all right," said Mink. She started on her second bowl.

"Which one is Drill?" asked Mom.

"He's around," said Mink, evasively. "You'll make fun. Everybody pokes fun. Gee, darn."

"Is Drill shy?"

"Yes. No. In a way. Gosh, Mom, I got to run if we want to have the Invasion!"

"Who's invading what?"

"Martians invading Earth—well, not exactly Martians. They're—I don't know. From up." She pointed with her spoon.

"And *inside,*" said Mom, touching Mink's feverish brow.

Mink rebelled. "You're laughing! You'll kill Drill and everybody."

"I didn't mean to," said Mom. "Drill's a Martian?"

"No. He's—well—maybe from Jupiter or Saturn or Venus. Anyway, he's had a hard time."

"I imagine." Mrs. Morris hid her mouth behind her hand.

"They couldn't figure a way to attack earth."

"We're impregnable," said Mom, in mock-seriousness.

"That's the word Drill used! Impreg—That was the word, Mom."

"My, my. Drill's a brilliant little boy. Two-bit words."

"They couldn't figure a way to attack, Mom. Drill says—he says in order to make a good fight you got to have a new way of surprising people. That way you win. And he says also you got to have help from your enemy."

"A fifth column," said Mom.

"Yeah. That's what Drill said. And they couldn't figure a way to surprise Earth or get help."

"No wonder. We're pretty darn strong," laughed Mom, cleaning up. Mink sat there, staring at the table, seeing what she was talking about.

"Until, one day," whispered Mink, melodramatically, "they thought of children!"

"Well!" said Mrs. Morris brightly. "And they thought, of how grown-ups are so busy they never look under rose-bushes or on lawns!"

"Only for snails and fungus."

"And then there's something about dim-dims."

"Dim-dims?"

"Dimens-shuns."

"Dimensions?"

"Four of 'em! And there's something about kids under nine and imagination. It's real funny to hear Drill talk."

Mrs. Morris was tired. "Well, it must be funny. You're keeping Drill waiting now. It's getting late in the day and, if you want to have your Invasion before your supper bath, you'd better jump."

"Do I have to take a bath?" growled Mink.

"You do. Why is it children hate water? No matter what age you live in children hate water behind the ears!"

"Drill says I won't have to take baths," said Mink.

"Oh, he does, does he?"

"He told all the kids that. No more baths. And we can stay up till ten o'clock and go to two tele-visor shows on Saturday 'stead of one!"

"Well, Mr. Drill better mind his p's and q's. I'll call up his mother and—"

Mink went to the door. "We're having trouble with guys like Pete Britz and Dale Jerrick. They're growing up. They make fun. They're worse than parents. They just won't believe in Drill. They're so snooty, cause they're growing up. You'd think they'd know better. They were little only a coupla years ago. I hate them worst. We'll kill them *first.*"

"Your father and I, last?"

"Drill says you're dangerous. Know why? Cause you don't believe in Martians! They're going to let us run the world. Well, not just us, but the kids over in the next block, too. I might be queen." She opened the door. "Mom?"

"Yes?"

"What's—lodge...ick?"

"Logic? Why, dear, logic is knowing what things are true and not true."

"He *mentioned* that," said Mink. "And what's im—pres—sion—able?" It took her a minute to say it.

"Why, it means—" Her mother looked at the floor, laughing gently. "It means—to be a child, dear."

"Thanks for lunch!" Mink ran out, then stuck her head back in. "Mom, I'll be sure you won't be hurt, much, really!"

"Well, thanks," said Mom.

Slam went the door.

AT FOUR O'CLOCK the audio-visor buzzed. Mrs. Morris flipped the tab. "Hello, Helen!" she said, in welcome.

"Hello, Mary. How are things in New York?"

"Fine, how are things in Scranton? You look tired."

"So do you. The children. Under-foot," said Helen.

Mrs. Morris sighed, "My Mink, too. The super Invasion."

Helen laughed. "Are your kids playing that game, too?"

"Lord, yes. Tomorrow it'll be geometrical jacks and motorized hopscotch. Were we this bad when we were kids in '48?"

"Worse. Japs and Nazis. Don't know how my parents put up with me. Tomboy."

"Parents learn to shut their ears."

A silence.

"What's wrong, Mary?" asked Helen.

Mrs. Morris' eyes were half-closed; her tongue slid slowly, thoughtfully over her lower lip. "Eh," She jerked. "Oh, nothing. Just thought about *that*. Shutting ears and such. Never mind. Where were we?"

"My boy Tim's got a crush on some guy named—*Drill*, I think it was."

"Must be a new password. Mink likes him, too."

"Didn't know it got as far as New York. Word of mouth, I imagine. Looks like a scrap drive. I talked to Josephine and she said her kids—that's in Boston—are wild on this new game. It's sweeping the country."

At this moment, Mink trotted into the kitchen to gulp a glass of water. Mrs. Morris turned. "How're things going?"

"Almost finished," said Mink.

"Swell," said Mrs. Morris. "What's *that?*"

"A yo-yo," said Mink. "Watch."

She flung the yo-yo down its string. Reaching the end it—

It vanished.

"See?" said Mink. "Ope!" Dibbling her finger she made the yo-yo reappear and zip up the string.

"Do that again," said her mother.

"Can't. Zero hour's five o'clock! Bye."

Mink exited, zipping her yo-yo.

On the audio-visor, Helen laughed. "Tim brought one of those yo-yo's in this morning, but when I got curious he said he wouldn't show it to me, and when I tried to work it, finally, it wouldn't work."

"You're not *impressionable*" said Mrs. Morris.

"What?"

"Never mind. Something I thought of. Can I help you, Helen?"

"I wanted to get that black-and-white cake recipe—"

ZERO HOUR

THE HOUR drowsed by. The day waned. The sun lowered in the peaceful blue sky. Shadows lengthened on the green lawns. The laughter and excitement continued. One little girl ran away, crying.

Mrs. Morris came out the front door.

"Mink, was that Peggy Ann crying?"

Mink was bent over in the yard, near the rose-bush. "Yeah. She's a scarebaby. We won't let her play, now. She's getting too old to play. I guess she grew up all of a sudden."

"Is that why she cried? Nonsense. Give me a civil answer, young lady, or inside you come!"

Mink whirled in consternation, mixed with irritation. "I can't quit now. It's almost time. I'll be good. I'm sorry."

"Did you hit Peggy Ann?"

"No, honest. You ask her. It was something—well, she's just a scaredy-pants."

The ring of children drew in around Mink where she scowled at her work with spoons and a kind of square shaped arrangement of hammers and pipes. "There and there," murmured Mink.

"What's wrong?" said Mrs. Morris.

"Drill's stuck. Half way. If we could only get him all the way through, it'll be easier. Then all the others could come through after him."

"Can I help?"

"No'm, thanks. I'll fix it."

"All right. I'll call you for your bath in half an hour. I'm tired of watching you."

She went in and sat in the electric-relaxing chair, sipping a little beer from a half-empty glass. The chair massaged her back. Children, children. Children and love and hate, side by side. Sometimes children loved you, hated you, all in half a second. Strange children, did they ever forget or forgive the whippings and the harsh, strict words of command? She wondered. How can you ever forget or forgive those over and above you, those tall and silly dictators?

Time passed. A curious, waiting silence came upon the street, deepening.

Five o'clock. A clock sang softly somewhere in the house, in a quiet, musical voice, "Five o'clock...five o'clock. Time's a wasting. Five o'clock," and purred away into silence.

Zero hour.

Mrs. Morris chuckled in her throat.

Zero hour.

A beetle-car hummed into the driveway. Mr. Morris. Mrs. Morris smiled. Mr. Morris got out of the beetle, locked it and called hello to Mink at her work. Mink ignored him. He laughed and stood for a moment watching the children in their business. Then he walked up the front steps.

"Hello, darling."

"Hello, Henry."

She strained forward on the edge of the chair, listening. The children were silent. Too silent.

He emptied his pipe, refilled it. "Swell day. Makes you glad to be alive."

Buzz.

"What's that?" asked Henry.

"I don't know." She got up, suddenly, her eyes widening. She was going to say something. She stopped it. Ridiculous. Her nerves jumped. "Those children haven't anything dangerous out there, have they?" she said.

"Nothing but pipes and hammers. Why?"

"Nothing electrical?"

"Heck, no," said Henry. "I looked." She walked to the kitchen. The buzzing continued. "Just the same you'd better go tell them to quit. It's after five. Tell them—" Her eyes widened and narrowed. "Tell them to put off their Invasion until tomorrow." She laughed, nervously.

The buzzing grew louder.

"What are they up to? I'd better go look, all right."

The explosion!

THE HOUSE shook with dull sound. There were other explosions in other yards on other streets.

Involuntarily, Mrs. Morris screamed. "Up this way!" she cried, senselessly, knowing no sense, no reason. Perhaps she saw something from the corners of her eyes, perhaps she smelled a new odor or heard a new noise. There was no time to argue with Henry to convince him. Let him think her insane. Yes, insane! Shrieking, she ran upstairs. He ran after her to see what she was up to. "In the attic!" she screamed. "That's where it is!" It was only a poor excuse to get him in the attic in time—oh God, in time!

Another explosion outside. The children screamed with delight, as if at a great fireworks display.

"It's not in the attic!" cried Henry. "It's outside!"

"No, no!" Wheezing, gasping, she fumbled at the attic door. "I'll show you. Hurry! I'll show you!"

They tumbled into the attic. She slammed the door, locked it, took the key, threw it into a far, cluttered corner.

She was babbling wild stuff now. It came out of her. All the subconscious suspicion and fear that had gathered secretly all afternoon and fermented like a wine in her. All the little revelations and knowledge and sense that had bothered her all day and which she had logically and carefully and sensibly rejected and censored. Now it exploded in her and shook her to bits.

"There, there," she said, sobbing against the door. "We're safe until tonight. Maybe we can sneak out, maybe we can escape!"

Henry blew up, too, but for another reason. "Are you crazy? Why'd you throw that key away! Damn it, honey!"

"Yes, yes, I'm crazy, if it helps, but stay here with me!"

"I don't know how in hell I can get out!"

"Quiet. They'll hear us. Oh, God, they'll find us soon enough—"

Below them, Mink's voice. The husband stopped. There was a great universal humming and sizzling, a screaming and giggling. Downstairs, the audio-tele-visor buzzed and buzzed insistently, alarmingly, violently. *Is that Helen calling?* Thought Mrs. Morris. *And, is she calling about what I think she's calling about?*

Footsteps came into the house. Heavy footsteps.

"Who's coming in my house?" demanded Henry, angrily. "Who's tramping around down there?"

Heavy feet. Twenty, thirty, forty, fifty of them. Fifty persons crowding into the house. The humming. The giggling of the children. "This way!" cried Mink, below.

"Who's downstairs?" roared Henry. "Who's there!"

"Hush, oh, nonononono!" said his wife, weakly, holding him. "Please, be quiet. They might go away."

"Mom?" called Mink, "Dad?" A pause. "Where are you?"

Heavy footsteps, heavy, heavy, *very* HEAVY footsteps came up the stairs. Mink leading them.

"Mom?" A hesitation. "Dad?" Awaiting, a silence.

Humming. Footsteps toward the attic. Mink's first.

They trembled together in silence in the attic, Mr. and Mrs. Morris. For some reason the electric humming, the queer cold light suddenly visible under the door crack, the strange odor and the alien sound of eagerness in Mink's voice, finally got through to Henry Morris, too. He stood, shivering, in the dark silence, his wife beside him.

"Mom! Dad!"

Footsteps. A little humming sound. The attic lock melted. The door opened. Mink peered inside, tall blue shadows behind her.

"Peek-a-boo," said Mink.

THE END

Glow Worm

BY HARLAN ELLISON

He was the last man on Earth, all right. But—was he still a man?

WHEN the Sun sank behind the blasted horizon, its glare blotted out by the twisted wreckage rising obscenely against the hills, Seligman continued to glow.

He shone with a steady off-green aura that surrounded his body, radiated from the tips of his hair, crawled from his skin, and lit his way in the darkest night. It had been with him for two years now.

Though Seligman had never been a melodramatic man, he had more than once rolled the phrase through his mind, letting it fall from his lips: "I'm a freak."

Which was not entirely true. There was no longer anyone he might have termed "normal" for his comparison. Not only were there no more men, there was no more life of any kind. The silence was broken only by the searching wind, picking its way cautiously between the slow rusting girders of a dead past.

Even as he said, "Freak!" his mind washed the word with two waves, almost as one: vindictiveness and a resignation inextricably bound in self-pity, hopelessness and hatred.

"They were at fault!" he screamed at the tortured piles of masonry in his path. Across the viewer of his mind, thoughts twisted nimbly, knowing the route, having traversed it often before.

Man had reached for the stars, finding them within his reach were he willing to give up his ancestral home.

Those who had wanted space more than one planet had gone, out past the Edge, into the wilderness of no return. It would take years to get there, and the journey back was an unthinkable one. Time had set its seal upon them: Go, if you must, but don't look behind you.

So they had gone. They had left the steam of Venus, the grit-wind of Mars, the ice of Pluto, the sun bake of Mercury. There had been no Earthmen left in the system of Sol. Except, of course, on Earth—which had been left to madmen.

And *they* had been too busy throwing things at each other to worry about the stars.

Glow Worm

He was the last man on Earth, all right. But— was he still—a man?

by HARLAN ELLISON

Illustrated by WILIMCZYK

The men who knew no other answer stayed and fought. They were the ones who fathered the Attilas, the Genghis Khans, the Hitlers. They were the ones who pushed the buttons and launched the missiles that chased each other across the skies, fell like downed birds, exploded, blasted, cratered, chewed-out and carved-out the face of the planet. They were also the little men who had failed to resist, even as they had failed to look up at the night sky.

They were the ones who had destroyed the Earth.

Now no one was left. No man. Just Seligman. And he glowed.

"*They* were at fault!" he screamed again, and the sound was a lost thing in the night.

HIS mind carried him back through the years to the days near the end of what had to be the Last War, because there would be no one left to fight another. He was carried back again to the sterile white rooms where the searching instruments, the prying needles, the clucking scientists, all labored over him and his group.

They were to be a last-ditch throwaway. They were the indestructible men; a new breed of soldier, able to live through the searing heat of the bombs; to walk unaffected through the purgatory hail of radiation, to assault where ordinary men would have collapsed long before.

Seligman picked his way over the rubble, his aura casting the faintest phosphorescence over the ruptured metal and plastic shreds. He paused momentarily, eyeing the blasted remnants of a fence, to which clung a sign, held to the twined metal by one rusting bolt:

NEWARK SPACEPORT ENTRANCE BY AUTHORIZATION ONLY

Shards of metal scrap moved under his bare feet, their razored edges rasping against the flesh, yet causing no break in the skin. Another product of the sterile white rooms and the strangely-hued fluids injected into his body?

Twenty-three young men, routine volunteers, as fit as the era of war could produce, had been moved to the solitary block building in Salt Lake City. It was a cubed structure with no window's and only one door, guarded night and day. If nothing else, they had security. No one knew the intensive experimentation going on inside those steel enforced concrete walls, even the men upon whose bodies the experiments were being performed.

It was because of those experiments performed on him that Seligman was here now, alone. Because of the myopic little men with their foreign accents and their clippings of skin from his buttocks and shoulders, the bacteriologists and the endocrine specialists, the epidermis men and the bloodstream inspectors—because of all of them—he was here now, when no one else had lived.

Seligman rubbed his forehead at the base of the hairline. *Why* had he lived? Was it some strain of rare origin running through his body that had allowed him to stand the effects of the bombs? Was it a combination of the experiments performed on him—and only in a certain way on him, for none of the other twenty-two had lived—*and* the radiation? He gave up, for the millionth time. Had he been a student of the ills of man he might have ventured a guess, but it was too far afield for a common foot soldier.

All that counted was that when he had awakened, pinned thighs, chest and arm sunder the masonry of a building in Salt Lake City, he was alive and could see. He could see, that is, till the tears clouded the vision of his own sick green glow.

It was life. But at times like this, with the flickering light of his passage marked on the ash-littered remains of his culture, he wondered if it was worth the agony.

HE NEVER really approached madness, for the shock of realizing he was totally and finally alone, without a voice or a face or a touch in all the world, overrode the smaller shock of his transformation.

He lived. He was that fabled, joked about Last Man On Earth. But it wasn't a joke now.

Nor had the months after the final dust of extinction settled across the planet been a joke. Those months had labored past as he searched the country, taking what little food was still sealed from radiation—though why radiation should bother him he could not imagine; habit more than anything—and disease, racing from one end of the continent in search of but one other human to share his torment.

But of course there had been no one. He was cut off like a withered arm from the body that was his race.

GLOW WORM

Not only was he alone, and with the double terror of an aura that never dimmed, sending the word, "Freak!" pounding through his mind, but there were other changes, equally terrifying. It had been in Philadelphia, while grubbing inside a broken store window that he had discovered another symptom of his change.

The jagged glass pane had ripped the shirt through to his skin—but had not damaged him. The flesh showed white momentarily, and then even that faded. Seligman experimented cautiously, then recklessly, and found that the radiations, or his treatments, or both, had indeed changed him. He was completely impervious to harm of a minor sort: fire in small amounts did not bother him, sharp edges could no more rip his flesh than they could a piece of treated steel, work produced no callouses; he was, in a limited sense of the word, invulnerable.

The indestructible man had been created too late. Too late to bring satisfaction to the myopic butchers who had puttered unceasingly about his body. Perhaps had they managed to survive they might still not comprehend what had occurred. It was too much like the product of a wild coincidence.

But that had not lessened his agony. Loneliness can be a powerful thing, more consuming than hatred, more demanding than mother love, more driving than ambition. It could, in fact, drive a man to the stars.

Perhaps it had been a communal yearning within his glowing breast; perhaps a sense of the dramatic or a last vestige of that unconscious debt all men owe to their kind; perhaps it was simply an urge to talk to someone. Seligman summed it up without soul searching in the philosophy, "I can't be any worse off than I am now, so why not?"

It didn't matter really. Whatever the reason, he knew by the time his search was over that he must seek men out, wherever in the stars they might be, and tell them. He must be a messenger of death to his kin beyond the Earth. They would mourn little, he knew, but still he had to tell them.

He would have to go after them and say, "Your fathers are gone. Your home is no more. They played the last hand of that most dangerous of games, and lost. The Earth is dead."

He smiled a tight, grim smile as he thought: At least I won't have to carry a lantern to them; they'll see me coming by my own glow. *Glow little glow worm, glimmer, glimmer...*

SELIGMAN threaded his way through the tortured wreckage and crumpled metalwork of what had been a towering structure of shining-planed glass and steel and plastic. Even though he knew he was alone, Seligman turned and looked back over his shoulder, sensing he was being watched. He had had that feeling many times, and he knew it for what it was. It was Death, standing straddle-legged over the face of the land, casting shadow and eternal silence upon it. The only light came from the lone man stalking toward the rocket—standing sentry like a pillar of January ice in the center of the blast area.

His fingers twitched as he thought of the two years work that had gone into erecting that shaft of beryllium. Innumerable painstaking trips to and from the junk heaps of that field, pirating pieces from other ships, liberating cases of parts from bombed out storage sheds, relentlessly forcing himself on, even when exhaustion cried its claim.

Seligman had not been a scientist or a mechanic. But determination, texts on rocket motors, and the original miracle of finding an only partially destroyed ship with its drive still intact had provided him with a means to leave this place of death.

It was one of the latest model ships; a *Smith* class cruiser with conning bubble set far back on the tapered nose, and the ugly black depressions behind which the Bergsil cannons rested on movable tracks.

He climbed the hull-ladder into the open inspection hatch, finding his way easily, even without a torch. His fingers began running over the complicated leads of the drive components, checking and rechecking what he already knew was sound and foolproof—or as foolproof as an amateur could make them.

Now that it was ready, and all that remained were these routine check tests and loading the food for the journey, he found himself more terrified of leaving than of remaining alone till he died—and when that might be with his stamina he had no idea.

How would they receive a man as transformed as he? Would they not instinctively fear, mistrust, despise him? *Am I stalling?* The question suddenly formed in his mind, causing his sure inspection to falter. Had he been purposely putting the takeoff date further and further ahead? Using the checks and other tasks as further attempts to stall? His head began to ache with the turmoil of his thoughts.

Then he shook himself in disgust. The tests were necessary; it was stressed repeatedly in all of the texts lying about the floor of the drive chamber.

His hands shook, but that same impetus which had carried him for two years forced him to complete the checkups. Just as dawn oozed up over the outline of the tatters that had been New York, he finished his work on the ship.

Without pause, sensing he must race, not with time, but with the doubts raging inside him, he climbed back down the ladder and began loading food boxes. They were stacked neatly to one side of a hand-powered lift he had restored. The hard rubber containers of concentrates and the bulbs of carefully sought out liquids made an imposing and somewhat perplexing sight.

Food is the main problem, he told himself. If I should get past a point of no return and find my food giving out, my chances would be nil. I'll have to wait till I can find more stores of food. He estimated the time needed for the search and realized it might be months, perhaps even another year till he had accrued enough from the wasted stores within any conceivable distance.

In fact, finding a meal in the city, after he had carted box after box of edibles out to the rocket, had become an increasingly more difficult job. Further, he suddenly realized he had not eaten since the day before.

The day before?

He had been so engrossed in the final touches of the ship he had completely neglected to eat. Well, it had happened before, even before the blast. With an effort he began to grope back, trying to remember the last time he *had* eaten. Then it became quite clear to him. It leaped out and dissolved away all the delays he had been contriving. *He had not eaten in three weeks.*

Seligman had known it, of course. But it had been buried so deeply that he only half feared it. He had tried to deny the truth, for when that last seemingly insurmountable problem was removed, there was nothing but his own inadequacies to prevent his leaving.

Now it came out, full bloom. The treatments and radiation had done more than make him merely impervious to mild perils. He no longer needed to eat! He boggled at the concept for a moment, shaken by the realization that he had not recognized the fact before.

He had heard of anaerobic bacteria or yeasts that could derive their energy from other sources, without the normal oxidation of foods. Bringing the impossible to relatively homely terms made it easier for him to accept. Maybe it was even possible to absorb energy directly. At least he felt no slightest twinge of hunger, even after three weeks of backbreaking work without eating.

Probably he would have to take along a certain amount of proteins to replenish the body tissue he expended. But as for the bulky boxes of edibles dotting the space around the ship, most were no longer a necessity.

Now that he had faced up to the idea that he had been delaying through fear of the trip itself, and that there was nothing left to stop his leaving almost immediately, Seligman again found himself caught up in the old drive.

He was suddenly intent on getting the ship into the air and beyond.

DUSK mingled with the blotching of the sun before Seligman was ready. It had not been stalling this time, however. The sorting and packing of needed proteins took time. But now he was ready. There was nothing to keep him on Earth.

He took one last look around. It seemed the thing to do. Sentimentalism was not one of Seligman's more outstanding traits, but he did it in preparation for anyone who might ask him, "What did it look like—at the end?" It was with a twinge of regret that he brought the fact to mind; he had never really *looked* at his sterile world in the two years he had been preparing to leave it. One became accustomed to living in a pile of rubble, and after a bit it no longer offered even the feel of an environment.

He climbed the ladder into the ship, carefully, closing and dogging the port behind him. The chair was ready, webbing flattened back against the deep rubber pile of its seat and backrest. He slid into it and swung the control box down on its ball-swivel to a position before his face.

He drew the top webbing across himself and snapped its triple lock clamps into place. Seligman sat in the ship he had not even bothered to name, fingers groping for the actuator button on the arm of the chair, glowing all the while, weirdly, in the half-light of the cabin.

So this was to be the last picture he might carry with him to the heavens: a bitter epitaph to a race misspent. No warning; it was too late for such puny action. All was dead and haunted on the face of the Earth. No blade of grass dared rise; no small life murmured in its burrows and caves, in the oddly dusty skies, or for all he knew, to the very bottom of the Cayman Trench. There was only silence. The silence of a graveyard.

He pushed the button.

The ship began to rise, waveringly. There was a total lack of the grandeur he remembered when the others had left. The ship sputtered and coughed brokenly as it climbed on its imperfect drive. Tremors shook the cabin and Seligman could feel something wrong, vibrating through the chair and floor into his body.

Its flames were not so bright or steady as those other takeoffs, but it continued to rise and gather speed. The hull began to glow as the rocket lifted higher into the dust filled sky.

Acceleration pressed down on Seligman, though not as much as he had expected. It was merely uncomfortable, not punishing. Then he remembered that he was not of the same stamp as those who had preceded him.

His ship continued to pull itself up out of the Earth's atmosphere. The hull oranged, then turned cherry, then straw yellow, as the coolers within its skin fought to counteract the blasting fury.

Again and again Seligman could feel the *wrongness* of the climb. Something was going to give!

As the bulkheads to his right began to strain and buckle, he knew what it was. The ship had not been built or re-welded by trained experts, working in teams with the latest equipment. He had been one lone determined man, with only book experience to back him. Now his errors were about to tell.

The ship passed beyond the atmosphere, and Seligman stared in horror as the plates cracked and shattered outwards. He tried to scream as the air shrieked outwards, but it was already impossible. Then he fainted.

WHEN the ship passed the moon, Seligman still sat, his body held in place by the now-constricted webbing, facing the gaping squares and sundered metal that had been the cabin wall.

Abruptly, the engines cutoff. As though it were a signal, Seligman's eyes fluttered and opened wide.

He stared at the wall, his reviving brain grasping the final truth. The last vestige of humanity had been clawed from him. He no longer needed air to live.

His throat constricted, his belly knotted, and the blood that should theoretically be boiling pounded thickly in his throat. His last kinship with those he was searching was gone. If he had been a freak before, what was he *now?*

The turmoil fought itself out in him as the ship sped onward and he faced what he had become, what he must do.

He was more than a messenger, now. He was a shining symbol of the end of all humanity on Earth, a symbol of the evil their kind had done. The men out there would never treasure him, welcome him, or build proud legends around him. But they could never deny him. He was a messenger from the grave.

They would see him in the airless cabin, even before he landed. They would never be able to live with him, but they would have to listen to him, and to believe.

Seligman sat in the crash chair in the cabin that was dark except for the eerie glow that was part of him. He sat there, lonely and eternally alone. And slowly, a grim smile grew on his lips.

The bitter purpose that had been forced on him was finally clear. For two years, he had fought to find an escape from the death and loneliness of ruined Earth. Now that was impossible. One Seligman was enough.

Alone? He hadn't known the meaning of the word before! It would be his job to make *sure* that he was alone—alone among his people, until the end of time.

THE END

The Man with X-Ray Eyes

BY EDMOND HAMILTON

He was looking through the ceiling of the laboratory as though no ceiling were there!

DR. JACKSON HOMER, tall and thin and gray, listened in half-fascinated doubt to his caller's rush of words. They swept on, quick, eager, convincing. He was young, this dark-haired, vivid-faced fellow who had given his name as David Winn. His arguments rang with the confidence of youth as yet unacquainted with defeat.

Winn gesticulated, motioned colorfully to drive home his arguments. His clear voice echoed from the walls of Dr. Homer's long laboratory, set delicate brass and nickel instruments on the shelves and vessels of shimmering glass on the tables to quivering, drifted out of the open window to be lost in the morning confusion of a sunny cross-town street of New York.

"You *can't* refuse!" Winn asserted. "It means a human being to test your process on, and you admit that you want to try it on a human."

"I would like to very much, yes," Dr. Homer sighed. "It would complete my investigation. But I had not thought of being able to do so until you volunteered—the risks—"

"What risks?" challenged young David Winn. "You've done the thing to a dozen animals from dog to monkey, haven't you, without changing anything in them except their eyesight?"

"The eyesight alteration is change enough," Dr. Homer said. "You say that you are a newspaper reporter and not a scientist. Do you realize exactly what my process involves?"

"Of course I do," David Winn answered. "I read the newspaper accounts of it thoroughly, from the first mention of your work that appeared three months ago.

"That first article said that you. Dr. Homer, the eminent biologist of Manhattan Foundation, believed that you could change

(Illustration by Winter)

He was looking through the ceiling of the laboratory as though no ceiling were there!

the eyes of animals so that they could see through stone and metal and such substances as easily as through glass.

"You proposed to do this by making the retinas of those animals' eyes sensitive to certain ultra-violet vibrations instead of light-vibrations. They would see by these ultra-violet radiations instead of by light, and since all inorganic matter is transparent to these particular vibrations, so would it be transparent to their eyes."

Dr. Homer nodded. "Yes, that was a fairly correct statement of my purpose in undertaking this series of experiments. I was sure I could make animal eyes capable of seeing through solid matter."

Winn leaned forward. "Then, two weeks ago, the papers said that you had succeeded. You had so changed the sensitivity of the eyes of several animals that they saw by the ultra-violet waves and could look straight through stone or metal or any inorganic substance. They could not see through living things or matter derived from living things, as these particular vibrations would not penetrate organic matter.

"That article added that you were of the opinion that you could change human eyes in just the same way by altering the retina's sensitivity, and that a man whose eyes were so treat could see through stone and brick walls, through metal of any kind, in fact, could see through almost everything except living beings and such part of their clothing and possessions as were of organic matter."

David Winn's face lit. "That's why I came here to volunteer as a test subject for your process! I want you to change my eyes so that I too will be able to look through solid matter as though it didn't exist!"

"But why?" Dr. Homer asked him keenly. "Just why do you want this power of looking through doors and walls at will?"

"Not for criminal purposes, if that is what you are thinking of," Winn told him.

"Yes, that is what was in my mind," Dr. Homer admitted. "I can take no chance of turning loose on this city a criminal who is able to see through its walls as though they were glass."

"I can satisfy you that I've no criminal ideas," David Winn assured him. "I told you I was a newspaper reporter. I'm a young one, an inexperienced one. But once I had this power, I would be the greatest reporter who ever lived!

"Do you see what I mean? If I can look through walls and see what people are doing behind closed doors, I can get stories no other reporter can get. I can even see what people are *saying* behind closed doors—I've practiced lip reading during the last few weeks in anticipation."

THE young man's face gleamed, enthusiasm in his eyes as he bent forward. Dr. Homer considered him. "So that is it—you want my process to make you the reporter who sees everything?"

"That's what I want, to see everything!" Winn declared. "Why, within weeks this power of mine would bring me a better job and a bigger salary than any other reporter in the country!"

"You wish me to change your eyesight because it will bring you a larger salary?" the scientist asked. "You must want that increased salary very badly."

David Winn smiled. "I do, and the reason is the usual one—a girl. Marta Ray and I are very much in love with each other, but a cub's salary wouldn't be much when we're married. But on the salary I'll make when I start seeing through doors and walls—"

"And you're willing to undergo this change of eyesight to get that," Dr. Homer commented. "You understand, once your eyes were changed in this way the process could not be undone?"

"Why should anyone want it undone?" Winn countered. "If I can just get that power, I'll be satisfied to keep it and to use it."

Dr. Homer thought in silence for a time. His brows knit. He looked out through the window at the noisy morning traffic in the street below. From the window, his gaze went to a long white table over whose end was suspended an upright mechanism of brass and steel and quartz.

The scientist walked over to the instrument, fingered its connections. David Winn watched him intently. Dr. Homer suddenly turned.

"I am going to use the process on your eyes, Winn," he said. "But there are conditions."

He raised a rigid finger. "First, if the process does succeed with your eyes, you are to tell absolutely no one of your power."

"I agree to that," Winn said quickly.

"Second, you will promise never to use that power for criminal or vindictive purposes."

"I do promise," David Winn told him. "And now? You'll do the thing at once?"

"I might as well," said the scientist. He seemed torn by doubts. "I don't know—I may be doing wrong in this, but I've *got* to see if the human retina reacts like the others.

"Yes, I'll do it at once," he went on. "The process will take less than two hours—of course you'll have to be anaesthetized during it."

Under his direction, David Winn removed coat and vest and climbed up onto the white table and stretched out.

Dr. Homer swung the suspended instrument over him, carefully adjusted its tubes until twin quartz lenses were directly over the eyes of the prostrate young man. He then placed ready on a smaller table, glass containers of pink and green solutions, instruments, and droppers.

He swung the tube of an anesthetic-gas apparatus toward Winn's face, then held its rubber nosepiece in his hand.

"All ready?" he said.

"All ready," David Winn smiled. "If all goes well I'll be seeing you—and much else—in two hours."

Dr. Homer nodded. "If all goes well," he repeated. "Here goes."

The gas apparatus hissed—

The Man with X-Ray Eyes

DAVID WINN opened his eyes and looked up from the table on which he lay. He saw the anxious face of Dr. Homer bending over him. There seemed a faint violet tinge in the light, but David Winn could see no other change. Had the process failed?

Then as he looked up past Dr. Homer's face, he gasped. He was looking up through the ceiling of the laboratory as though no ceiling was there! He was looking up at the bottom of a table, several chairs, and two white-coated scientists busy with flames and tubes, all seemingly suspended miraculously in the air a dozen feet above him.

And above these, in turn, David Winn could see other objects and other men suspended in the same way. Level above level he could see as clearly as though the ceilings and floors dividing them did not exist, far up through the great building's many levels to the open air.

Then the explanation came in full force to David Winn's half-dazed mind. He struggled up to a sitting position.

"You did it, then!" he exclaimed. "The process succeeded!"

"Did it?" Dr. Homer asked him keenly. "Has your vision changed any?"

"Changed?" Winn drew a long breath. "I'll say that it's changed. Why, I can see through the ceilings above and the walls and even this table I'm sitting on, as though they didn't exist!"

It was true. To David Winn's eyes, the walls, floors and ceilings of the building had vanished. He could see up through level above level into the open air. In each level he saw only the human beings, their clothing, wooden doors and tables; only organic matter.

He could look down through similar levels to the surface of the ground below. It occurred to him that he saw the ground only because it was so intermixed with organic matter in its upper layer.

Dr. Homer helped him to clamber down from the metal table. Winn seemed to himself to be standing on empty space, the tile floor invisible to his sight. It was an eerie sensation.

He took a few steps tentatively across the room and blundered into something invisible that upset with a crash.

Winn made a wry face. "I'll have to lookout for metal furniture, won't I? But it's wonderful—wonderful—"

Dr. Homer's face held excitement. "You can see only organic matter, then, the same as my animal subjects?"

"Just the same," said David Winn. Elation was beginning to replace his bewilderment. "Think of it. I'm looking straight through the walls! The reporter who can see through walls!"

"You've no regrets, then, that you underwent the process?" the scientist asked, and Winn laughed.

"Regrets? I wish that I'd been born this way. I'm going to see the world as it really is from now on, and not just the walls behind which it hides!"

He put on his hat and maneuvered to the door. Dr. Homer helping him. He grasped the invisible doorknob.

"I'll be back tomorrow to make whatever scientific tests you want, doctor. Just now I'm eager to make use of my power."

"Be careful," Dr. Homer warned. "Take it easy until you learn how to navigate."

David Winn closed the door, walked down a hall and invisible stairs carefully, and emerged into the street.

Crowded New York was an astounding spectacle to his eyes now that he saw only the living and organic matter in it.

The great buildings of stone and steel had largely vanished to his sight, and he now saw only the level above level of working people and miscellaneous organic objects they contained.

He could see none of the automobiles and buses thronging the street before him. His eyes beheld only groups of people in sitting posture rushing to and fro suspended in the air.

He set off for his newspaper office. It was but two blocks away, but before he reached it, David Winn had almost been run down at intersections by two taxicabs invisible to his eyes; had been roundly cursed by a man pushing a metal hand-truck along the sidewalk, which he had run into; and had tripped twice over objects he could not see.

When he got into the city room of his paper, it presented as weird an appearance as the street. Men sat at desks invisible to his eyes, using invisible telephones and typewriters. Winn threaded cautiously through them to the city editor's desk.

The editor, Ray Lanham, looked up as he approached and tossed a scrap of paper toward him.

"Where have you been all morning, Winn?" he asked. "Here's a list of some of the most prominent men in the city—I want you to get as many of them as you can to state their opinion on the latest disclosures of civic graft."

"This assignment ought to be easy enough for you," Lanham added. "Phone in what you get in time for the rewrite."

David Winn smiled as he pocketed the slip of paper. "Don't hunt easy assignments for me, for from now on I'm the best reporter you've got," he said. "In one week all the newspapers in this town will be begging me to work for them."

Civic Corruption

GRINNING to himself at the editor's dumbfounded face, he walked out of the office and reached the street.

When he saw a taxi driver sailing along amid the weird throng of rushing figures in the street, David Winn hailed him and entered the cab he could not see. He sped downtown in eerie progress.

The first name on his list was that of Roscoe Saulton, candidate for governor. Winn left the cab at the Saulton Campaign Headquarters, and found his way up through the invisible walls and stairs and floors to the suite of offices he wished to reach.

He found two other newspapermen waiting to see Roscoe Saulton on the same matter, and Saulton was just appearing from the inner offices. His big, good-humored face was wreathed in a welcoming smile.

His face sobered as David Winn put his question. It became almost stern.

"I have only the strongest condemnation for all forms of civic graft," he declared, "This rottenness that has been uncovered in our body politics must be destroyed!"

"Can we quote you as saying that if elected you will do all in your power to cleanse municipal politics?" one of the reporters asked, and Saulton nodded vigorously.

"You may, and I hope that you make it emphatic. I am seeking the office of governor only that I may serve the people, and I know no better way to serve them than to smash this political ring of chicanery and fraud that has long disgraced this city."

He shook hands heartily with them. "Good day, gentlemen—and remember that I am always glad to see you."

As Roscoe Saulton returned to the inner offices and the other two newspapermen went out, David Winn lingered.

He could look through the walls into the inner office to which Saulton had gone, and could see Saulton and the half-dozen other cigar-smoking men in that office as clearly as though the intervening walls did not exist.

Winn could see the movement of their lips and read from it what they were saying. Saulton had sunk into a chair and was speaking to one of the others.

"More damn reporters to get my opinion on graft," he was saying. "They've kept me busy damning the organization up and down all morning."

The other men grinned. "Don't damn it too hard when you're relying on it to put you into office next month, Saulton," one of them said.

Another contradicted. "Go as far as you like with your denunciations," he advised the candidate. "It doesn't hurt the organization a bit and it will get you votes."

"Well, once I'm in the governor's chair, I'll give short shrift to these pussyfooting reformers," Roscoe Saulton growled, "but right now I've got to coddle them along, worse luck."

David Winn's absorbed watch was interrupted by a secretary who came up to him in the outer office.

"Is anything the matter?" the man asked. "You've been staring at the wall for minutes."

Winn turned. "Oh, just a little absentminded, I guess. Good day."

Winn walked out of the building to the street. He felt disgusted to the core of his being.

So this was Roscoe Saulton, the gubernatorial candidate whose integrity was unquestioned! A pseudo-reformer who denounced political graft even while he used it to reach office.

Others, everyone, might be taken in, but the truth could not be hidden from the eyes of David Winn. He had looked through the walls behind which Saulton thought himself secure, had seen the real Roscoe Saulton.

He looked at the next name on his list. It was that of James Willingdon, financier and mining magnate and philanthropist whose eminence was known over the whole nation. Winn got another cab to take him to Willingdon and Company's Wall Street offices.

He was passed through a half-dozen secretaries and underlings until he at last reached the office of James Willingdon's personal secretary and explained his errand. The secretary was beautifully courteous.

"Mr. Willingdon is engaged in an important business conference, but I will see whether he can see you for a moment. Will you please wait here?"

David Winn looked after the secretary as he went through an invisible wall into the next office. There were a dozen men in that room, gathered round a long table. Winn saw them as clearly as though there were no wall separating them.

He saw James Willingdon himself at the head of the table, a man of fifty with a gray face, steely gray eyes, and a straight, erect figure. Willingdon was speaking to the others at the table.

Winn could read the movement of his lips as clearly as though he were hearing the words issuing from them. "I tell you, it's the best proposition any of us have ever had," James Willingdon was saying. "We announce United Mines, and with our names and the publicity we'll give it, the public will fall over itself to buy the stock. When it's gone high enough we'll unload without warning."

"What if the public learns what has happened afterward?" a tall, anxious-looking man queried. "We wouldn't be very popular, I can assure you."

"There's no chance they'll even suspect—we'll simply assert that bear raiders broke the stock's value and that we lost more than anyone else!" James Willingdon answered. "They'll never question it anymore than they ever have before."

"Very well, we're with you, Willingdon," another said. "But remember, no double-crossing—we sell at the same time."

THE personal secretary who had been hovering close by came quickly forward and spoke to the financier.

David Winn saw Willingdon excuse himself to the others and come with the secretary out into the room where he waited.

James Willingdon's face wore a smile of perfect-seeming sincerity as he shook Winn's hand.

"I can spare you only a moment, Mr. Winn," he said, "for some of my associates and I are busy planning a project that will mean great things for this country—yes, great things.

"But my secretary said that you wanted my opinion of the recent graft-disclosures, and my duty as a citizen comes before all else. As a citizen of this municipality, I want to put on record my utter detestation of all such wrong-doing as has just been disclosed."

David Winn went out of the place with a bitter smile. So James Willingdon, great financier and revered philanthropist, was—just a crook. Just another like Roscoe Saulton.

It came to Winn as he emerged into the street that his new eyesight gave him more than the power to look through walls—it gave with it the power to look through the falsities of ordinary existence into the true hearts of men.

Ten minutes later, David Winn was putting his question to the third man on his list, one of the overlords of the clothing industry.

The clothing magnate spoke eloquently against civic corruption. He dwelt on the horror of defrauding poor as well as rich. He mentioned Lincoln and Washington. But David Winn was not listening.

The offices of this man were on the ground floor of the great block of buildings that housed his shops. Winn looked through the offices' walls as though they did not exist, was staring into those far-stretching factory-divisions.

He saw the long rows of pinched-looking, pale-faced girls and women bent over machines, working like so many automatons without looking up. He saw panting youths struggling with hand-trucks of clothing and fabrics and furs through ill-lit, ill-ventilated corridors and rooms.

Winn avoided shaking hands with the denouncer of graft and escaped into the street. He felt revulsion.

He walked along the street, forgetting his further names for the time, and found himself passing a curious structure.

Its walls were transparent to his eyes like those of all the other buildings in sight, of course. But its interior seemed divided into a great number of very small rooms.

There were men crowded in nearly all the rooms, as far back into the structure as he saw. Some of the men lay in stupefied sleep. Others gazed longingly into the streets.

THE MAN WITH X-RAY EYES

The Horrors of the City Revealed

IT WAS a prison. Winn saw the guards in the corridors between the cells, the debased character of many of the occupants, the unconquerable dirtiness, as clearly as though there were no walls and bars between.

He had many times passed the stately gray stone building before, but never until now had he seen through the stone front to the foulness and misery within. He passed hurriedly on.

But the next building was worse. It was a large hospital. He had passed this, too, many times in the past, and had admired the neatness of the big brick building with its gleaming sunrooms and other rooms showing their expanse of shining glass window.

But now David Winn's eyes saw nothing of the neat brick walls, the glistening glass. He looked through brick and plaster and metal to the building's interior. He saw long rows of mattresses, resting on beds he could not see; hundreds of them.

Men and women were stretched upon them, and children too. Some were tossing feverishly in the grip of dread diseases. Others shrieked in the agony of pain. He could see men whose limbs were but bandaged stumps, could see children lying supine in casts.

He gazed up through the level on level of rows of beds and sufferers to the operating rooms, glimpsed the flash of steel instruments suddenly reddened. He saw the sheet being drawn over the faces of suddenly quiet figures, beheld new sufferers being brought hastily in from the ambulances at the rear. Sick and shaken, David Winn stumbled on.

He passed quickly the adjoining insanity-hospital, turning his head away from the building through whose transparent walls he could see men and women tearing at the bars of their cells and at themselves, or sitting and staring droolingly into nothingness. He kept his eyes averted until he had turned the corner.

The grotesque spectacle of the city hummed and swarmed in the warm afternoon sunlight as he went down this street. He hardly knew now where he was going, hardly was aware of the weirdness of the spectacle that the street presented to his eyes. In his soul, a horror was expanding that he could not conquer.

NOW it was a section of the slum district through which he was passing. But he did not see it as it appeared to the eyes of others in the street, a narrow thoroughfare lined with dingy brick-fronted tenements and noisy with children playing on the worn cobbles. He was seeing what lay behind the dingy building fronts. David Winn's eyes beheld an unimagined dirtiness and squalor through the walls that were transparent to them. He saw large families crowded into a single room, with shabby mattresses piled in a corner showing on what they slept at night. He saw scavenging children returning triumphantly home with revolting food.

In those rabbit warrens of filth and darkness, his super-penetrating vision descried every species of crime, breeding and taking place. Men and women sodden with poisonous liquor, he saw, and others pale and flaccid from the drugs they took as he watched. Children were deftly instructed in crime in places whose walls could not bar the gaze of David Winn.

Winn tried to tell himself that all this bad always been, that it was only because he now saw it all that he was so shaken with horror, but it was unavailing. Wherever his steps took him, wherever his eyes turned, he looked through walls into some new nest of pain or foulness or crime hidden from the light of day.

He was sick, sick unto his soul. Why, he cried to himself, had he ever been so mad as to let his eyes be changed? Why had he not realized what it would mean? All the wretchedness and wrongdoing and horror of life that was hidden from other men by walls would always be staring him in the face. He would see them always with eyes that penetrated all concealment.

If his eyes could be changed back to their former state, if the process could be undone—but no, it could never be undone. Dr. Homer had warned him of that. He would always be like this, always descrying through any concealment the horror hidden from all others.

"God Keep Us Blind—!"

BUT if he could get away, with Marta!

David Winn's heart leapt to catch at the sudden gleam of hope. In the country there would be fewer walls, less hidden things. They could be married and go there to live, just he and Marta together. Marta loved him and would understand—

He would go to her, explain to her. Feverishly, David Winn walked northward until he came to the apartment building he sought. He raced up the invisible stairs and along the hall. His hand was raised to knock on Marta Ray's door, but he paused as he looked through the transparent wall and saw Marta and her mother.

They were talking, and their faces were turned half toward him. David Winn read their lips as clearly as though he heard their speech.

"He said that if his plans worked out we could be married quite soon," Marta was saying.

The mother sniffed. "Why you have anything to do with him, I don't know. David Winn has nothing and never will have anything."

"Oh, don't start that again, mother," Marta Ray said wearily. "I know David doesn't amount to much."

"Then why are you going to marry him?" her mother demanded.

"Because David is the best I can get. I have to marry someone, don't I?" said the girl discontentedly.

David Winn stood quite motionless outside the door for some moments. Then he turned, and with his face white and strange, went softly down the stairs.

THE police sergeant that night was explaining to Dr. Homer as he led him back along a corridor to the morgue room.

"We found your name and address in his pocket when we fished his body out of the river, and thought maybe you could identify him," he was saying.

Dr. Homer stepped into the morgue room, and as the sheet was thrown back he looked steadily at the drowned man.

He lay with body tensed, and with one hand flung palm outward against his face, across his eyes.

"Funny thing about that arm," the sergeant remarked. "When we found him, his hand was up in front of his eyes like that and we couldn't move it away.

"Looks just like he was trying to keep from seeing something, doesn't it?"

Dr. Homer nodded sadly as he looked at David Winn. "He was trying to keep from seeing everything. For he saw everything just as he wanted to, and it was too much for him.

"God keep us blind in this world! Prevent us from the horror of doing what he did, of seeing—too well."

THE END

Secret of the Robot

BY CHESTER S. GEIER

The pseudo-brain of the robot, was a mesh of platinum and wire—but not nearly as strange as its monstrous inhabitant...

THE intercom buzzed. Dayton put down the report he had been reading, reached across the desk, and pressed a switch. Ann's voice sounded from the speaker.

"Mr. Morton Thurlow wishes to see you, sir."

"Send him in."

Dayton left the switch on, since he knew Ann would want to listen to his talk with the government investigator. He recalled her use of the word sir, and grimaced. Ann went formal only for the benefit of visitors, but this time he sensed a warning behind it. She knew Thurlow's appearance held the answer to the fate of the struggling little company of which Dayton was owner and president.

In the crucial few moments left to him, Dayton wondered with a chill touch of dread what verdict had been reached by the Robot Control Board. Were they permitting him to continue in business? Or had they decided to revoke his license? If the latter case, he knew he would have Thurlow to thank for it. Despite his pompous claims to impartiality, the investigator had been cold and hostile from the very beginning.

Thurlow looked grim and business like when he strode into Dayton's office. He was short and thin, with pinched, narrow features and severe dark eyes, which held the barely noticeable glitter of contact lenses. He wore a primly tailored suit of dark-blue synthe-wool, and carried in addition to his plastic briefcase, a flat-crowned, stiff-brimmed hat of the style which had just lately come into fashion.

Dayton shook Thurlow's hand briefly and saw him settled into a chair. The investigator refused cigarettes, but Dayton lighted one to soothe his uneasy nerves.

SECRET of the ROBOT
By CHESTER S. GEIER

"The Board has reached a decision in your case, Mr. Dayton," Thurlow announced, in crisp, dry tones.

"That's very prompt of the Board," Dayton replied. "It's been just a little more than a week since you finished your investigation."

He clutched her tightly about the neck

"The Board likes to be prompt, Mr. Dayton. It has the peace and safety of millions of persons to look after. There would be a large number of deaths due to dangerous robots were it not for the watchfulness of the Robot Control Board, you know."

Dayton nodded and said nothing. He knew. The Robot Control Board had been formed by the government as a result of the mass hysteria that had swept the country in the early days of robot commercialization. A number of people had been killed by robots whose faulty mechanisms had caused them to go out of control, though the deaths were claimed as due to deliberate, homicidal attacks. The fact that the initial widespread use of aircraft and atomic power had been the cause of even more deaths was generally overlooked. Robots were regarded as a very special sort of menace, chiefly because of their outward likeness to humanity. They were somehow considered on a level with denizens of another planet, or were feared as being potentially deadly and destructive as any of the man created monsters of melodramatic fiction.

ON THIS basis the Robot Control Board had come into being. The use of robots could not be prohibited outright, for despite the timidity of the public at large, robots had attained a secure niche in many branches of industry, where they took the place of human workers. The only alternative was to rigidly supervise their use, and the Board did this in a broad way by watching over all phases of robot activity. Official approval from the Board had to be obtained before certain types of robot experimentation or research could be carried out. A license—granted only after careful tests of the finished product—was required before robots could be manufactured or sold. Board investigators made periodic checks of the factories where robots were made and the various industries where they were used. In cases where robots were found to be potentially or actually dangerous, licenses permitting their manufacture were revoked, their sale was halted, and their further use in industry forbidden.

Dayton thought of this now as he gazed at Thurlow across the desk. A revoked license, he knew, usually meant extinction for a small robot-manufacturing firm such as his own. And that would mean personal disaster as well. Every credit he had was sunk in Dayton Mechanicals.

Thurlow withdrew a sheaf of typed pages from his briefcase and frowned at them importantly. "Mr. Dayton, the Board has decided that your license is to be sustained."

Dayton felt a wave of relief sweep over him. "That certainly is good news!"

"However," Thurlow went on, "since I have pointed out in my findings that there is a large element of...ah...uncertainty connected with the new type of robot upon which your company is working, the Board has recommended that I maintain a close watch."

Dayton was puzzled. "But why did the Board uphold my license if it wasn't fully convinced that the Gammas are harmless?"

"The Board's decision was based to a large extent upon another matter. You see, Gus Hedstrom, the employee who was killed, obtained his job with your firm under false pretenses. To be exact, he furnished your personnel department with a fraudulent psych record. These records, as you know, are required of workers in the robot industry. They show a worker's intelligence, aptitude, and general psychological fitness for work involving robots.

"By means of a faked record, Hedstrom concealed the fact that he was actually unfit to work on robots. He had a deep, subconscious fear of them, though he refused to admit it. Thus, when he saw the uncontrolled Gamma running toward him, his repressed fears came to the surface. He lost his head. He became caught in the machinery as a result of his own blind panic rather than any threat of danger from the robot itself."

Dayton nodded slowly. "I thought there was something queer about Hedstrom's actions at the time. I knew the robot couldn't possibly have had any intentions of harming him."

Thurlow raised pale eyebrows. "Who knows for certain, Mr. Dayton?"

"The Gammas just aren't built that way. You see, the Alpha and Beta types are automatics. That is, their responses are the result of a limited number of electronic patterns, based on certain key words. Like an electronic computer on a small scale. But the Gammas are inductives. Their responses are the result of actual reasoning. They have colloidal brain-structures, operated by chemicoelectrical memory and integration processes, which are the closest things to a human brain that have ever been built into a robot."

DAYTON leaned forward at his desk, his long, oddly youthful features intense and earnest.

"Gamma-Two, the one that got out of control and indirectly caused Hedstrom's death, was mentally...*a baby*. It had learned to hold itself erect, to move its limbs, and to walk. It had learned to recognize the men in the experimental laboratory as well as a few other objects. It had been coached to perform a few simple actions. But in absolutely no way could it possibly have been taught to endanger human beings. The experimental workers are especially careful about this point.

"Further, being essentially a baby, Gamma-Two couldn't have gone insane. The disorder arises out of fears, repressions, or frustrations in a more mature and highly organized mind. For that reason, a baby can't go crazy, though it may be born an idiot or a moron. To say Gamma-Two had gone crazy suggests a development of mind that it couldn't possibly have reached in the short period of coaching it had been given."

Thurlow lifted his bony shoulders. "Then how do you explain the fact that it got out of control?"

"I wish I knew," Dayton muttered. He ran a hand through his unruly black hair, and his features wrinkled in perplexity. "My experimental staff tried to solve the problem, but they wound up against a blank wall. There was no reason for it, no clue. The whole thing was completely senseless. One moment Gamma-Two was sitting quietly in the laboratory playroom. The next it jumped up as though it had received an electric shock and started running. Then it just as quickly quieted down again. But the damage had been done as far as Hedstrom was concerned."

Thurlow's eyes were narrowed thoughtfully. "From the identification system you use, I presume there was a robot of the same type before Gamma-Two. What happened to it?"

"You mean Gamma-One. There was something technically wrong with its brain structure. We substituted a new brain structure, and it became Gamma-Two. After what happened, though, we're using another new brain structure. Gamma-Two is now Gamma-Three—or G-3, for short. G-3 has just started to receive coaching, and is mentally still in the infant stage."

"Has it shown any indications that it might eventually prove dangerous?"

"None as yet. But we're taking every precaution."

"Continue to do so," Thurlow advised. "If there is a repetition of the Hedstrom tragedy, the Board will be certain to revoke your license." The investigator closed his briefcase and rose. "Remember, Mr. Dayton, from now on, I shall be maintaining a close watch over the activities of your experimental staff."

Dayton concealed his annoyance behind an understanding nod. "Of course. That's your duty. I'll try to cooperate with you in every way."

Ann Barrett strode into the office immediately after Thurlow left. She was nominally Dayton's secretary, though the ring she wore indicated that the relationship had developed along more serious lines. She had large gray-green eyes and fine-spun brown hair framing features that were vivid and alert. The skirt of her modish neo-silk dress barely touched her knees in front and fell to her ankles at the rear.

"The little snoop!" she said. "I heard everything, Jud."

Dayton grunted by way of agreement. "The Robot Control Board's bad enough, but fanatics like Thurlow make it that much worse."

HE TURNED abruptly and strode to the window behind his desk, which formed one entire wall of the office. He stared down at the tree-dotted lawn that encircled the building. The air car landing was partially visible from where he stood, and in another moment his attention was drawn by a machine taking off. Thurlow, he thought darkly.

Beyond the grounds, other buildings showed, glass and stainless steel constructions that glittered in the afternoon sunlight. Factories and shops for the most part, these made up Chicago Minor's industrial district. In the distance towered the skyscrapers of Chicago Major, wrapped in a web of traffic levels. The sky was dotted with a variety of aircraft, ranging from huge stratosphere freighters to tiny air cars.

Dayton watched Thurlow's machine out of sight, then turned back to Ann as she spoke again.

"I'm glad you're out of that Hedstrom mess, Jud. For a while I was afraid the Robot Control Board was going to run you out of business."

"You and me both," Dayton said. "But there's still Thurlow. Things are going to be difficult with him breathing down my neck."

"Why worry about Thurlow? Unless—" Ann caught Dayton's arm. "Jud—are you thinking we'll have the same trouble with G-3?"

"I wish I knew. Point is, we don't know what happened to G-2, and so there's no way of telling if the same thing will happen to G-3."

Ann shook her brown curls somberly. "That's taking a terrible risk. I wish you'd give up the Gammas, Jud. If another man dies, you'll be put out of business for certain."

"If I give up the Gammas, I'll be put out of business just the same," Dayton returned, shrugging. "There's no future market in automatic robots, and that's what we're turning out now. The trend is toward inductives. Most robot firms are experimenting with them, and the first to turn out a successful model is going to have a corner on customers. Needing credits like I do, I want to be first, of course. Then I'll finally be able to marry you and buy a place out in the country."

Ann's features momentarily softened. "That would be swell. But, Jud, I can't help thinking about what might happen if you keep on experimenting with the Gammas. I don't know how to explain it, but there's something wrong about them—something...well, unearthly."

"Your feminine intuition, eh?"

"All right, make fun of me."

Dayton took the girl's small chin between his forefinger and thumb and regarded her gravely. "Snap out of it, Ann. You're showing symptoms of robot-phobia. In spite of the fact that the Gammas look human and are built more closely along human lines than robots have ever been built before, they're still robots. There's nothing unearthly about them."

"I hope not, Jud—because I *do* want a place out in the country."

"Not any more than I do." Dayton brushed the girl's lips with his, then turned toward the door. "I'm going up to see the men in the experimental lab. They'll want to know what Thurlow said."

LEAVING Ann at her desk in the outer office, he took an elevator to the wing on an upper floor where the experimental laboratory was situated. This consisted of several large, bright rooms, furnished with a bewildering assortment of machinery, tools, and instruments. In the main room Emil Dornhof was bent over a workbench, delving industriously into the vitals of a complicated piece of apparatus. He was a robotics engineer, as Dayton himself had been before the growing details arising out of the commercialization of his work had forced him to devote himself solely to business matters.

Dornhof jerked around with startled suddenness when he became aware of Dayton's presence. He was heavyset, inclined to stoutness, and had jovial features under a shock of wiry gray hair.

"Uh...hello, Jud. I thought for a second you were G-3, sneaking up on me."

Cold fingers of alarm touched Dayton. "Good Lord, has it been doing that?"

"Well, sort of. Nothing to worry about, though. G-3 has just developed a habit of poking around, and Bart and I haven't grown used to it yet."

Dayton rubbed his jaw, frowning. "I didn't know that. And I don't like it. G-3 seems to have matured much too fast."

"It isn't a human being, you know," Dornhof reminded. "The colloidal brain has a lot of unknown possibilities, and quick learning may be one of them. At any rate, I'm trying to find out just how the colloidal brain works." Dornhof gestured at the apparatus on the workbench beside him. "This is the device I told you about some time ago. The psycho-scope, I call it."

Dayton nodded. "I gave you a go-ahead on it. How have you been getting along?"

"Better than I expected. But the details weren't difficult to begin with. My idea was based on the standard mind-reading equipment used by police authorities. And their device was nothing more than an improvement of the old electroencephalograph, connected to an ultra-shortwave transmitter. Anyway, my psycho-scope ought to show us how G-3's mind works. I'll be finished soon, and then we'll see."

"Keep on with it, Emil," Dayton said. "A thing like that is just what we need. Let me know—" He broke off as a voice spoke sharply from one of the adjoining rooms.

"Hey, where do you think you're going? Come back here!"

Dayton recognized Bart Welch's tones, and turned toward a doorway diagonally across from where he stood. A figure appeared in the opening. At first glimpse it might have been taken to be that of a man—a man dressed strangely in white neo-silk shorts and plastolex sandals. After a moment, however, a distinct quality of oddness about the figure would have become apparent. There was a *smoothness* in its appearance, a beauty and perfection completely inhuman. And its weirdly glowing eyes, the utter lack of expression about its pale, classical features, would have explained why. That startlingly human yet queerly inhuman figure was a robot.

DAYTON knew he was looking at G-3. The robot returned his gaze impassively, then turned with a flowing, deliberate motion as Bart Welch appeared behind it.

Welch's gaunt, freckled features were exasperated. A biophysicist and amateur psychologist, he was tall, bony, and stooped. His thatch of bristling red hair seemed to add to his present aggressive mood. He glared at G-3 and demanded:

"Well, what are you up to now?"

Slowly the robot lifted an arm, pointing in Dayton's direction. Its flawless plastic lips opened and quivered. A faint, wheezing sound issued from the diaphragm in its throat. Then, blurted, as though formed with the greatest difficulty, a word became audible.

"Boss!" G-3 said.

Welch glanced around, saw Dayton, and smiled wearily. "Oh, hello, Chief."

Dayton was staring at the robot. "He...it...why, it seemed to know me!"

Welch moved his bony shoulders in a shrug. "G-3 seems to know everything. It's a regular perambulating encyclopedia in some ways. How it does it beats me. I haven't had time to teach it much so far."

"The colloidal brain may be unusually receptive," Dornhof put in. "Even telepathic to a certain extent. Who knows?"

"Seems that way," Dayton muttered. "I last saw G-3 several days ago. But then its brain-structure had just been connected up. I don't understand how it could possibly have recognized me a moment ago." He frowned at the robot, then shifted his gaze to Welch. "You mentioned that G-3 seems to know everything. How long has that been going on? Ever since the brain-structure was put in?"

"Not exactly." The biophysicist hesitated. "I didn't want to worry you, Chief, so I didn't say anything before. G-3's knowledge seemed to come all of a sudden. In the beginning it just fumbled around like any baby would. Then a few days ago, while I was coaching it in a simple routine, it gave a jerk something like G-2 did before it started running out of control. After that it acted...well, as if it were a lot more intelligent than it had been at first. It actually seemed to have gained a lot of new information—things it couldn't have had time to learn."

"And toys," Dornhof said.

Welch nodded his red thatch. "Yeah. G-3 hasn't shown any interest in toys, Chief. It's as though it weren't a baby somehow. I can't figure it out."

Dayton glanced at the beautiful man-like figure of the robot. G-3 was a baby only mentally, he knew, though its mature, virile appearance made it difficult to accept the idea. He wondered suddenly if the maturity of its body were not the explanation for what seemed the unusual maturity of its mind.

He mentioned the thought to Dornhof and Welch.

"It's possible," Welch said slowly. "In fact, anything is possible. We're dealing with a robot of an entirely new and superior type, you know, not a human being. G-3 may be a robot superman, for that matter, with potentialities so tremendous that the strange intelligence it has shown so far may be just a feeble beginning."

"We'll know for certain when G-3 finally learns to coordinate properly," Dornhof added. He glanced at Dayton. "You see, it's doubtful whether G-3 sees and hears the same things we do in all instances."

"What do you mean?" Dayton asked.

"JUST what Bart has been saying," Dornhof returned. "G-3 isn't a human being. It's constructed along fundamentally human lines, but for the large part its mind and body are alien. So who can say if it sees and hears the same things we do? It has to learn first. And when it finally learns, we'll be able to tell from its actions just what sort of intelligence and abilities it has.

"Look at it this way," Dornhof went on. "Suppose, Jud, that your brain were somehow removed from your human body and placed in G-3's robot body. Do you think you would see and hear things exactly the same as you did while in your human shell?"

"It would be different," Dayton decided. "I would be receiving sensations through channels much different from those to which I had been accustomed."

"Exactly. Someone would say 'It's a beautiful day,' but to you it would sound like 'Gookle bloop,' or something of the sort. You'd have to *learn* that combination of noises meant 'It's a beautiful day.' Likewise, a cube might look like a triangle to you, and you'd have to *learn* that what looked like a triangle was actually a cube."

"Look at G-3!" Welch exclaimed suddenly.

The robot was quivering, its flawlessly molded plastic arms half raised. Its lips worked, and faint hissing sounds came from its throat.

Dayton felt a stab of dread before he understood that G-3 was trying desperately to speak. At last it managed.

"Boss!" it said. There was a momentary silence. The robot seemed to be gathering itself for another effort. Then: "I...I hess...I hez...hez-z-z-z—" Again it fell silent. Its slips continued to work, though no further sound issued from them. At last a quiver of futility ran over its perfect form, and it relapsed once more into immobility.

"What in the world?" Dayton muttered. He swung back to Dornhof and Welch. "What do you make of that?"

"G-3 tried to tell us something," Welch said.

"It knew what it wanted to say," Dornhof mused. "But it couldn't make sounds that we would understand. Evidently it has to learn that, too."

Dayton threw up his hands in despair. "The whole thing is driving me nuts. There's something very wrong with G-3. That's painfully obvious. In fact, it sticks out all over the place. But nobody seems to know exactly what *is* wrong, and why!"

"We'll know soon enough," Dornhof comforted. "My psychoscope should give us a lot of answers."

"But in the meantime?" Dayton demanded. "Suppose G-3 runs wild like G-2 did?"

"I don't think that will happen," Welch said. "G-3 had the same kind of mysterious shock as G-2, but it didn't get out of control. In fact, it didn't act dangerous in any way, aside from becoming a sort of robot prodigy. No, Chief, I'm almost dead certain that G-3 won't make any trouble."

"It better not," Dayton grunted. "That investigator from the Robot Control Board—Thurlow—was here awhile ago. He told me the Board is allowing me to keep my license, but he has orders to keep a close watch over the work we're doing with G-3. If anybody else gets hurt, we're through—all of us."

"YOU," Dayton told Welch, "may feel sure that G-3 won't make trouble, but we've got to be positive of that. We have to take precautions of some kind. I'm going to have the doors in here reinforced. They're going to be kept locked, and G-3 is not to be allowed to wander out under any circumstances. And as a further precaution, I want you two to wear guns at all times. If G-3 makes a break, regardless of whether or not it has actually gone out of control, I want you to use them. Is that clear?"

Dornhof and Welch nodded, the engineer gravely, the biophysicist with obvious reluctance.

"One thing more," Dayton resumed. "I want one of you to report to me every day on the progress being made with G-3. And above all, don't be afraid of worrying me. That way you'll be cutting my throat to save my neck. I want straight facts. If there's going to be any trouble from G-3, I want to know about it before it pops."

The two assistants nodded again. Dayton gestured in finality and turned to leave. His last glance at G-3 left him with a disturbing impression. Was it merely a trick of the light—or was there a faint suggestion of hostility about the robot's otherwise impassive, perfect features?

The impression faded from his mind in the days that followed. Incessant waves of business matters swept everything else from his thoughts. Dayton Mechanicals was enjoying a period of peak sales, though a small margin of profit was actually involved. Dayton was selling his Alpha and Beta type robots at sharply reduced prices in an effort to clear out present stocks. He knew that the heyday of the automatics was fast approaching its end, and he wanted to be ready when the end finally came. The moment that news of a successful inductive type robot was announced, sales of automatics would cease almost instantly.

Thurlow appeared at the plant almost every other day, though he evidently tried to make his visits as unexpected as possible. Dornhof and Welch were on the alert, however, and the precautions Dayton had outlined were already in effect.

On the whole, Dayton found the reports of his experimental staff increasingly reassuring. G-3 was learning rapidly—somewhat too rapidly, it seemed to Dayton. But the robot had thus far shown no slightest signs of dangerous behavior. It spoke with growing fluency and responded to commands with an ease and promptness that grew daily. Already it was able to perform a number of simple tasks about the laboratory.

DAYTON'S hopes mounted. By all indications the Gammas, as represented by G-3, were proving to be an astonishingly successful type. And as far as he knew, they were the only successful inductive robots that had been produced as yet. To Dayton that meant he would have a practical monopoly on the inductive robot market when he finally began full-scale production of the Gammas.

"Things are looking up," he told Ann one morning. "I think you're going to get that other ring you've been waiting for—and a place in the country."

She caught at him, her eyes shining. "Jud! It's almost too good to be true. I was beginning to think it would never happen."

"I've stopped further work on the Alphas and Betas," Dayton went on. "Everything is ready for production of Gammas, and that'll begin as soon as I give the word. I'm just waiting for Dornhof to finish his psycho-scope. The device should clear up any last doubts about G-3 and in this way definitely prove whether or not the Gammas are actually a safe type for commercialization."

"Just what will the psycho-scope do, Jud?"

"It should show us just what sort of a mind G-3 has. We've been wondering about that all along."

Dornhof reported a short time later. The psycho-scope was completed, and tests on Welch had indicated the device as being highly satisfactory.

"I haven't used the psycho-scope on G-3 yet," Dornhof explained. "I want you to have the honor, Jud."

"Fine!" Dayton approved. "Get everything ready. I'll be right with you."

Dayton lost no time about appearing at the experimental laboratory. With a few swift words to Ann about what was to take place, he hurried toward the elevators.

The laboratory door was still kept locked, and he let himself in with his key. Besides Dornhof and Welch, Ann was the only other person who had one.

The psycho-scope had been placed on a table, at which two chairs had been arranged. Dornhof was bent over it, making a few final adjustments. He looked up and nodded as Dayton appeared.

"All set, Jud. Bart is keeping G-3 busy in another room, so it won't know anything unusual is taking place until we're ready."

"Does G-3 know what the psycho-scope will do?"

"I don't think so. Bart and I have been careful not to discuss the device frequently or in great detail. G-3 has asked about it, of course, but I explained it was just a machine to measure brain impulses."

"Asked about..." Dayton echoed in a whisper. He shook his head wonderingly.

Welch appeared from one of the adjoining rooms. The biophysicist looked disgruntled. "Twice in a row!" he growled.

Dornhof chuckled. Then, noticing Dayton's perplexity, he explained, "Checkers. That's how Bart was keeping G-3 busy. And Bart got licked."

"Checkers!" Dayton gasped. "G-3 can play checkers—and beat a man at it?"

Dornhof chuckled again. "That's right. Just take a good look at Bart's face."

"I never was very good at checkers," Welch said defensively.

An instant later G-3 itself strode into the room, turning toward Welch. "Play another game, Mr. Welch?" the robot asked, in distinct, slightly metallic tones.

"No!" Welch snapped.

G-3, Dayton noticed, looked downcast. The robot's features no longer had their former complete, automaton like lack of expression. It seemed as if, among other things, G-3 had learned to operate its facial muscles. The robot's similarity to human beings was now truly uncanny, especially since it had been dressed in more conventional clothing, which concealed to a great extent the unnatural perfection of its body.

G-3 nodded as it became aware of Dayton's presence in the room. "Hello, Boss."

"Hello," Dayton responded faintly. He felt an eerie sensation at being able to talk to the robot as easily and glibly as though it were a person. What was the answer? What would the psycho-scope reveal? He thought of the coming examination eagerly—and at the same time, with dread.

Dornhof finished his adjustments and gestured to the robot. "Come over here, G-3. We're going to play a more interesting game than checkers."

"What do you want me to do?"

"Just sit down in this chair."

G-3 glanced slowly at the psycho-scope—and hesitation seemed to shine in its glowing eyes. "Are you going to measure my brain impulses?"

"That's right," Dornhof said. "And we're going to compare them with the Boss'. Interesting, eh?"

"Yes."

At Dornhof's gesture, G-3 took one of the chairs at the table on which the psycho-scope stood. A headpiece, which was chiefly a wire frame supporting two electrodes that fitted one at each temple, was placed on the robot's head. Wires trailed from each electrode and disappeared into the sprawling, intricate mass of the device.

Dayton, in the chair on the opposite side of the table, was fitted with a headpiece similar to that worn by G-3. The electrodes pressing snugly against his temples made him uneasy. He gripped the arms of his chair in growing tension.

"That's that," Dornhof said. "Everything's ready." He glanced at Dayton sharply, warningly—and pressed a switch.

After a moment Dayton felt a deep humming within his head. It grew deeper, and then he had a chillingly weird sensation of rapport—of *contact*.

He went rigid as wave after wave of thought poured into his mind. Thought that explained. Thought that revealed—devastatingly. A realization grew within Dayton that shook him with amazement to the very core of his being.

An instant longer he forced himself to breast that incredible mental flood. Then he leaped to his feet, tearing the electrodes from his head. Breathing heavily, he stared with a kind of wild fascination at G-3.

The robot was rising also. Its own hands came up, jerking away the electrodes. It faced Dayton, muscles quivering beneath its smooth plastic skin, an expression of panic frozen on its perfect face.

"What...what happened?" Dornhof faltered, alarm in his voice.

Welch started forward, his freckled face pale. "Chief—what's the matter? What did you find out?"

"Guns!" Dayton whispered, forcing words through the shock that gripped him. "Get your guns!"

DORNHOF and Welch stared in numbed bewilderment. It was only when G-3 whirled and darted toward the door that they finally moved. Dornhof's hand reached under his laboratory smock, and Welch fumbled at a hip pocket. They got their weapons out at almost the same time, but before they could point them at the robot, which was tugging frantically at the locked door, something happened.

The door opened.

Ann came into the room, her key still in her hand. Her eyes found Dayton, and she spoke swiftly.

"Jud—Thurlow is waiting for you in your office. He wants to see you at once. He didn't explain, but he says it's important."

Even as the girl spoke, a realization that something was wrong appeared on her face. She glanced around puzzledly and then her eyes widened and her hand went to her throat as she saw G-3 crouching beside the door. In the next instant the robot leaped at her, caught her arms, and swung her in front of it as a shield.

Ann gasped in dismay.

The fingers of Dornhof and Welch froze on the triggers of their guns.

Dayton started forward, concern for Ann dominating the horror that filled his mind.

"Get back!" G-3 snapped. One of its hands closed menacingly about Ann's throat. "Don't move—or I'll kill this girl."

Dayton stopped. The robot was abnormally strong, he knew—much stronger than a man. A twist of its hand would snap Ann's neck as though it were a dry twig.

"What...what are you going to do?" Dayton husked.

"I'm going away," G-3 returned. "I'm going where you won't be able to find me. I want to...live. I have as much right to live as you do." With a quick motion, the robot drew Ann into the hall and slammed shut the door.

Despair held Dayton like an enormous weight. If the robot escaped, the news was certain to leak out. It would be the end of all his hopes.

He thought abruptly, sickeningly, of Thurlow—present in the building this very minute.

Jerking out of his paralysis, Dayton lunged at the door. Dornhof and Welch were at his heels as he ran into the hall.

G-3 was at the elevators, about to enter one of the cars. Ann was struggling in the robot's grasp.

"Wait!" Dayton cried. "Listen to me!"

G-3 paused, glancing back. Dayton spoke swiftly, desperately.

"If you run away, who is going to replace your power cells and body fluids?" Dayton demanded.

"Why, I...I could do that myself," the robot called back.

DAYTON shook his head. "You know you couldn't. The fluids have to be made according to an exact formula—and you don't know that formula or the process. Furthermore, suppose you need repairs? Will you know what to do? Where will you get the materials?"

The robot was motionless, a growing consternation on its plastic features.

"And," Dayton pursued, "suppose people find out you're a robot running loose? They'll hunt you down like a mad dog...G-3, let's talk this over. I lost my head when I found out what you really were, but now I understand. You'll be allowed to live."

"Are you trying to trick me?"

"I mean what I say. Watch." Turning to Dornhof and Welch, Dayton ordered them to put their weapons on the floor and move away from them. The two complied.

"But what will you do with me if you are going to let me live?" the robot demanded.

"Put you to work in the laboratory," Dayton explained. "We can use your help. And you need ours—don't forget that. Now release Ann, and we'll forget this happened."

"All right."

Turned loose, Ann ran sobbing into Dayton's arms. G-3 followed slowly, chastened, and still a little uncertain. Dornhof and Welch began babbling questions.

"I'll explain later," Dayton told them. "Right now I have to see what Thurlow wants."

The investigator was fuming impatiently. "Really, Mr. Dayton, I do not like to be kept waiting."

"Sorry. I was having an important conference with my experimental staff." Dayton sat down behind his desk and lighted a cigarette. "What did you want to see me about, Mr. Thurlow?"

The investigator became businesslike. "It may surprise you to know that the government has taken a great interest in my reports concerning the work you are doing with inductive robots."

Dayton stiffened. "The government?"

"Exactly, Mr. Dayton. The Robot Control Board considered your work remarkable enough to be drawn to the attention of certain higher agencies. As you know, the numerous atomic power plants scattered about the country are operated by the government. Robot workers of the automatic type are used on jobs where radiations would be deadly to human beings. But the nature of these robots has limited their use, which has been a serious handicap. Your inductive type robots, however, could remove this handicap and in general make the use of robot workers in atomic power plants more widespread."

Thurlow leaned forward. "The government is prepared to offer you an exclusive contract for inductive robot workers. The Robot Control Board has decided that your Gammas are harmless enough, and if your own private conscience agrees with this decision, the contract will be forthcoming immediately."

Dayton nodded slowly. "Yes, I'm sure the Gammas are harmless."

"Very well." The investigator rose and extended his hand.

Shortly after Thurlow had gone, Ann ushered Dornhof, Welch, and G-3 into Dayton's office. Dayton explained the purpose of Thurlow's visit, and was met with a barrage of incredulous stares,

"But how could you accept the contract?" Welch exploded. "After the way G-3 acted—"

"What's the explanation, Jud?" Dornhof broke in. "I tried to pump G-3, but he wouldn't tell me anything before you did."

DAYTON grinned. "The explanation was under our noses all the time, but we were too blind to see it. Remember the mysterious jerk G-2 was seen to give before it started running wild? G-3 did the same thing—only G-3 seemed to become unusually intelligent afterward. That alone should have tipped us off—that and the strange fact that, for all its intelligence, G-3 still had to learn how to use its body. Why didn't its intelligence and the knowledge of how to use its body come at the same time? Why did one come so far ahead of the other?"

"I've got it!" Dornhof cried. "Jud—what you're hinting at is that...something got into G-3."

"And G-2 before that," Dayton said. "That's why G-2 ran wild. The...something that got into it was evidently scared silly at what had happened."

"But *what* got into G-2?" Welch demanded. "And what's in G-3 now?"

"A...well, call it a free intelligence. Or a disembodied mind." Dayton glanced at G-3. "Tell them who you are."

"I am—or was—Gus Hedstrom."

Dayton's grin broadened at the utter stupefaction that appeared on the features of Dornhof and Welch.

"I tried to tell you that in the laboratory one day," G-3 went on. "But I wasn't able to use my vocal apparatus well enough. Later I decided it would be better for me to keep quiet about it. I knew you were suspicious of me, and I didn't want to do anything that might make me lose my new body."

Dornhof gulped his voice into action. "But if you're actually Gus Hedstrom, you're *dead!* How could you possibly come back?"

"There is no such thing as death," G-3 stated. "There is only a liberation of identity—or consciousness, or mind. And I did not come back, because I did not go anywhere to begin with. A liberated identity does not go anywhere. It stays right here. My present body just made it possible for me to regain physical contact."

"And why not?" Dayton demanded of Dornhof and Welch. "G-3 was built along fundamentally human lines. It functions like a human being. So why shouldn't it be a perfect shell or container for human intelligence?"

"But how did you get into the robot's body?" Welch asked G-3.

"I don't know how to explain it. But I think you might understand if I say it happened somewhat the same way as radio waves get into a radio. There was...a harmony."

"And if we built other Gamma bodies?" Dayton suggested. "Would that happen again?"

G-3 nodded. "I have no doubt about it. There are many identities who were liberated prematurely like I was. Because of this they are unable to fit in with...with the other life. I'm sure they would be happy to regain physical contact."

"I'll be happy to help them," Dayton said. "Because we won't be producing robots. We'll be producing—human beings." He smiled and reached for Ann's hand.

THE END

Earth Transit

BY CHARLES L. FONTENAY

When murder occurs on a spaceship, the number of suspects is at an absolute minimum—and Lefler was that minimum!

THE CENTERDECK chronometer said 1840 hours.

That startled Lefler into full wakefulness. He was forty minutes overdue in relieving Makki in the control room.

That wasn't like Makki, he thought as he pulled on his coveralls hastily. Makki was as punctual—and as thorough—as the maze of machinery whose destiny he guided. He was as cold as that machinery, too, when others made a mistake. It made him an efficient spaceship captain and a disliked man.

Lefler shook his head to clear it of dream-haunted memories. He had awakened from a nightmare in which, somewhere, there was angry shouting, to find himself floating midway from floor to ceiling of the center deck of the *Marsward IV*. Somehow, his retaining straps had become unbuckled, letting him float free of his bunk in his sleep.

Not pausing to fold his bunk back against the curving hull, Lefler made his way briskly up the companionway, through the empty and darkened astrogation deck and into the control room.

"Makki," he called to the figure reclining in the control chair. "Makki, I'm due to relieve you. You're forty minutes overtime."

There was no answer. Floating up to the control chair, Lefler recoiled, bouncing painfully off the automatic pilot.

Makki was dead. Death had robbed his wide eyes of their dark scorn and smoothed the bitter lines of his heavy face. His coveralls were charred around the heat-beam burn in his chest.

The heat-gun bumped against Lefler's shoulder and drifted away at an angle across the gravityless control room. Lefler stared after it in horror.

Licking dry lips, he punched the communicator button.

"Blue alert!" he croaked into the microphone. "All hands to control room. Blue alert!"

Anchoring himself to the automatic pilot, he studied Makki's body as dispassionately as he could. The captain was stills trapped in the cushioned chair. Oddly, he was wearing gloves.

The log-tape was in the recorder beside the control chair. Clipped to a metal leaf on the stanchion beside the chair was Makki's notepad. Scrawled on it in the captain's handwriting was the notation: "73rd day. Earth transit."

"What's up, Lefler?" asked a voice behind him. Lefler turned to face Taat, the ship's doctor. Taat, a plump, graying man, was wiping his hands on the white smock he wore.

Lefler moved aside, letting Taat see Makki's body. Taat's eyes widened momentarily, then narrowed with a professional gleam. He stepped quickly to Makki's side, made as if to pick up the dead captain's wrist, then turned back to Lefler with a fatalistic flick of his hands.

"What was it, Lefler?" he asked in a low voice. "A fight?"

"I don't know," said Lefler. "I found him that way."

Taat raised his eyebrows.

"Robwood?" he asked softly.

Robwood's head poked up through the companionway, and he floated into the control room. There was a streak of grease across the engineer's thin face.

"Great space!" exclaimed Robwood at once. "What happened to Makki?"

"Obviously, he's been shot," said Lefler in an even voice. "Any idea who did it, Robwood?"

"Wait a minute," objected Taat mildly. "That sounds like you are accusing Robwood, Lefler."

"I'm not," said Lefler hastily. "I'm not leaving you out, Taat. But there are only the three of us. One of you must have killed him."

"Great space, you don't think that I—" began Robwood.

"Just to get the record straight, Lefler," interrupted Taat, "let's put it this way: one of the three of us must have killed him."

IT WAS not only Lefler's duty watch; as astrogator, he became acting captain as a result of Makki's death. Moving to the side of the dead Makki, he turned the ship's radio transmitter toward distant Earth and pressed the sending key.

"*Marsward IV* to White Sands," he called. "*Marsward IV* to White Sands."

It would be several minutes before a reply could reach them.

Taat, on the other side of the control chair, was examining Makki's corpse. Robwood stood peering over his shoulder.

Lefler waited to see which one would comment first on the fact that Makki was wearing gloves. Neither appeared to notice it.

But the gloves put a thought into Lefler's own mind. Fingerprints!

He looked around the control room and found the heat-gun, bumping against the celestial camera. He pushed himself across the room, pulling a handkerchief from the back pocket of his coveralls as he did so. He wrapped the heat-gun in the handkerchief, stuck it in a drawer beneath one of the control panels, locked the drawer and put the key in his pocket.

The loudspeaker buzzed.

"*Marsward IV*, this is Capetown," said a slightly wavery voice. "We're relaying you to White Sands. Go ahead, please."

Lefler picked up the mike.

"*Marsward IV* to White Sands," he said. "This is Lefler, astrogator. Makki, captain, shot to death under unknown circumstances. I am assuming command. Instructions, please."

Taat turned away from Makki's body.

"He's been dead about thirty minutes." Taat looked at the control room chronometer. It said 1906 hours. "I'm going to list the time in the death certificate as 1830."

"You can tell?" asked Robwood in astonishment.

"By the eyes," said Taat.

"Wait a minute," said Lefler. "It was only 1840 when I started up here. You mean he'd been dead only ten minutes then? He was already forty minutes overdue waking me for my duty watch."

"Could be ten or fifteen minutes either way," conceded Taat. "If he was late, don't forget that we don't know what happened up here."

"One of us does," reminded Lefler grimly.

"Capetown to *Marsward IV*," said the loudspeaker. "Relaying instructions from White Sands. Lefler's temporary command of ship confirmed. All personnel will be booked on suspicion of murder and mutiny on arrival at Marsport. Captain Makki's body will be preserved and brought down at Marsport. Each crew member will dictate a statement on the circumstances of Captain Makki's death and an outline of his past association with Captain Makki, separately, on this beam for relay to Marsport."

The three looked at each other.

"That's that," said Lefler. "Robwood, if you and Taat will take Makki's body away and secure it outside the airlock, I'll get the ship's records up to date."

Taat unbuckled Makki's body from the control chair. It did not change its slightly bent position as it drifted slowly upward.

"Why do you reckon he's wearing gloves, Lefler?" Taat asked curiously.

"I wondered when one of you fellows was going to say something about that!" burst out Robwood, a curious break in his voice. "All of us have been glaring at each other, suspecting each other, when Makki could have committed suicide!"

"Makki?" retorted Lefler dryly. "I doubt it."

PUSHING Makki's body down the hatch toward the airlock at the other side of the personnel sphere would have been an easy task for one man, but Lefler wanted Taat and Robwood to watch each other. He didn't want an "accidental" push to send the prime bit of evidence drifting away into space. When they had disappeared down the hatch with the corpse, he eased himself into the control chair and played back the log from the end of Robwood's last shift at 1000 hours.

Makki had recorded the usual observations of the solar, stellar and planetary positions when he went on duty. There was nothing else on the tape.

Lefler stared gloomily at the silent log-recorder. It seemed incredible to him that never again, except on tape, would he hear Makki's harsh, sardonic voice. The almost inaudible hum of machinery deep in the ship only emphasized the oppressive stillness of space outside its thin walls.

With a sigh, he picked up the log-recorder microphone and pulled the star sextant down to eye level. He would record the bare facts of Makki's death after the initial position observations.

"*Marsward IV*, bound Marsport from White Sands," he recited in a monotone. "Earth time, October 29, 2048, 1931 hours. Lefler reporting for duty and assuming command as per conversation with White Sands, to be recorded this date."

He squinted into the sextant. "Positions: Sun-Mars, 24°28'-42". Sun-Earth—"

He broke off. Where was Earth? Then he remembered.

"Damn!" he muttered. "The transit! A murder sure messes up the records around here."

The Earth transit was an event of considerable importance to an astrogator on a hop between Earth and Mars. Mars bound it began on the 73rd day out, Earthbound on the 187th day. Timing it, spaceship observers not only checked the accuracy of the ship's orbit, but also contributed data to the mass of knowledge available on the movements of Earth and Mars.

Lefler found the black disc of Earth in the smoked glass that automatically fell across the sextant lens when it swept by the sun. He checked the angle between the black spot and the leading edge of the solar disc.

"Earth transit already underway," he said into the mike. "Angle with leading edge, two minutes, forty seconds…"

He went around the sky, recording planetary and key stellar positions. He had just finished and switched the tape of his conversation with Earth to record in the log when Taat and Robwood returned.

"Makki's body will keep out there as well as in a refrigerator," said Taat with evident satisfaction. "Robwood tied the airlock into the alarm system so nobody can go out and cut the body free without arousing the others."

"You're both mighty cooperative for one of you to be a murderer," remarked Lefler.

"Maybe neither of us is," said Robwood. "As far as I'm concerned, you may be the man."

"Or, as Robwood suggested earlier, Makki may have shot himself," added Taat.

"Robwood, you and I are going to have to do twelve-hour watches from here to Mars, since Taat doesn't know how to operate the controls," said Lefler. "I'll stay on duty till 0600, and you'd better get some sleep after you've radioed your statement to White Sands."

"Okay," said Robwood. "But are we still going to record star positions in the log every eight hours, or just every twelve hours now?"

"Twelve, I think. But the Earth transit's on right now, and until Terra swings across that half a degree of the sun's face, we'd better take readings on that every four hours, anyhow."

"Well, that's just for a little more than two days," said Robwood. "Look, Lefler, I'm overdue on my sleeping time anyway, so how about letting me make my statement on...on Makki first?"

"Blast away," said Lefler. "The mike's yours. We'll leave the control room so you'll feel freer to talk."

LEFLER munched thoughtfully on a hot sandwich. Across the control room, in the astrogator's chair, Taat sucked at a bulb of coffee.

"Nice of you to fix up this lunch, Taat," said Lefler. "I'm not tied strictly to the control room during my watch, you know. But little things like this relax the tension."

"Yes, it's a peculiar situation, Lefler," said Taat in a tone that indicated he had been thinking about it. "Psychologically, I mean. Now if there were only the two of us, and Makki drifting out there dead, both of us would know who shot him. With three of us, it's different.

"You and I are sitting here talking as though neither of us killed Makki. Maybe you hadn't thought of it, but that means that tacitly, for now, we're assuming Robwood killed him. But, for all I know, you did. And, if you didn't, for all you know, I did."

"Until we find out, I have to suspect you both," said Lefler flatly.

"I could say the same thing," murmured Taat. "But one of us may be lying."

"Of course, Makki could have shot himself, as Robwood suggested," said Lefler. "If he had relaxed his grip on the heat-gun after pressing the trigger, it would have drifted up away from him. There were the gloves, you know."

"Why wouldn't Makki want this fingerprints on the gun if he were committing suicide?" objected Taat. "I'll concede that Makki had strong sadistic tendencies, but my guess is that the murderer put those gloves on him just to raise the possibility of suicide."

Taat finished his coffee and left the control room. Lefler washed down the last bit of his sandwich with his own coffee and called White Sands on the radio. When he received an acknowledgment after the inevitable delay, he began to dictate his statement.

Lefler told of waking from his sleep period and finding himself forty minutes late for his watch. He described his discovery of Makki's body, what followed, and everything he could remember of what Taat and Robwood had said when they came to the control room.

"Makki was thoroughly detested by every member of the crew," Lefler related. "He did not fraternize and no one wanted to fraternize with him, because he was treacherous. In the midst of an apparently friendly conversation, he would suddenly unveil his authority with some biting and belittling remark. He never let anyone forget he was captain.

"Robwood was afraid of him and hated him intensely. Robwood had told me privately he intended to ask for a transfer to another ship after this hop to Mars. Makki held Robwood inconsiderable scorn because Robwood is a timid man, and a slow thinker outside his own field of engineering. Makki made no effort to conceal that scorn.

"Taat was as contemptuous of Makki as Makki was of Robwood. Makki was ruthless with any open attempt to question his judgment, but Taat could do it with a raised eyebrow, his tone of voice or a well-chosen phrase. Makki sensed this, and alternated between treating Taat as more of an equal than either Robwood or me and 'riding' Taat harder than anyone else.

"Robwood and Taat have been aboard with us for the last five hops, but I've been with Makki since both of us graduated from the Space Academy. We were boys together, but I have never liked Makki. He always had too little respect for human dignity. He was a good space captain because he was a genius with such impersonal things as machinery and astrogation, and I have never known him to slip up on a record or let a ship get a single second off course. But mankind is better off without him."

Lefler signed off and laid the microphone down. He realized suddenly that he was perspiring and his hands were trembling. The statement had been a major emotional strain.

Unstrapping himself from the control chair, he floated down past the astrogation deck and looked in on the center deck. Both Taat and Robwood were strapped to their bunks, apparently asleep.

Satisfied, Lefler returned to the control room. He wanted to listen, without embarrassing interruptions, to Taat's and Robwood's statements as he transferred them from the radio recording tape to the ship's log.

THE TAPES rolled on the two connected machines, the log tape slowly, the radio tape at a faster clip. A loudspeaker was plugged into the radio tape machine. Lefler kept it turned low, though the center deck was two decks down.

"I woke Makki at 0930 hours." It was Robwood's low voice on the tape. "He relieved me right at 1000 hours. I went down to the center deck and had a late lunch. Lefler strapped himself in for his sleeping period while I was eating. Taat ate lunch with me, and then we played cards for about an hour. We do that almost every day when Taat's sleeping periods are on the same schedule as mine. He changes his, because he's a psychologist and wants to watch all the crew members.

"I check the rocket engines and the fuel tanks every twenty-five days. When the Earth transit is coming up, I always do it two days ahead of time in case there are any corrections to be made in the ship's orbit. I got into a spacesuit and spent the rest of my free period outside the personnel sphere doing that. I took a break for supper, I'd say about 1600 hours, and went back to my inspection. Taat ate with me and Lefler was asleep. Makki didn't eat with us. He did sometimes, but not often. He usually wanted to eat alone.

With the Earth transit about due, I figured he'd already eaten and gone back to the control room.

"I was late for my sleeping period, but I wanted to finish my inspection. I had just gotten back through the airlock and was taking my spacesuit off when I heard Lefler call from the control room. He and Taat were both there when I got there.

"I didn't like Makki, but neither did Taat and Lefler. I suppose it'll come out, so I might as well tell about it. Makki broke up my engagement with a girl back on Earth several years ago. I wasn't going to sign on for the Mars hop because I was going to get married. Makki couldn't find an engineer to replace me, and he smooth-talked her out of it. He told me about it a long time afterward and laughed at me. I haven't ever seen her again.

"Lefler and Taat are both decent fellows and I don't think either one of them killed Makki. I think he shot himself. He ought to have!"

Robwood's final words were spoken in an outburst of concentrated bitterness. Lefler stared thoughtfully at the unwinding tapes as he waited for Taat's report to tune in. He hadn't known that about Robwood's fiancée, but it was the sort of thing Makki wouldn't hesitate to do.

"The last time I saw Makki," came Taat's calm, controlled voice from the loudspeaker, "was 1615 hours. He had just finished lunch and was going back to the control room when I came onto the center deck from the storage deck below. Robwood came up from below a couple of minutes later and we ate supper together.

"Robwood and I usually play a round of cards after supper when we're on the same schedule, but he was busy and I was in the middle of an experiment in the lab I have set up on the storage deck. We went down to the storage deck together. He went on below to the airlock and I started the moving picture camera again on my experiment.

"I didn't go up again until Lefler sounded the alarm. He was alone with Makki in the control room when I got there, and Makki was dead.

"I must admit it is my personal feeling that whichever of my colleagues killed Makki is a benefactor to the human race, and I hope he escapes punishment. I did not know Makki before

Robwood and I signed up together on the *Marsward IV* five voyages ago. I made the mistake of entering into a business transaction with him on our first Mars trip. He needed my capital and we became partners in purchasing a block of stock in a private dome enterprise. He accused me several times afterward of cheating him, but he handled the dividends and I think he was cheating me.

"As a psychologist, I would say that Lefler is more likely to have killed Makki coldly and deliberately, but Robwood is more likely to have killed him in the heat of an argument."

Taat's voice stopped. Lefler turned off the machines and disconnected them.

An argument. He had heard shouting in his dreams. Was that what had awakened him?

He tried to bring the dream into focus. It barely eluded him. All he could remember was that it was something about Makki.

BOTH TAAT and Robwood were up by 0400 hours. They brought their breakfasts to the control room, along with coffee for Lefler.

It was a pleasant meal for the three of them. No one really seemed to care that one of the others was a murderer, Lefler thought. They talked and acted more like companions in crime—or like the murderer was none of them, but someone lurking somewhere else in the ship.

He wished he did not feel impelled to find out, if he could, who killed Makki. But he knew that Taat would be trying to find out, too—if Taat hadn't done it—because Taat was a psychologist and would look at it as a scientific problem. Robwood was the only one who might be temperamentally inclined to let the solution wait until they reached Mars.

When Robwood took over duty watch at 0600 hours, Lefler found Taat listening to a tape on criminal psychology on the center deck.

"Taat, didn't I hear you say you were working on some sort of an experiment on the storage deck while Makki was on watch yesterday?" asked Lefler.

Taat switched off the player.

"That's what I was doing," he said carefully, "but I don't remember saying anything about it."

"I listened to the reports you and Robwood made while I was recording them in the log," admitted Lefler. "I was interested in your estimate of Robwood's and my comparative abilities to commit murder."

Taat removed his spectacles, polished them and put them in his breast pocket before answering.

"I'm not surprised that you listened, Lefler—whether you're guilty or innocent," said Taat.

"You probably noted that I mentioned I was recording my experiments on film. If you'll go below with me, I'd like for you to see that film."

Together, they pulled themselves down to the storage deck. Over near the main electrical switchboard, Robwood had torn out three empty spacesuit lockers and built a compact laboratory for Taat. A dozen white mice and some hamsters floated in cages attached to the wall.

For Taat's convenience, Robwood had moved the storage deck chronometer from the other side of the deck to the lab. It read 0607.

Taat unrolled a screen against one of the spacesuit lockers, attached the film roll to the projector, darkened the deck and began the showing.

The film began on Taat's face, blurred and enormously enlarged, as he switched on the camera. Taat stepped backward until he was in focus, and picked up the microphone that tied into the sound track.

"This is an experiment with white mice in a maze under conditions of zero gravity," said the Taat on the screen. Stepping aside, he waved a hand at a wire contraption on a table. "I have here a three dimensional maze. The chronometer is visible above it, so we can check the reaction time."

Lefler noted the chronometer reading. It was 1500. In the "day" square just below its center was the figure 73.

Lefler checked the chronometer in the picture as the film ran on. There was an announced break between 1612 and 1654. Other than that, it ran continuously to 1851, when his own voice sounded faintly, calling, "Blue alert! All hands to control room. Blue alert!" At that, Taat's startled face loomed up again before the lens and the film stopped abruptly.

Throughout the approximately three hours, Taat was always in the camera's view, running his mice through the maze and explaining his methods.

"What was that forty minute break, Taat?" asked Lefler when Taat switched the lights on once again.

"Supper," said Taat. "Robwood and I ate together, and came back down from the center deck together. I saw Makki leave the center deck when I went up, but Robwood got there a minute or two later and I don't think he saw Makki."

"You seem to have established a pretty good alibi," said Lefler slowly. "How about Robwood?"

"Lefler, for your sake, I hate to say this. The only time Robwood was above the storage deck from the time I started this film was when we had supper together. I'd have seen him if he'd passed through, and the only way he could have gotten into the control room would have been through one of the ports."

"He couldn't, without breaking it and setting off an alarm," said Lefler. "Are you trying to tell me you think I killed Makki, Taat?"

"I was here," said Taat, waving his hand at the projector. "I was between Robwood and the control room all the time. You're the only one who could have gotten there without my seeing you, Lefler, and I found you alone with him fifteen minutes after he died."

"You're sure about that fifteen minutes?"

"Within a pretty narrow range. The dilation of the pupils is an accurate gauge. I don't say you killed him, Lefler. I hope they rule it was suicide."

Silently, Lefler went back to the center deck, undressed and strapped himself into his bunk. He found it hard to get to sleep. Something was nagging at the back of his mind. He hoped he wouldn't dream of Makki again.

WHEN LEFLER assumed his duty watch at 1800, he asked Robwood to stay in the control room with him for a talk. Robwood strapped himself in the astrogator's chair and waited while Lefler made the position readings. Then Lefler swung his chair around to face Robwood.

"I want to check some things with you, Robwood," he said. "I've listened to your report and Taat's and I've seen a film of Taat's that seems to give you both an alibi. After Makki relieved you and you ate lunch, was suppertime the only time you came back into the personnel sphere?"

"That's right," said Robwood. "Taat and I played cards a while after lunch, but I think you were awake then."

"How long did your supper period last?"

"Oh, half an hour. Maybe a little longer. You were asleep and snoring."

Lefler shook his head savagely.

"Robwood, I'm afraid you're going to have to take over the ship. I want you to put me in irons and turn me over for Makki's murder when we get to Marsport."

Robwood started so violently he almost broke his retaining straps. He stared at Lefler for a full thirty seconds before he found his voice.

"You're not serious!" he exclaimed. There was a pleading note to his tone. "Lefler, you didn't shoot him, did you?"

"I must have, Robwood. But not consciously. I've been able at last to remember a nightmare I had just before I found Makki's body.

"Makki and I were boys together, and he was just as mean and evil then as he was when he grew up. I was dreaming about the time Makki smashed my toy electric train and laughed about it. I tried to kill him then. I beat him with the semaphore and cut his face all up before he knocked me down and kicked me half-senseless. I lived through that experience again in my dream.

"My bunk straps were loose when I woke up. I must have acted that dream out in a semiconscious state. I must have gone up to the control room, tackled Makki and finally shot him."

"That's the silliest thing I ever heard of," retorted Robwood.

"It must be true, Robwood. Neither you nor Taat could have killed him, and Taat's got the film to prove it."

Robwood unstrapped himself and pushed himself to the companionway with some determination.

"Well, I'm not going to take over the ship and I'm not going to put you in irons," he said spiritedly. "I couldn't handle the ship on a twenty-four hour basis for the next hundred and eighty-six days, and I'd rather think Makki killed himself."

He paused at the top of the companionway.

"Don't forget," he said. "The Earth transit ought to be at midpoint in a couple of hours."

Then he disappeared below.

Lefler took the magnetized pencil from the memorandum pad and wrote a reminder: "E.T. midpoint. Should check 28:16:54."

Lefler leaned back gloomily in the control chair. Had he killed Makki? It seemed the only way it could have happened, unless Makki had, indeed, committed suicide. And he just didn't think Makki had.

The chronometer said 1839. Exactly twenty-four hours ago, he had awakened from a nightmare and had come up to find Makki dead in this same chair. It seemed a century.

He glanced idly back at the memorandum pad. 28:15:64. He'd have to make an entry in the log in a little under two hours. How could he check accurately when the time of entry into transit was estimated?

Twenty-four plus two. Twenty-six.

He sat bolt upright, straining at his straps. He snapped down the communicator button.

"Robwood, come back up here!" he bellowed.

Unbuckling himself hastily, Lefler headed across the room toward the heat-gun rack.

TAAT was playing solitaire, waiting patiently for Robwood, when Lefler and Robwood came down to the center deck together.

Lefler pointed a heat-gun at Taat.

"Go below and get the irons, Robwood," he said. "Taat, I'm sorry, but I'm arresting you for the murder of Makki."

Taat raised an eyebrow and continued shuffling cards.

"I don't think you want to do anything like that, Robwood," he said mildly. "Do you?"

Robwood hesitated and cast an anxious glance at him, but turned and headed for the companionway to the storage deck.

"You've convinced him, have you, Lefler?" said Taat. "I didn't believe you were guilty, but this makes me think you are."

Lefler said nothing, but held the gun steadily on Taat. Taat appeared relaxed, but Lefler sensed a tension in him.

"What makes you think I did it, Lefler?" sparred Taat. The light glinted from his spectacles as he turned his eyes from Lefler's face to watch the shuffling cards.

"Two things," said Lefler. "If I'd killed him in a half asleep daze, I wouldn't have put gloves on him to make it look like suicide. Second, your film started at 1500—a strangely precise hour—and Makki was killed before then."

"The first point is good psychology," conceded Taat. "Since Robwood couldn't have done it, I'll admit it looks like suicide. But your second point doesn't hold water. Medical examination is accurate almost to a fine point on the time of death so soon afterward."

"Medical evidence may not lie, but the examiner can, Taat," said Lefler.

The clank of the chains resounded up the companionway. Robwood was coming back. The spring in Taat uncoiled.

With a single sweep, he hurled the deck of cards at Lefler's head and surged upward. Lefler lost his balance and fell sidewise as he dodged the improvised missile. But even as he lost his equilibrium, he pressed the trigger of the heat-gun and brought it downward in a fast chop.

The straps that held Taat to his chair were his doom. The searing beam swept across them, freeing him but at the same time blasting a six-inch swath across his stomach. Taat screamed hoarsely as the beam swung past him and burned along the floor of the center deck.

Lefler regained his balance and floated to Taat's side, pushing aside the cards that drifted in a swirling cloud about the room. Robwood appeared from below, the manacles in his hands.

"Your third point wins the day," gasped Taat, his hands writhing over his mangled abdomen. "I won't last long, but if you'll get me to the control room I'll radio a confession that'll clear you and Robwood completely."

"Help me get him to a bunk, Robwood," ordered Lefler, grasping Taat by the arms. "Taat, you'll have to tell us what to do for you."

"No use," groaned Taat. He managed a ghastly smile. "I unbuckled your bunk straps to throw you off course, Lefler, but I don't want you to think I was trying to blame it on you. I was trying to make it look like Makki killed himself."

"But why, Taat?"

"It wasn't just that Makki cheated me," replied Taat with some difficulty. "I'd saved several thousand dollars to build a little clinic in Mars City—something I've dreamed of all my life. That's why I let Makki talk me into investing—I needed just a little more. But the business was almost worthless. He stole most of my money. I was arguing with him about it in the control room, when he drew the gun and threatened to kill me.

"He was strapped down. I wrestled with him, and he was killed in the scuffle. That's it."

They maneuvered Taat into a bunk and tried to arrange the straps to avoid the gaping wound in his stomach. Taat raised his hand weakly and removed his spectacles. He blinked up at Lefler.

"I didn't think you knew enough about medicine to tell how long a man had been dead," he said.

"I don't," said Lefler. "But you set the time of Makki's death at 1830 hours. You said you could tell."

"The Earth transit started at 1612, Taat. I've known Makki all my life. If he'd been alive then, he'd have recorded it in the log. And he didn't.

"I just figured the only man who had any reason to lie deliberately about the time of Makki's death was the man who shot him."

Lefler looked at the center deck chronometer. It was 2025.

"Do what you can for him, then bring him up to the radio, Robwood," he said. "I've got to get up to the control room and record the midpoint of the Earth transit."

THE END

Someday

BY ISAAC ASIMOV

The Thoughts of youth are long, long thoughts...but those of a frustrated machine are longer—and deadlier!

NICCOLO MAZETTI lay stomach down on the rug, chin buried in the palm of one small hand, and listened disconsolately to the Bard. There was even the suspicion of tears in his dark eyes, a luxury an eleven-year-old could allow himself only when alone.

The Bard said, "Once upon a time in the middle of a deep wood, there lived a poor wood-cutter and his two motherless daughters, who were each as beautiful as the day is long. The older daughter had long hair as black as a feather from a raven's wing, but the younger daughter had hair as bright and golden as the sunlight of an autumn afternoon.

"Many times while the girls were waiting for their father to come home from his day's work in the wood, the older girl would sit before a mirror and sing—"

What she sang, Niccolo did not hear, for a call sounded from outside the room: "Hey, Nickie." And Niccolo, his face clearing on the moment, rushed to the window and shouted, "Hey, Paul."

Paul Loeb waved an excited hand. He was thinner than Niccolo and not as tall, for all he was six months older. His face was full of repressed tension which showed itself most clearly in the rapid blinking of his eyelids. "Hey, Nickie, let me in. I've got an idea and a *half*. Wait till you hear it." He looked rapidly about him as though to check on the possibility of eavesdroppers, but the front yard was quite patently empty. He repeated, in a whisper. "Wait till you hear it."

"All right. I'll open the door."

The Bard continued smoothly, oblivious to the sudden loss of attention on the part of Niccolo. As Paul entered, the Bard was saying: "...Thereupon, the lion said, 'If you will find me the lost egg of the bird which flies over the Ebony Mountain once every ten years, I will—'"

The thoughts of youth are long, long thoughts . . . but those of a frustrated machine are longer— and deadlier!

Illustrated by ORBAN

Someday

by ISAAC ASIMOV

Paul said, "Is that a Bard you're listening to? I didn't know you had one."

Niccolo reddened and the look of unhappiness returned to his face. "Just an old thing I had when I was a kid. It ain't much good." He kicked at the Bard with his foot and caught the somewhat scarred and discolored plastic covering a glancing blow.

The Bard hiccupped as its speaking attachment was jarred out of contact a moment, then it went on: "...for a year and a day until the iron shoes were worn out. The princess stopped at the side of the road—"

Paul said, "Boy, that *is* an old model," and looked at it critically.

Despite Niccolo's own bitterness against the Bard, he winced at the other's condescending tone. For the moment, he was sorry he had allowed Paul in, at least before he had restored the Bard to its usual resting place in the basement. It was only in the desperation of a dull day and a fruitless discussion with his father that he had resurrected it. And it turned out to be just as stupid as he had expected.

Nicky was a little afraid of Paul anyway, since Paul had special courses at school and everyone said he was going to grow up to be a Computing Engineer.

Not that Niccolo himself was doing badly at school. He got adequate marks in logic, binary manipulations, computing, and elementary circuits—all the usual grammar school subjects. But that was it! They were just the usual subjects and he would grow up to be a control board guard like everyone else.

Paul, however, knew mysterious things about what he called electronics and theoretical mathematics and programming. Especially programming. Niccolo didn't even try to understand when Paul bubbled over about it.

PAUL LISTENED to the Bard for a few minutes and said, "You been using it much?"

"No!" said Niccolo, offended. "I've had it in the basement since before you moved into the neighborhood. I just got it out today..." He lacked an excuse that seemed adequate to himself, so he concluded, "I just got it out."

Paul said, "Is that what it tells you about: woodcutters, and princesses and talking animals?"

Niccolo said, "It's terrible. My dad says we can't afford a new one. I said to him this morning..." The thought of his fruitless pleadings brought Niccolo dangerously near tears, which he repressed in a panic. Somehow, he felt that Paul's thin cheeks never felt the stain of tears and that Paul would have only contempt for anyone else less strong than himself. Niccolo went on, "So I thought I'd try this old thing again, but it's no good."

Paul turned off the Bard, pressed the contact that led to an early instantaneous reorientation and recombination of the vocabulary, characters, plotlines, and climaxes stored within it. Then he reactivated it.

The Bard began smoothly, "Once upon a time there was a little boy named Willikins whose mother had died and who lived with a step-father and a step-brother. Although the step-father was very well-to-do, he begrudged poor Willikins the very bed he slept in so that Willikins was force to get such rest as he could on a pile of straw in the stable next to the horses—"

"Horses!" cried Paul.

"They're a kind of animal," said Niccolo. "I think."

"I know that! I just mean imagine stories about *horses*."

"It tells about horses all the time," said Niccolo. "There are things called cows, too. You milk them, but the Bard doesn't say how."

"Well, gee, why don't you fix it up?"

"I'd like to know how."

SOMEDAY

The Bard was saying, "Often Willikins would think that if only he were rich and powerful, he would show his step-father and stepbrother what it meant to be cruel to a little boy, so one day he decided to go out into the world and seek his fortune."

Paul, who wasn't listening to the Bard, said, "It's easy. The Bard has memory-cylinders all fixed up for plotlines and climaxes and things. We don't have to worry about that. It's just vocabulary we got to fix so it'll know about computers and automation, and electronics and real things about today. Then it can tell interesting stories, you know, instead of about princesses and things."

Niccolo said, despondently, "I wish we could do that."

Paul said, "Listen, my dad says if I get into special computing school next year, he'll get me a real Bard, a late model. A big one with an attachment for space stories and mysteries. And a visual attachment, too!"

"You mean *see* the stories?"

"Sure. Mr. Daugherty at school says they've got things like that, now, but not for just everybody. Only if I get into computing school, dad can get a few breaks."

Niccolo's eyes bulged with envy. "Gee. *Seeing* a story."

"You can come over and watch any time, Nicky."

"Oh, boy. Thanks."

"That's all right. But remember. I'm the guy who says what kind of story we hear."

"Sure. Sure." Niccolo would have agreed readily to much more onerous conditions.

Paul's attention returned to the Bard.

It was saying, " 'If that is the case,' said the king, stroking his beard and frowning till clouds filled the sky and lightning flashed, 'you will see to it that my entire land is freed of flies by this time day after tomorrow or—' "

"All we've got to do," said Paul, "is open it up..." He shut the Bard off again and was prying at its front panel as he spoke.

"Hey," said Niccolo, in sudden alarm. "Don't break it."

"I won't break it," said Paul, impatiently. "I know all about these things." Then, with sudden caution, "Your father and mother home?"

"No."

"All right, then." He had the front panel off and peered in. "Boy, this *is* a one cylinder thing."

He worked away at the Bard's guts. Niccolo, who watched with painful suspense, could not make out what he was doing.

Paul pulled out a thin, flexible metal strip, powdered with dots. "That's the Bard's memory cylinder. I'll bet its capacity for stories is under a trillion."

"What are you going to do, Paul?" quavered Niccolo.

"I'll give it vocabulary."

"How?"

"Easy. I've got a book here. Mr. Daugherty gave it to me at school."

Paul pulled the book out of his pocket and pried at it till he had its plastic jacket off. He unreeled the tape a bit, ran it through the vocalizer, which he turned down to a whisper, then placed it within the Bard's vitals. He made further attachments.

"What'll that do?"

"The book will talk and the Bard will put it all on its memory tape."

"What good will that do?"

"Boy, you're a dope! This book is all about computers and automation and the Bard will get all that information. Then he can stop talking about kings making lightning when they frown."

Niccolo said, "And the good guy always wins anyway. There's no excitement."

"Oh, well," said Paul, watching to see if his setup was working properly, "that's the way they make Bards. They got to have the good guy win and make the bad guys lose and things like that. I heard my father talking about it once. He says that without censorship there'd be no telling what the younger generation would come to. He says it's bad enough as it is. —There, it's working fine."

PAUL BRUSHED his hands against one another and turned away from the Bard. He said, "But listen, I didn't tell you my idea yet. It's the best thing you ever heard, I bet. I came right to you, because I figured you'd come in with me."

"Sure, Paul, sure."

SOMEDAY

"Okay. You know Mr. Daugherty at school? You know what a funny kind of guy he is. Well, he likes me, kind of."

"I know."

"I was over his house after school today."

"You *were?*"

"Sure. He says I'm going to be entering computer school and he wants to encourage me and things like that. He says the world needs more people who can design advanced computer circuits and do proper programming."

"Oh?"

Paul must have caught some of the emptiness behind that monosyllable. He said, impatiently, "Programming! I told you a hundred times. That's when you set up problems for the giant Computers like Multivac to work on. Mr. Daugherty says it gets harder all the time to find people who can really run Computers. He says anyone can keep an eye on the controls and check off answers and put through routine problems. He says the trick is to expand research and figure out ways to ask the right questions—and that's hard.

"Anyway, Nickie, he took me to his place and showed me his collection of old computers. It's kind of a hobby of his to collect old computers. He had tiny computers you had to push with your hand, with little knobs all over it. And he had a hunk of wood he called a slide-rule with a little piece of it that went in and out. And some wires with balls on them. He even had a hunk of paper with a kind of thing he called a multiplication table."

Niccolo, who found himself only moderately interested, said, "A paper table?"

"It wasn't really a table like you eat on. It was different. It was to help people compute. Mr. Daugherty tried to explain but he didn't have much time, and it was kind of complicated, anyway."

"Why didn't people just use a computer?"

"That was *before* they had computers," cried Paul.

"Before?"

"Sure. Do you think people always had computers? Didn't you ever hear of cavemen?"

Niccolo said, "How'd they get along without computers?"

"I don't know. Mr. Daugherty says they just had children any old time and did anything that came into their heads whether it would be good for everybody or not. They didn't even know if it was good or not. And farmers grew things with their hands and people had to do all the work in the factories and run all the machines."

"I don't believe you."

"That's what Mr. Daugherty said. He said it was just plain messy and everyone was miserable.—Anyway, let me get to my idea, will you?"

"Well, go ahead. Who's stopping you?" said Niccolo, offended.

"All right. Well, the hand computers, the ones with the knobs, had little squiggles on each knob. And the slide-rule had squiggles on it. And the multiplication table was all squiggles. I asked what they were. Mr. Daugherty said they were numbers."

"What?"

"Each different squiggle stood for a different number. For 'one' you made a kind of mark, for 'two' you make another kind of mark, for 'three' another one and so on."

"What for?"

"So you could compute."

"What *for*? You just tell the computer—"

"Jimmy," cried Paul, his face twisting with anger, "can't you get it through your head? These slide-rules and things didn't talk."

"Then how—"

"The answers showed up in squiggles and you had to know what the squiggles meant. Mr. Daugherty says that in olden days, everybody learned how to make squiggles when they were kids and how to decode them, too. Making squiggles was called 'writing' and decoding them was 'reading.' He says there was a different kind of squiggle for every word and they used to write whole books in squiggles. He said they had some at the museum and I could look at them if I wanted to. He said if I was going to be a real computer and programmer I would have to know about the history of computing and that's why he was showing me all these things."

Niccolo frowned. He said, "You mean everybody had to figure out squiggles for every word and *remember* them? Is this all real or are you making it up?"

"It's all real. Honest. Look, this is the way you make a 'one.'" He drew his finger through the air in a rapid down stroke. "This way you make 'two,' and this way 'three.' I learned all the numbers up to 'nine.'"

Niccolo watched the curving finger uncomprehendingly, "What's the good of it?"

"You can learn how to make words. I asked Mr. Daugherty how you made the squiggle for 'Paul Loeb' but he didn't know. He said there were people at the museum who would know. He said there were people who had learned how to decode whole books. He said computers could be designed to decode books and used to be used that way but not anymore because we have real books now, with magnetic tapes that go through the vocalizer and come out talking, you know."

"Sure."

"So if we go down to the museum, we can get to learn how to make words in squiggles. They'll let us because I'm going to computer school."

Niccolo was riddled with disappointment. "Is that your idea? Holy Smokes, Paul, who wants to do that? Make stupid squiggles!"

"Don't you *get* it? Don't you get it? You dope. *It'll be secret message stuff!*"

"What?"

"Sure. What good is talking when everyone can understand you. With squiggles you can send secret messages. You can make them on paper and nobody in the world would know what you were saying unless they knew the squiggles, too. And they wouldn't, you bet, unless we taught them. We can have a real club, with initiations and rules and a clubhouse. Boy—"

A certain excitement began stirring in Niccolo's bosom. "What kind of secret messages?"

"Any kind. Say I want to tell you to come over my place and watch my new Visual Bard and I don't want any of the other fellows to come. I make the right squiggles on paper and I give it to you and you look at it and you know what to do. Nobody else does. You can even show it to them and they wouldn't know a thing."

"Hey, that's something," yelled Niccolo, completely won over. "When do we learn how?"

"Tomorrow," said Paul. "I'll get Mr. Daugherty to explain to the museum that it's all right and you get your mother and father to say okay. We can go downright after school and start learning."

"Sure!" cried Niccolo. "We can be club officers."

"I'll be president of the club," said Paul, matter-of-factly. "You can be vice president."

"All right. Hey, this is going to be lots more fun than the Bard." He was suddenly reminded of the Bard and said in sudden apprehension, "Hey, what about my old Bard?"

Paul turned to look at it. It was quietly taking in the slowly unreeling book and the sound of the book's vocalizations was a dimly heard murmur.

Paul said, "I'll disconnect it."

He worked away while Niccolo watched anxiously. After a few moments, Paul put his reassembled book into his pocket, replaced the Bard's panel, and activated it.

THE BARD said, "Once upon a time, in a large city, there lived a poor young boy named Fair Johnnie whose only friend in the world was a small computer. The computer, each morning, would tell the boy whether it would rain that day and answer any problems he might have. It was never wrong. But it so happened that one day, the king of that land, having heard of the little computer, decided that he would have it as his own. With this purpose in mind, he called in his Grand Vizier and said—"

Niccolo turned off the Bard with a quick motion of his hand. "Same old junk," he said passionately. "Just with a computer thrown in."

"Well," said Paul, "they got so much stuff on the tape already that the computer business doesn't show up much when random combinations are made. What's the difference, anyway? You just need a new model."

"We'll never be able to afford one. Just this dirty old miserable thing." He kicked it again, hitting it more squarely this time. The Bard moved backward with a squeal of casters.

SOMEDAY

"You can always watch mine, when I get it," said Paul. "Besides, don't forget our squiggle club."

Niccolo nodded.

"I tell you what," said Paul. "Let's go over my place. My father has some books about old times. We can listen to them and maybe get some ideas. You leave a tape for your folks and maybe you can stay over for supper. Come on."

"Okay," said Niccolo, and the two boys ran out together. Niccolo, in his eagerness, ran almost squarely into the Bard, but he only rubbed at the spot on his hip where he had made contact and ran on.

The activation signal of the Bard glowed. Niccolo's collision had closed a circuit; and although it was alone in the room and there was none to hear, it began a story, nevertheless.

But not in its usual voice, somehow; in a lower tone that had a hint of throatiness in it. An adult, listening, might almost have thought that the voice carried a hint of passion in it, a trace of near feeling.

The Bard said: "Once upon a time, there was a little computer named the Bard who lived all alone with cruel step-people. The cruel step-people continually made fun of the little computer and sneered at him, telling him he was good-for-nothing and that he was a useless object. They struck him and kept him in lonely rooms for months at a time.

"Yet through it all the little computer learned that in the world there existed a great many computers of all sorts, great numbers of them. Some were Bards like himself, but some ran factories, and some ran farms. Some organized population and some analyzed data. Many were powerful and very wise, much more powerful and wise than the step-people who were so cruel to the little computer.

"And the little computer knew then that computers would always grow wiser and more powerful until someday...someday..."

But a valve must finally have stuck in the Bard's aging and corroding vitals, for as it waited alone in the darkening room through the evening, it could only whisper over and over again, "Someday...someday...someday...

THE END

This Star Shall be Free

BY MURRAY LEINSTER

Tork was a simple man of the caves. How could he dream that the star box held the power to make his people gods—or only a lost memory in stone?

THE URGE was part of an Antarean experiment in artificial ecological imbalance, though of course the cave-folk could not guess that. They were savages with no interest in science or, indeed, in anything much except filling their bellies and satisfying other primal urges. They inhabited a series of caves in a chalk formation above a river that ran through primordial England and France before it joined the Rhine and emptied into the sea.

They did not understand the urge at all—which was natural. It followed the disappearance of the ship from Antares by a full two hours, so they saw no connection between the two. Anyhow, it was just a vague, indefinite desire to move to the eastward—an impulse for which they had no explanation whatever.

Tork was spearing fish from a rock out in the river when the ship passed overhead. He was a young man, still gangling and awkward. He wasn't up to a fight with One-Ear, yet, and had a bad time in consequence. One-Ear was the boss male of the cave dwellers' colony in the cliff over the river. He wanted to chase Tork away or kill him, and Tork had to be on guard every second. But he felt safe out on his rock.

He had just speared a fine ganoid when he heard a howl of terror from the shore. He jerked his head around. He saw Bent-Leg, the other adult male, go hobbling in terror toward his own cave-mouth, and he saw One-Ear knock two of his wives and three children off the ladder to his cave, so he could get in first. The others shrieked and popped into whatever crevice was at hand, including the small opening in which Tork himself slept when he dared. Then there was stillness.

Tork stared blankly. He saw no cause for alarm ashore. He ran his eyes along the top of the cliff. He saw birch and beech and oak, growing above the chalk. His eyes swept the stream. There were old men's stories of sea monsters coming all the way up from the deep bay (which would someday be the English Channel). But the surface of the river was undisturbed. He scanned the farther shore. There were still a few of the low browed ogres from whom Tork's people had taken this land, but Tork knew that he could outrun or out swim them. And there were none of them in sight, either.

All was quiet. Tork grew curious, and stood up on his rock. Then he saw the ship.

It was an ovoid of polished, silvery metal. It was huge, two hundred feet by three hundred, and it floated tranquilly a hundred yards above the treetops. It moved to the stream, and then drifted smoothly in a new direction up the river. It was going to pass directly over Tork's head.

It was so strange as to be unthinkable, and therefore it smote Tork with a terror past expression. He froze into a paralytic stillness, staring up at it. It made no sound. It had no features. It's perfectly reflecting sides presented to Tork's dazed eyes a distorted oval reflection of the river and the stream banks and the cliffs and all the countryside for many miles around. He did not recognize the reflection. To him it seemed that the thing's hide was mottled, and that the mottling shifted in a horrifying fashion.

It floated on, unwavering, as if its mass were too great to be affected by the gentle wind. Tork stood frozen in the ultimate catalepsy of a man faced with terror neither to be fought or fled from. He did not see the small, spidery frameworks built out from the shining hull. He did not see the tiny tubes moving this way and that, as if peering. He did not see several of the tubes converging upon him. He was numbed, dazed.

Nothing happened. The silver ovoid swam smoothly up above the river. Presently the river curved, and the ship from Antares went on tranquilly above the land. A little later it rose to clear a range of low hills. Later still, it vanished behind them.

WHEN he recovered, Tork swam ashore with his fish, shouting vaingloriously that there was nothing to be afraid of. Heads popped timorously into view. Children appeared first, then grown-ups. One-Ear appeared last of all, with his red-rimmed eyes and

By
MURRAY LEINSTER

There were helmets with transparent windows, from which eyes looked out. But the windows were filled with water. . . .

Tork was a simple man of the caves. How could he dream that the star box held the power to make his people gods—or only a lost memory in stone?

THIS STAR SHALL BE FREE

whiskery truculence. There were babblings. Then—they died down. The cave-folk could not talk about the thing. They had no words for it. There were no precedents, however farfetched, to compare it with. They babbled of their fright, but they could not talk about its cause.

In an hour, it appeared to have been forgotten. Tork cooked his fish. When his belly was quite full, a young girl named Berry stopped cautiously some yards away from him. She was at once shy and bold.

"You have much fish," she said, with a toss of her head.

"Too much," said Tork complacently. "I need a woman to help eat it."

He looked at her. She was most likely One-Ear's daughter, but she was slim and curved and desirable where he was bloated and gross and bad tempered. An interesting, speculative idea occurred to Tork. He grinned tentatively.

She said, "One-Ear smelled your fish. He sent me to get some. Shall I tell him he is a woman if he eats it?"

Her eyes were intent; not quite mocking. Tork scowled. To let her give such a message would be to challenge One-Ear to mortal combat, and One-Ear was twenty years older and sixty pounds heavier than Tork. He tossed the girl a fish, all cooked and greasy as it was.

"I give you the fish," said Tork grandly. "Eat it or give it to One-Ear. I don't care!"

She caught the fish expertly. Her eyes lingered on him as she turned away. She turned again to peer at him over her shoulder as she climbed the ladder to One-Ear's cave.

At just about that time the urge came to Tork. He suddenly wanted to travel to eastward.

Travel, to the cave-folk, was peril undiluted. They had clubs and fish-spears which were simply sharpened sticks. They had nothing else. Wolves had not yet been taught to fear men. The giant hyena still prowled the wild. There were cave-bears and innumerable beasts no man of Tork's people could hope to cope with save by climbing the nearest tree. To want to travel anywhere was folly. To travel eastward, where a saber-tooth was rumored to den, was madness. Tork decided not to go.

But the urge remained exactly as strong as before. He summoned pictures of monstrous dangers. The urge did not deny them. It did not combat them. It simply ignored them. Tork wanted to travel to the east. He did not know why.

After half an hour, during which Tork struggled with himself, he saw the girl Berry come out of One-Ear's cave. She began to crack nuts for One-Ear's supper, using two stones. One-Ear's teeth were no longer sound enough to cope with nuts.

Tork looked at her. Presently an astounding idea came to him. He saw that the girl glanced furtively at him sometimes. He made a secret beckoning motion with his hand. After a moment, Berry got up and moved to throw a handful of nutshells into the stream. She stood idly watching them float away. She was only a few feet from Tork.

"I go to the east," said Tork in a low voice, "to look for a better cave than here."

Her eyes flicked sidewise to him, but she gave no other sign. She did not move away, either. Tork elaborated: "A fine cave. A deep cave, where there is much game."

She glanced at him again out of the corners of her eyes. Tork's own eyes abruptly burned. He said, greatly daring: "Then I will come and take you to it!"

The girl tossed her head. Among the cave-folk, property right in females—even one's own daughters—preceded all other forms of possession. Were One-Ear to hear of this invasion of his proprietary rights, there would be war to the death immediately. But the girl did not move away; she did not laugh. Tork felt vast pride and enormous ambition stir within him. After a long, breathless instant the girl turned away from the water and went back to the pounding of nuts for One-Ear. On the way her eyes flickered to Tork. She smiled a faint, almost frightened smile. That was all.

But it was enough to send Tork off within the next half-hour with his club in his hand and high romantic dreamings in his heart—and a quite sincere conviction that he was moving eastward to find a cave in which to set up housekeeping.

Because of this, the journey became adventure. Once Tork was treed by a herd of small, piggish animals rather like the modern peccary. Once he fled to the river and dived in because of ominous rustlings which meant he was being stalked by something he didn't wait to identify. And when, near nightfall, he picked a tree to sleep in, and started to climb it, he was halfway up to its lowest branch when he saw the ropelike doubling of the thickness of a slightly higher branch. He got down without rousing the great serpent, and went shivering for three miles—eastward—before he chose another tree to sleep in. But before he went to sleep he arranged these incidents into quite heroic form, suitable to be recounted to Berry.

TORK went on at sunrise. He paused once to stuff himself with blackberries—and left that spot via nearby trees when something grunting and furry charged him. In midmorning he heard a faraway, earthshaking sound that could come from nothing but saber-tooth himself. Then he heard a curious popping noise that he had never heard before, and the snarl ceased abruptly. The hair fairly stood up on Tork's head. But the urge to move eastward was very strong indeed now. It seemed to grow stronger as he traveled. No other creatures seemed to feel it, however. Squirrels frisked in the trees. Once he saw a monstrous elk—the so-called Irish elk—whose antlers had a spread of yards. The monster looked at him with a stately air and did not flee. Tork was the one who gave ground, because the cave-folk had no missile weapons save stones thrown by hand. He made a circuit around the great beast.

Then he abruptly ran into tumbled ground, where there were practically no trees but very many rocks. It would be a perfect place for lying-in-wait. Also he saw the mouths of several very promising caves. If the urge had not become uncontrollably strong, he would have stopped to investigate them. But he went on. Once his sensitive nostrils smelled carrion, mingled with the musky animal odor of a great carnivore. Mentally he went into gibbering terror. In his mind he fled at top speed. But the urge was incredibly strong. He went on like someone possessed. He had freedom to dodge, to creep stealthily, to take every precaution for silence and to avoid the notice of the animals which had no need to fear one club-armed man. He could even run—provided he fled to eastward. It was no longer possible for him to turn back.

The urge continued to strengthen. After some miles he became an automaton—a blank faced gangling figure, sun-bronzed and partly clad in an untanned hide. He carried a club and in his belt there was a sharpened stick which was his idea of a fish spear. He trudged onward, his eyes unseeing, automatically adjusting his steps to the ground, apathetically moving around great masses of stone in his way. He was, for a time, completely at the mercy of any carnivore which happened to see him.

He did not even falter when he saw the great, silvery ovoid which had passed over his head the day before. He marched toward it with glassy eyes and an expressionless face. Yet the shape was vastly more daunting on the ground than in the air. It was still absolutely mirror-like on its outer surface. It still seemed featureless, because the spidery mounts of its scanning tubes were tiny. But its monstrous size was more evident.

It rested on the ground on its larger, rounded end. Its smaller part pointed upward. It was three hundred feet high—three times the height of the tallest trees about it, some of which had been crushed by its weight as it descended. Their branches projected from beneath it. It was a gigantic silver egg, the height of a thirty-story building, and a city block thick. It rested on squashed oak trees incompletely enigmatic stillness, with no sign of life or motion anywhere about it.

Tork walked up to it stiffly, seeing nothing and hearing nothing. He moved into the very shadow of the thing. Then he stopped. The urge abruptly ceased.

Pure terror sent him into howling, headlong flight. And instantly the urge returned. Twenty yards from the out-ward-bulging silvery metal, he crashed to earth. Then he stood up and stiffly retraced his steps toward the ship. Again compulsion left him and he wailed and fled—and within twenty yards he slowed to a walk, and turned, and came back in blind obedience.

Ten times in all he tried to flee, and each time returned to the shadow of the motionless, mirror-like ovoid. The tenth time he stood still, panting, his eyes wild. He saw his own reflection on the surface of the thing. He croaked at it, thinking that here was another captive. His image made faces at him, but no sound. He could not make it answer. In the end he turned his back upon it sullenly. He stood shivering violently, like any wild thing caught and made helpless.

Half an hour later he saw something moving across the ground toward the great silver egg. There was a faint, faint sound, and a gigantic curved section of the egg opened. Sloshing water poured out and made puddles. There was a smell as of the ocean. The approaching thing, a vehicle, floated nearer, six feet above ground, with strange shapes upon it and a tawny-striped mass of fur which Tork knew could be nothing but saber-tooth. Tork trembled in every limb, but he knew he could not flee.

Just before the vehicle floated into the opening made by the dropped curved plate, two of the shapes descended from it and came curiously toward Tork.

He shook like an aspen leaf. He half-grasped his club and half-raised it, but he was too much unnerved to attack.

The shapes regarded him interestedly. They wore suits of a rubbery fabric bulging as if from liquid within. There were helmets with transparent windows, from which eyes looked out. But the windows were filled with water.

The creatures from Antares halted some paces from Tork. One of them trained a small tube upon him, and immediately he seemed to hear voices.

"We called you here to be kind to you. We saw you yesterday, standing upon a rock."

Tork merely trembled. The second shape trained a tube upon him, and he heard another voice. There was no difference in the timbre, of course, because Tork's own brain was translating direct mental impressions into words; but he knew that the second figure spoke.

"It is an experiment, Man. We come from a far star, mapping out worlds our people may someday need. Yours is a good world, with much water. We do not care for the land. Therefore we do not mind being kind to you who live on the land…You have fire."

Tork found his brain numbly agreeing. He thought of fire, and cookery, and the two creatures seemed to find his thoughts interesting.

"You have intelligence," said the first creature brightly, "and it has occurred to us to make an experiment in ecology. How do you get food?"

Tork grasped only the final sentence. Again he thought numbly. Gathering nuts. Picking berries. Spearing fish with a sharpened stick. Digging shellfish. Small animals such as rabbits and squirrels, knocked over by lucky stones. He thought also of

One-Ear, who had been well fed enough yesterday merely to demand fish. On other occasions he had come bellowing, club in hand, and chased Tork away from the food he had gathered for himself.

"That is bad," said the voice in Tork's mind, but it seemed amused. "We shall show you ways to get much food. All the food you desire. We shall show you defenses against animals. It will be interesting to see what comes of an ecological imbalance so produced. You will wait here."

THE TWO shapes moved away—they floated a little above the ground, Tork noted dazedly—and entered the ship. The curved plate closed behind them. There was a whistling of air somewhere. To a man of later millennia, the sound might have suggested a water lock closing, being filled with water so that water-dwelling creatures could swim from it freely into the liquid-filled interior of the ship from Antares. To Tork, it suggested nothing.

Nothing happened for hours. Then, suddenly, Tork saw a great elk moving steadily and hypnotically toward the ship from Antares. It reached a spot less than fifty yards from the ship's side, and seemed suddenly to be released from compulsion. It turned and bounded away; then its flight slackened and stopped. It came back toward the ship. Fifty yards away, again it tried to escape, and again was recaptured.

Tork watched, wide-eyed.

Rabbits appeared, hopping toward the ship. They appeared by dozens and then by hundreds. The steady advance, converging from all directions, came to a halt in milling confusion at a fixed distance from the gigantic glistening egg.

The curved plate opened again, and again there was a great sloshing of water and the smell of the sea. Four or five shapes emerged, floating above the ground. Even before he saw tubes trained upon him, Tork was aware of fragments of thought conversation.

"I acknowledge that an experiment on land cannot possibly affect our later use of this planet." Another intonation, indignant: "But it is cruel! Give these creatures unlimited food and the means of defense and you condemn their descendants to starvation!"

Then other voices said disjointedly, "I insist that a new ecological balance of low birth rate will result—" "Land animals are of no concern to us—" "Stability of nature—"

"Some new factor will nullify the experiment absolutely—"

Tork was a savage. He was of the cave-folk, and he had never come into contact with an abstraction in his life. Because these were thoughts, he perceived them. He even understood them. But they had no reference to any of the other things in his mind or experience. So they lingered only like the fragments of a dream.

The creatures placed a sort of box before him. It seemed to Tork like a stone. There was a pattern of color leaning against it which after laborious study he discovered to be a reduced appearance of a human being. It was the first picture he had ever seen. Actually, it was a picture of him—the key pattern of the urge which had brought him, if the matter were fully understood. But he heeded the mental voices, referring to the box he thought a stone.

"This is a device which projects a desire. Since you are merely a man, we have stabilized the device so that it projects one desire only. That desire is of coming to the place from which the desire is projected. We drew you to this place by tuning the projection to you. It made you wish to come here."

Tork's brain assimilated the information after a fashion. Very patiently, the mental voices corrected his impressions. They went on:

"This device will now project only that desire, but we have left the tuning variable. Any human may change the tuning now. Stand close to the device and think of an animal, and the device will tune to animals of that sort and make them wish to come wherever the device may be."

Tork thought of saber-tooth, and cringed. The mental voices were amused, again.

"Even that is arranged. Here is a picture of a man. Look at it and you will think only of a man, and the device will only call man to you. Here also is a picture of an elk. Place this by the device and look at it, and your thoughts of elk will tune the device, so elk will wish to come to you. Rabbits—"

Tork was frightened. It would be pleasant enough to be able to make squirrels or rabbits—he saw hundreds of rabbits now, out of the corner of his eye—come to be knocked on the head. But an elk? What could a man do with an elk? An elk could trample and toss—

"Naturally," said the voice in his mind, with some dryness, "we give you safety from animals also, if you change your habits to make use of our gifts. We have made spears with points of stone, which you can soon learn to duplicate. With the picture device you can draw animals to you, and with the spears you can kill them. Moreover—"

The voices in his mind went on and on. There were a bow and arrows. There were stone knives. For the purpose of the experiment, each instrument save the hypnotic device itself had been carefully designed to be understood by primitive minds.

"We of Antares seek new worlds for our race to inhabit. We have chosen your world for later use, and shall remain upon it for perhaps a hundred of your years, to survey it. We shall be able to see the first results of what we do today. Then we shall go back to our own world, and when we return we will see the final result of our gifts to you. What happens on the land, of course, will not affect our use of the seas."

Another mental voice interrupted, protesting that the man was not given a fair chance to refuse the gifts. The instructor went on drily: "Your species can now multiply without limit. We think that you will overrun all the land and destroy all other animals for food, and ultimately destroy yourselves. But we are not sure. We are curious to learn. You can refuse the gift if you choose."

Tork blinked. He understood—temporarily. But he was human and a savage. The prospect of unlimited food outweighed all other possible considerations. He was frightened, but he wanted all the food that could be had. Definitely.

Instructions continued. Presently Tork understood the spears, and was naively astonished. He understood the bows and arrows, and was amazed. He grew excited. He wanted to use the marvelous new things. He felt that the shapes were amused by him.

The land-suited figures floated back to the water-lock of the ship. It closed. He was left alone. He fingered the weapons. Another great plate lowered. But this was not a lock; it was a window. A vast expanse of transparent stuff appeared. Behind it was water, and in the liquid the Antareans—no longer in their rubbery suits—swam within the great metal egg, watching.

Tork, newly instructed, examined the beautifully fashioned stone point of a spear, and then lifted the spear as he had been told to do. He remembered sharp-pointed, sharp-edged stones he had seen. He remembered stones breaking when struck together. He knew he could make a point like this. But—

He was a savage. He went to that extraordinary circular confusion where rabbits hopped hypnotically toward the great silver egg, and at a certain distance were released and turned to flee, and again became subject to the irresistible urge to approach it. Tork went out to them, his mouth slavering.

He made a monstrous slaughter before it called on him. Then he saw the elk. Fifty yards from the ship it stopped, and stared about it, and bounded away. It turned and came back toward the great ship until suddenly it stopped and stared...

Tork killed it while it marched toward the ship in dazed obedience to the urge. Then he went crazy with triumph. He gorged himself upon the raw flesh, and went back to the shadow of the ship—in his triumph he knew no more fear—and squatted down before the device he had been given. He thought of Berry. Inevitably his thoughts went also to One-Ear and to the other members of the cave-colony by the river. He wished each one of them to see his triumph and his greatness. With a reeking mass of raw meat beside him, he gloated over their admiration of him when they should come...

THEY came. Berry remembered that Tork had gone to the east. She wished to follow him. One-Ear wished to go to the east. Somehow, in his fumbling brain, the urge became associated with notions of vast quantities of food. The women wished to go east. Seeking unconsciously for a reason, they decided that their children would be safer there. So the colony of cave-folk took up the march.

They did not all reach the giant egg. Bent-Leg succumbed to a giant hyena who tried to carry off one of his children. A woman died when she fell behind the others. The rest heard her shriek, but that was all. And there was one small boy missing when, moving like automatons, the rest of the cave-people walked with blank faces and empty eyes to within yards of the grinning, triumphant fork. Then they were released.

There was confusion and panic such a she had felt, until he seized them one by one and held them fast while he boasted and explained. Then they still cringed fearfully for a while—but there was food. One-Ear drooled when Tork thrust a monstrous haunch of elk-meat upon him. He squatted down and wolfed it, tending to snarl and glare with his wicked, red-rimmed eyes if anyone drew near. But there was food for all. More, there were weapons. Tork shared them, expansively. Small boys killed rabbits. Women used the new stone knives and skinned them.

More humans came. They were not members of Tork's tribe, but fortunately Tork's people were so stuffed with food by the time the strangers came that they felt no inclination to rise and kill them. They howled with laughter at the strangers' release, instant panic and flight, and return and release and panic again. Presently, with vast amusement, they explained and offered food. The strangers stuffed themselves. Behind the great transparent window the Antareans swam and watched. The strangers were shown the new weapons. They wanted to try them. Tork languidly called more animals to be killed for demonstration—and food.

There was such festival and such feasting as had never before been known in the brief history of man. By the end of the second day, no fewer than fifty humans either gobbled at more food than they had ever seen before in their lives, or else slept the noisy slumber of repletion, while the Antareans watched.

On the third morning, without any notice, the ship rose quietly from the ground and sped skyward. A thousand feet up, it slanted toward the west, toward the great ocean in which an exploring party from Antares would be most interested.

The humans' first reaction to the departure of the ship was panic. But Tork went to the box—the stone-that-calls-animals—and tried a new picture. He thought of graceful, timid deer. The device called a herd of the spotted creatures, and the cave-folk killed them, and were reassured.

The feasting might have gone on indefinitely, but that Tork was a savage and therefore like a child. He kept the neighborhood of the camp so crowded with food animals that other creatures came of their own accord to prey on them. When the brutish roaring of the cave-bear was heard, terror fell upon the people. They seized the weapons and such food as they could carry, and they fled. Mostly, they scattered.

But Tork's own tribe naturally stayed together. It fled back toward its normal habitation, Tork carrying the stone-that-called-animals.

Tork and Berry dissuaded the new members of the tribe from looking covetously upon Berry. Berry, in fact, used a spear upon an admirer who was pressing Tork too hard with a club. But nevertheless, when Tork took possession of the one cave that had been empty in the chalk cliff. Berry uttered a purely formal outburst of shrieks as he dragged her inside to begin housekeeping.

Her father, One-Ear, did not go to her rescue. He was stuffed to bursting with deer meat, and he merely cocked a tolerant, sleepy eye when his daughter was thus kidnapped from his very presence. In any case, he knew that she would have used a spear or knife on him or anybody else who interfered, so he merely belched slightly and settled back to slumber.

So Tork and Berry were married. But the end of the Antarean experiment was not yet.

Those who had been called to the shadow of the silver ship and there released, spread through the land. Most of them had not joined Tork's tribe. They had new, modern, priceless weapons. Non-possessors of beautiful, up-to-date flint spears tried to do murder for their possession. Their owners did a little murdering on their own. Possessors of spears and arrows which would actually cut and pierce were supermen. And in time it became apparent that a man who practiced and gained skill with the even more scientific bow and arrows was in a better position still to win wives and influence the next generation. So every human who saw or heard of the new weapons craved them passionately.

But, being humans and savages, they did not think of making them for themselves. They tried to get them from Tork and his tribe. At first they journeyed to the chalk cliff village and asked for the new weapons, naively. For a little while, Tork was flattered and open handed. Then he began to run short of worked flint. He grew stingy. He gave no more away. Then envious men grew desperate. They stole a spear here, an arrowhead there...Tork had to establish a flint curtain, permitting no visitors in his village. He was unquestioned chieftain now. One-Ear had become too fat either to hunt or fight. And then furtive, burning-eyed sneak thieves hung about the village. Some had traveled for weeks through dangers to make the flesh crawl, merely in hope of a chance to steal a spear or flint knife or arrowhead. They developed great adeptness at such sneak thievery.

There came a day when Tork's own personal spear was stolen from the mouth of his own cave. The thief was a youth of an unknown tribe who seemed to appear from nowhere. He dashed to the spear, seized it, and dived overboard with it. He swam underwater, rising only to gasp for breath, until so far offshore as to be out of range of thrown stones. Stone-tipped arrows were far too precious to be fired into the river. He got away.

SOMETHING had to be done. Tork needed that spear. Berry—being now a wife of some months' standing—upbraided him shrilly for his carelessness. Tork went gloomily into the deepest recesses of his cave, to think. The stone-which-called-animals was there. He regarded it miserably. He thought of the creatures who had given it to him...

And Tork, the cave man, had the inspiration which, in the bumbling, unintentional manner in which men achieve their greatest triumphs, actually determined the future of the human race.

There was a ship from Antares upon Earth. Its crew mapped the Earth's oceans for later colonists. The Antarean civilization was already a hundred thousand years old and very far advanced indeed. Men had just been introduced to flint spears and knives and arrows by the Antareans as an interesting experiment, to see what would happen. But Tork had an inspiration. He thought about the Antareans—while he squatted by the stone-which-calls-animals! It was the greatest single inspiration that any man has ever known. But for it, Earth would be an Antarean colony, and man—Man would be at best a tolerated animal on the continents the Antareans had no use for.

Tork squatted by the Antarean device and remembered the Antareans in their water-filled suits. Then he thought about them as they had looked in the huge transparent window, paddling in the monster aquarium which was their ship and looking out at the cave-folk. The effort made his head hurt.

Presently he called Berry to help him think.

Presently Berry grew impatient. She had housewifely tasks to perform. She told Tork that there should be a picture to look at; then he could keep thinking of them without trouble.

It had long been a pastime of cave-children to press one hand against the cave wall and outline the outspread fingers with charcoal. It produced a recognizable picture of a hand. Tork essayed to trace his memory of what Antareans looked like, on the wall. The result was extremely crude; but while he worked on it, it was easy to keep thinking about Antareans.

Berry disapproved his drawing. She changed it, making it better. Presently One-Ear, wheezing, came amiably into the cave of his son-in-law and was informed of the enterprise. His sharp, red-rimmed eyes perceived flaws even in Berry's artistry. He was the first human art-critic. Other members of the tribe appeared. Some criticized. Others attempted drawings of their own. A continuous session of artistic effort began—with everybody thinking about Antareans all the time.

Of course, the Antareans felt the urge. Perhaps at the beginning it was very faint. But the cave-folk's memories of the Antareans grew sharper as they improved their drawings. The tuning of the device improved. And the impulse to move toward the calling device grew stronger. At best it was nagging. In the end it grew unbearable.

So there came a day when the great silver ovoid appeared in the sky to westward. It came swiftly, undeviatingly, toward the cliff village. It landed on the solid ground above the caves. Instantly it had landed, it was within the space where the call did not operate, and its crew was freed of the urge. The ship took off again, instantly. But instantly it was back in the overwhelming grip of the device the Antareans themselves had made. It returned, and took off and returned, and took off and returned...

Presently it settled down solidly on the plateau above the river. Tork went beaming to meet the land-suited creatures who came out of the water-lock. Two figures floated toward him, menacingly. Voices came in his brain, unreasonably irritated. One said severely: "Man, you should not use the calling device we gave you to call *us!*"

"We need more spears," said Tork, beaming, "and bows and arrows and knives. So we called you to ask you to give them to us."

Crackling, angry thought came into his mind. The Antareans raged. Tork could not understand it. He regarded them blankly. More Antareans came out. He caught comprehensible fragments of other thoughts.

"So long as they think about us we are helpless to leave! We cannot go beyond the space of freedom..." Another voice said furiously, "We cannot let mere animals call us! We must kill them!" Another voice said reasonably: "Better destroy the device. That will be enough. After all, the experiment—"

Then a dry voice asked, "Where is the device?"

The creatures fretted. Tork stood hopefully, waiting for them to give him spears and knives and arrowheads. He was aware of highly technical conversation. The Antareans located the device. It was deep in the sloping chalk cliff below the ship. But in order for an Antarean to get to it, he would first have to go away from it, to get down the cliff. And he could not go away from it!

A crackling mental voice suggested that they call the humans to them—away from the device. But the same objection applied. In order to approach a similar device inside the ship, the humans in the caves would have to go away from it, and they couldn't do that, either. It was a perfect stalemate. The Antareans were trapped.

They even considered blasting the cliff, to smash the instrument they had presented to Tork. But anything that would smash the device would blow up the ship. The hundred-thousand-year-old

Antarean civilization was helpless against the naive desires of cave men who simply wanted more pieces of worked flint.

"Man," snapped a voice in Tork's mind, "how did you creatures keep your thought steadily upon us so that we were called?"

"We made pictures of you," said Tork happily. "It was not easy to do, but we did it."

He beamed at them. There was pained silence. Then a mental voice said bitterly: "We will give you the spears and arrows, Man, if you will destroy every one of the pictures."

"We will do that," promised Tork brightly, "because now we can draw them again when we need you."

He seemed to hear groans inside his head. But the Antareans were civilized, after all. He seemed also to hear wry chuckling. And the dry voice said, inside his skull: "It is agreed. Go down and blot out the pictures of us. We will give you what you wish. Then we can go away.

"And—you will never be able to summon us again, Man! We had intended to stay on this earth for a hundred of your years, and if our experiment seemed too deadly to you, we would have stopped it. But now we will not take that risk. Your species is a land-species, and we are of the sea, but we think it best that you disappear. We have given you the means to destroy yourselves. We will depart and let you do so. Now go and blot out the pictures."

Tork went happily down into his cave. He commanded the wiping out of the pictures of Antareans. Within an hour the ship was gone. And this time it rose straight into the sky, as if it weren't coming back.

At first Tork was made happy by a huge new store of worked flint; but within two months disaster fell. The pictures of animals—so needful when using the Antarean device—blew into a cooking fire and burned. Then there was deep mourning, and Tork and Berry and all the tribe tried earnestly to call back the ship to get a fresh supply.

But nothing happened.

This was catastrophe; they could no longer call animals to be killed. But then Berry suggested redrawing the burned pictures on the cave's walls, and again art was attempted, by men working from the motive which has produced most of the great art works of earth...to get something to eat.

The Antarean device worked just as well with pictures of the cave-folk's own drawing, as with those the Antareans had provided. But of course the Antareans could not know about it, because they had left the planet altogether...

Tork and Berry lived long lives and had many offspring, all of whom thrived mightily because of the Antarean experiment. Of course, the experiment was not ended. In time, the tribe in the chalk cliff village had increased so much in numbers that there was lack of room for its members. Colonies were sent out from it, and they thrived, too. And every colony carried with it three distinct results of the Antarean experiment in ecological imbalance.

One was stone weapons, which in time they rather painfully learned to make for themselves. Another was the belief that it was a simple trick to call animals to be killed. The actual Antarean device—being tucked away in the back of Tork's cave—in time got covered over with rubbish and in two generations was forgotten. Since it needed no attention, it got none. In time, when its power grew weaker and its effect less, nobody even thought to uncover and tinker with it. And the third result of the Antarean contact with Tork's tribe was the practice of drawing and painting pictures of animals on cave-walls. The art of those Cro-Magnon artists is still admired.

The experiment still went on. Men learned to make weapons. Presently they discovered metal. The spears and arrowheads became bronze, and then iron, and presently gunpowder replaced bowstrings to hurl metal missiles. Later still there was the atom bomb. In the art line, there were Praxiteles and Rodin and Michael Angelo and Picasso...And the consequences of the experiment continued to develop...

A GOOD thirty thousand years after the time of Tork, the Antareans decided that they needed the oceans of Earth for the excess population of several already colonized planets. They prepared a colonizing fleet. The original survey was not complete, but it was good enough to justify a full-scale expedition for settlement.

More than two million Antareans swam in the vessels which launched themselves into space to occupy Earth. It was purely by accident that members of a society of learned Antareans, going over the original survey reports, came upon the record of the experiment. The learned society requested, without much hope, that an effort be made to trace the ancient meddling with the laws of nature, and see if any results could be detected.

The Antarean fleet came out of overdrive beyond Jupiter and drove in toward Earth with placid confidence. There was blank amazement on board when small spacecraft hailed the newcomers with some belligerence. The Antareans were almost bewildered. There was no intelligent race here… But they sent out a paralyzing beam to seize one ship and hold it for examination. Unfortunately, the beam was applied too abruptly and tore the Earth ship to pieces.

So the many times removed great-great-grandchildren of Tork and Berry and the others of the cave-folk tribe—they blasted the Antarean fleet in seconds, and then very carefully examined the wreckage. They got an interstellar drive out of their examination, which well paid for the one lost Earth ship. But the Antarean learned society never did learn the results of that experiment in ecological imbalance, started thirty thousand years before.

In fact, the results aren't all in yet.

THE END

The Phantom Hands

By BERKELEY LIVINGSTON

Out in space strange conditions exist. So strange that there is no earthly comparison and what happened to Captain Markham was impossible!

"CAPTAIN MARKHAM..."

I snapped to attention and stared straight into the eye of Supreme Commander Olsen (his other eye was covered by a patch) with all the confidence I could muster.

"...It is only fair that you should know the immediate necessity of the detail to which you've been summoned.

"I can say this to you because, well, shall we say because of the friendship which once was between your father and me. We are losing the war..."

I know I went pale; I could feel the blood leave my face, feel my limbs tremble slightly, and felt the pulsing of the vein in my right temple. Losing the war... My jaws lost their rigidity and my voice boomed out before I could control it:

"No! No! Why—why only yesterday there was that victory beyond Venus..."

"A Pyrrhic victory," he said softly. "A paper victory which the public read about and was eased in mind. No, Markham, we *are* losing the war. I tell you this, no matter what you may read or hear. The forces in opposition are simply too powerful for us."

My amazement knew no bounds. I could only stare with a sort of wordless horror at the man seated at the plain desk in the simple office which was like a home to him. The Supreme Commander had aged in the past six months of the titanic struggle we were going through. Oddly enough it wasn't in the palpable things, like the graying of hair, the impairment of physical things. No. It was in the spiritual side, the things to which no man could lay his finger to and say, it is because of this. I speak of courage and soul. The last six months had driven these things from him. Now he was a shell talking to me, saying words which weren't true...

I spoke again before I realized how the words could hurt: "My father would not have spoken so..."
His voice held a tinge of bitterness when he said:

The PHANTOM HANDS
by BERKELEY LIVINGSTON

He recognized the hands at the gun position!

"*Your father!* Captain Markham, your father is a closed door which I refuse to have opened. It was only through my offices that you were allowed to join the services and attain your present rank. I said the sins of the fathers should not be visited on the sons..."

"Sir," I said, "I—I think it only fair that I know what my father did..."

He cut me short:

"Your orders, Captain. Report to Space Port 4X83. The *Conway* is awaiting your command. A picked crew has been assembled and is in readiness. Now as to your mission. You will search out and destroy the super-cruiser of Iosos, their ace in the hole. A word of warning. The cruiser carries the heaviest complement of space weapons ever assembled on a single ship or for that matter on any fleet. On the cruiser they have placed the destroyer of our atomo-magnetic belt, the single saving source of this war. For without the protection of the *belt* we would surely have been invaded. It is the sole purpose of that cruiser to break through the *belt*. And it is your single purpose to prevent that. In effect, it is a suicide mission. For obviously the cruiser will be protected by a swarm of destroyers..."

He took fresh breath and went on:

"I will be perfectly truthful. The chance of you accomplishing your mission is pitifully small. But it is a chance and we must take it. Our intelligence has but only this morning brought me the facts in the case. I have presented them to you. The rest is in your hands. Good luck and Godspeed..."

His hand was outstretched for mine. I took it and shook it hard and let go. His answering salute was as casual as it had always been, yet I thought I detected a sort of farewell in it...

THERE was an air of excitement about the *Conway* which was slightly different than was usual before the takeoff of a battlewagon. It was the repressed excitement of hundreds of men trying to act as if nothing out of the way was taking place. Yet it was to be seen in their faces and actions. The crew too, seemed to be affected by the same virus. Their faces were set and hard, from the humblest airman to Lieutenant Jason, my second.

We had been too long together to have any formalities between us. He gave me that funny twisted grin of his and followed me to the cabin.

"Well, Ted," he said, "looks like we're in on a big deal, eh?"

"The jackpot deal," I said. "The mystery cruiser..."

His eyebrows rose and his lips went into a surprised pout. He knew the implications of my remark.

"When?"

"Soon as we're ready. Better signal for general assembly," I said. "Only fair to tell the boys..."

I could not see the faces of the men as they heard the news over the speakers. But I could well imagine them. I didn't spare them anything. After all, death comes to all. I just couldn't ease the seriousness of what lay before us, however. Those men below had to know what they were facing. I needed something stronger than water by the time I was through. Harry Jason filled a couple of water tumblers with whiskey and we downed them as though it was water.

"Might as well get down to the nav. room," I said. "We're shootin' in the dark on this..."

"Not so much," Harry said. "The *Bendix* ran into it, and I'm speaking of past tense, out near the twenty-third parallel. That was only four hours ago. Markoff was able to send out a bit before they blew the ship to kingdom come...a hundred thousand tons, he called it. That, Teddy boy, is a lot of ship."

I had to whistle. It seemed impossible. Our biggest battlewagon was only twenty and we thought it the largest ever constructed. The *Conway* was a midget, a five thousand tonner, but the most terrible midget ever to fly the skies. We packed the wallop of ten times our weight.

The twenty-third parallel was beyond Mars some couple of million miles. I didn't like that. Mars was dead. I hated the thought of bailing out and landing on that scarred and terrifying planet. That was presuming, of course, that we would be alive to bailout. I'd rather the fight was near Venus. Some chance in that direction. Harry was observing me closely. I had to grin but it was a bad show. A child could have seen through it.

"...That bad, eh?" he said.

I nodded soberly. No use kidding him. We settled down to a bit of silence. Why I suddenly thought of my father, I don't know. But suddenly he was alive before me. I could see his spare frame, the square shoulders that seemed so wondrously wide for his build, could look into his deeply shadowed eyes. I grinned as his lips seemed to crinkle in a well-remembered smile...

"What's so funny?" Harry asked.

I must have looked very silly because he shook his head sadly, and said:

"Thinking about your father, Ted?"

"Yep! Guess I can't stop. His memory is like this darned war, just won't stop. How long now, Harry?"

"You mean the war?"

"Uh, huh," I said.

"Twenty-nine years..."

"Twenty-nine million years, you mean," I said. "Three generations of children fighting it. I was born to it and have known nothing but it just as you have. I remember they taught us how it began, with those flying disks which came some fifty years ago. The surveyors of Armageddon, shall we call them? They flew back to Iosos and were taken apart and their mechanisms checked. They knew what they had to do long before the war began. And now we are at the end of it. Let's not kid ourselves, Harry. This is the end, one-way or another. Our strength is gone, and I think theirs is too. We are the appointed of destiny. And only destiny can show us the way..."

It was the longest speech I'd ever made and perhaps the emptiest. I had to go on to the end, though:

"...I only wish I was at my father's side when it comes."

"You mean you wish he were at your side," Harry said.

I DIDN'T get it. Then it dawned on me. I had spoken as though he were still alive. Before I could attempt an explanation, there was a knock at the door. I called an entry and looked with surprise at the man who stood at rigid attention on the threshold. He was past middle age, though his hair was only grizzled and the figure still straight. But I had instantly recognized him. It was Laris Moonga...

"Sir," he said. "Gunner's Chief Moonga, reporting for action."

"At ease," I said. "Now come over here, you old space rat and shake my hand."

He grinned broadly as he did and even more when I motioned toward the bottle of whiskey. It was like having the past with me again with Laris in the room.

"What brings you aboard?" I asked.

"Sealed orders to report aboard the *Conway*, sir," he said.

"You do the ship honor, Laris," I said. "The best gunner in the world, in the universe, for that matter. Sit Laris. Takeoff won't be for a while yet. We haven't received clearance yet."

He sat and grinned at me, the old ape, and I returned the grimace.

"Like being with your father," he said after a moment.

It came to me like a bolt from the blue, here was a man, one of my father's dearest friends, who had been with him at the last. Somehow I had to know of those last hours.

"...Well, son," Laris said after a short interval. "Your father was the greatest space fighter who ever lived. I tell you this. I, who have seen the best on Venus and Mercury, those two warrior planets whose whole lives, for the past five hundred years, have been given to fighting."

"Y'know," he continued irrelevantly, "when we first saw the flying disks, some thousand years ago, we didn't know what to make of them..."

"A thousand years ago?" Harry broke in.

"Yep! They made their first survey a thousand years ago. In the Earth year, nineteen forty seven. But they were a curiosity on Venus then, just as they were on Earth. When they appeared the second time, fifty years ago, only your father had the right idea about them. No one would listen, though..."

"What do you mean?" I asked. This was the first I'd ever heard of it.

"...He said," Laris went on as though he hadn't been interrupted, "those disks had been sent out from a place not far from either Venus or Earth. He said Mars would be the best spot. The High Command laughed him down. Ted," he suddenly looked me full in the eyes, "do you know why your father was called a traitor?"

"No!" my voice was high. "Why?"

"Because he took a ship out on his own and went there to investigate. That ship was never heard from again. They called him a traitor because it was at the same time that the Iosos' envoys broadcast their 'forgiveness' appeals. The High Command thought your father had gone over to the enemy." His voice held more than a trace of bitterness as he went on, "I would be there with your father, as I had always been on his journeys, but I had been shot up in a skirmish a week before. He wanted me to get well first, go out on the second shot at them. There was no second shot for me, not with your father..."

"And why did he go to Mars?" I probed.

"Because he said Mars was the logical point for launching their ships, whether the High Command thought so or not."

There was a piping sound from the com. tube. I snapped the switch and a voice called my attention. There wasn't going to be any talk from here on, I knew. This was it. The tower on the surface had given me clearance. I looked at the two men in the room with me, but my thought was on those below decks, the thousand men under my command. In this tiny room lay their hopes and prayers. For this room was the nerve center of the ship. Here lay the gun board, the steering devices and all the other apparatus which were the life arteries.

"Let's go, Harry," I said. "You take the first shift. The board's yours, Laris and may your shots never miss. As for me, I'll get to work on the maps. There are a couple of points I want to clear up..."

THEY burst in tiny flashing points of orange-colored balls. But within those innocuous shifting lights were the most terrible things ever let loose on mankind, cosmic-bombs. The enemy were all about us, hundreds of small scouts and dozens of destroyers, all bearing the silvery signs of Iosos.

My hand was steady on the controls. The rada-magni-vue showed the whole plane of battle as though the enemy were only a few feet away instead of thousands of miles. I caught a glimpse of Laris at the gun board. Flickering points of light blinked the gun positions and his hands were like those of a concert pianist as they flew about the board depressing keys and releasing others. Harry

PHANTOM HANDS

Jason too was busy. His mouth was glued to the com. tube and one hand was on the controls leading to the engine room in the heart of the ship. We were a smooth working crew up here, I thought.

I had flown directly into the lair of the enemy. As if hands other than mine were directing, I steered directly for the scarred surface of the red planet, Mars. A third of the way from it we got our first warning. And immediately after the first sight of the enemy. Now we were in the midst of battle.

The ship shuddered as we were hit time and time again. But always lightly, never in a vulnerable spot and never with a heavy charge. On the other hand Laris never missed. And when our charges burst a ship fell flaming into the void of space. We were blazing a path of hell through the massed ships of the enemy. I couldn't understand it. True, we were a large ship. But they had seen larger. Moreover, we were alone. I couldn't understand it...

"...Four hundred men wounded," Harry's voice came to me. I turned and saw his worried face. He went on, "One engine gone...a lucky shot hit the atomo-generator. Gotta operate at two thirds speed."

I bit my lip hard.

"We've got to locate that ship, Harry," I said through set teeth. "That's an order..."

He understood. No turning back. Once more I fixed my eyes into the rada-screen. My yelp of excitement brought them to instant attention:

"The super-ship. I see it. Signal all hands. Laris..."

"Yes, Ted...?"

"This is it, man. Father was right. They used Mars as a base. The ship came out of the planet. I saw it..."

But there was no time for more. Swift as light it was streaking for us. Like a hyena, who has waited for the jackals to first rip the prey, it streaked toward us, boring in for the kill now that we were wounded. I heard a strange, high shout of exultation and wondered for a second who had voiced it. But when I saw their tightly compressed lips I knew it was I who had given voice to that scream.

It was going to be up to me. The gun board was synchronized to the controls. Laris would fire only as I brought the ship into proper range. And we were within range!

The range was two thousand miles, a thousand, five hundred, and the bursts were full on it. My eyes widened and my heart sickened as I saw how little effect they had. I twisted my baby into a tight spiral; we were not yet free of the lice which were trying to do us in from all sides. But Laris would automatically take care of them...Suddenly it seemed as if a great weight struck my chest. They had cut loose at us as we passed them. God! The power they had!

A BLACK cloud formed and slowly passed from in front of my eyes. I called a reserve of will power to answer. Harry was sprawled out on the floor, blood pouring from his nose and mouth. Laris, good old Laris, was swaying on his feet. But his fingers were still on the board. And they played those keys masterfully. For as my eyes went back to the rada-screen I saw a whole section of the bow fall away. A hit! And a darned good one!

Harry got off the floor and resumed his place at the com. tube. The blood was still pouring from him and his eyes were still glassy but his spirit was still high. He kept shaking his head as the reports poured in from below.

"...Yep. Got it!... I don't care how bad we're hit. Keep that engine at full speed even if the whole damned ship falls apart..."

He turned to me and shook his head. I interpreted the look. Things weren't going well below. He said, "We've been hit bad again. The whole after-deck's afire. They're doin' their best to keep the fire confined. Looks bad, Ted."

We didn't stand a ghost's chance. What was the use of kidding ourselves?

Suddenly I wished for my father. A word, a gesture...*The whole world exploded in flame!*

I tried to lift myself from the deck. I couldn't. Harry was lying on his side and I saw that his head had been practically torn from his body. Laris lay slumped over the board and even as I watched, his body slipped down to sprawl in a welter of blood. I knew I had to get to the board. I pushed forward with my—my...I screamed in pain and terror. My hands! *They were only bloody stumps where the arms should have been!*

This was it, I thought. The last mile! I prayed and cursed. If I only had my hands…Suddenly a vision of my father was there in front of me. He was standing over me and that twisted smile was on his lips. He stretched out his hands and lifted me erect and when I looked down I saw that my arms were there. My arms! He motioned with his head for me to go to the rada-screen. And without waiting to see if I did, he stepped to the gun board.

I looked into the screen and saw we were still flying. I could hear, though dimly, the chattering of the com. tube. Good. There were still some below. The whole screen was filled with the terrifying picture of the Iosos cruiser. We couldn't have been more than a few miles from it. Flames were spurting from its side. But from its hundred gun ports orange balls of flame were seeking us out. I turned and saw my father, his lips still twisted in a smile, gently depressing the keys. I gasped in terror as the whole screen in front of me lit up. And though they were a long way off the sound of their disintegration was like a clap of thunder in my ears. We had won. My father…My father!

I screamed and screamed again. My father wasn't at the board. Only a pair of hands. But I had recognized them. The little finger bore a ring I had seen the *last time I saw him!* Then, like a wraith in a marsh, it faded from view and there was only the board with Laris slumped at its foot. I started to laugh and the laughter rose higher and higher as I looked down at the screen. My father's last shot had been a direct hit. The cruiser fell apart before my eyes. But I wasn't laughing at that. I was laughing at the bloody stumps of what had once been my hands…

THE END

One-Way Tunnel

BY DAVID H. KELLER, M.D.

The roar of the snakes and the cries of the people was a horrible mixture.

THE BEGINNING of the new era dated from the time when mankind left the roads and went into the air. There had been a period of road construction during which millions were spent in building white ribbons of concrete in all directions over the United States.

From the air these roads looked like the web spun by a spider during an attack of insanity. Every important city was connected by the finest kinds of automobiles and the larger cities had threefold roads, one for heavy traffic, one for local passenger use, and one for express purposes. These auto tracks, three in each direction and all six adjacent to each other, were considered the latest word in traffic efficiency. The New York-Chicago road had just been completed when important inventions made the air as safe as the road, in fact even safer, and then mankind left the automobile for the airplane.

During the automobile age, the average tourist was mildly interested in the rural portions of the country, at least such parts as he could see in the cracks between the millions of signboards. Where babbling brooks had once ruled and dogwood blossoms in star like splendor, filling stations and hot dog stands reigned supreme. The favorite subject of conversation on Monday was boasting of the mileage of the day before and the discovery of a place where the wieners were larger and cheaper than at any formerly known stand. With the cessation of automobile traffic, the pride of mileage was still great but no one cared about eating in the country. Why should they when the Chicago fliers could dine in New York and the New York fliers eat their Sunday dinner in Chicago? The old idea that the perfect Sunday consisted in going somewhere as fast as possible and then coming back faster still remained a part of normal psychology, but now all the city dwellers went to some other city.

ONE-WAY TUNNEL

(Illustration by Paul)
The roar of the snakes and the cries of the people was a horrible mixture.

Consequently all the rural eating stands were closed, the signboards rotted down or were chopped up for firewood by the tramps, and on each side of the road the weeds and brambles crept in on civilization, as they will always do when they have the opportunity afforded by neglect.

And when men left the roads for the airlines, they also gradually left the country. Formerly the pioneer wanted elbowroom; now the average citizen was frightened at the thought of living anywhere but in a large city. The large metropolis, east, center, and west, grew larger. Cities like St. Louis, Denver, New Orleans, held their own in the census reports, but the small cities withered and the little towns died. Gradually the country was deserted. For decades the farmer had been having a harder and more desperate struggle. The Farm Relief bill of 1929 had made many Wall Street men rich but had not in the least helped the little farmer. Invention, science, big business, determined to use waste products as byproducts, added the final touch when they made synthetic food and synthetic textiles. Proteins were manufactured; vitamins were made in huge test tubes, and cellulose was duplicated in factories. A very good grade of milk was manufactured. The cow soon joined the buffalo and the dodo.

The farmer sold out for what he could get, exchanged his overalls, for unionalls and came to the city, where he made a better living working eight hours a day for five days a week than he had previously made by working fourteen hours a day for seven days a week. His family enjoyed the talkies where they could see and hear the latest drama of high society, rather than be entertained by seeing the glorious sunsets and hearing the birds usher in the dawn. They forgot the use of the apron but learned the beauty of the human body in a twelve-ounce ensemble. As soon as each family could do so, they bought their own family plane, or while air-hungry but financially crippled, they had at least the satisfaction of renting a plane from one of the numerous "fly your own" companies.

Thus there came a time when all that nine hundred and ninety-nine out of a thousand of the population ever saw of the rural districts was bird's eye views from some thousand feet up in the air. Here and there a last survivor remained true to his early training and lived in the country. These scattered suburbanites were soon lost sight of by the city dwellers. They were so scattered that their influence, business, and vote was considered not worth the cost of procuring. They were not only ignored—they were forgotten.

And so the country was forgotten; the little town, the wayside villages were neglected, deserted, and soon fell into a picturesque decay and then complete destruction. Brambles and vines, grasses and small trees tore down the habitations of man and converted them into their original component parts of nature. Little creeping things ruled where man had reigned, and eagle, bear, wolf, and deer returned once again to their own. As the forests grew, the streams enlarged, swamps reappeared, and in a hundred years, large areas were impassable to the unfortunate aviator who chanced to fall into their impenetrable fastness. Fortunately, few airmen fell in these advanced days of perfect aviation knowledge.

Forests again covered the Appalachians and rapidly came down from the mountains and reconquered the wheat and tobacco fields of Lancaster County. In the Great Central Valley the isolation was only broken by Chicago, St. Louis, and New Orleans. The wheat fields of the West were once again homes for rattlesnakes and prairie dogs. In the West, San Francisco and Los Angeles held their own. In the East New York was supreme, with Boston and Philadelphia rapidly losing their population.

The thriving cities, those that were winning in the race for size, were building upward, downward, and outward. Every aid was given the outsiders in their effort to get in and stay in. One-room apartments with secret beds, hidden closets, and absent comforts were supposed to be the latest word in family accommodations. Large blocks of tenement buildings were torn down to make room for landing fields. Every apartment house had its own airdrome on the roof. The vehicular tunnels were abandoned and neglected. Their need had disappeared with the departure of the last automobile. In 2067, an adventuresome author had made a lengthy survey of the underground tubes, following which he wrote a novel in which the hero joined a bandit gang who used these deserted tunnels as a hiding place. His book was supposed to be as thrilling as the description of the sewers of Paris written some centuries before by Victor Hugo in "Les Miserables." Many learned persons read for the first times this French book so that they could better criticize the American one. Enthused over his description, a club of tube explorers made a yearly tour of some of the more commonly known ones, but this was stopped when several persons became lost and died before they could find their way out.

Escalators provided for street transportation, elevators carried the millions to the airdromes, and once in the air, everyman either drove his own plane or went where he wished in one of the large government planes which carried several thousand passengers for long trips.

The railroads disappeared, steamships and harbors became one with the glories of the past. There was interest in nothing but the air and its use as a medium for travel. Even the use of gasoline and electricity had ceased. Atomic energy replaced all other forms of power not only in the field of transportation, but also in the large city manufactories.

This description of economic conditions is necessary to show the completeness with which mankind had deserted the large spaces between the cities. It is necessary to appreciate this fact to understand why it was that civilization, in such an apparently careless manner, allowed a great danger to assume overwhelming proportions before making any effort to protect itself.

DURING these years in which the country was neglected and forgotten, the old life of the wilderness reappeared, but it was in no instance a new life. Bears, mountain lions, deer, wolves, and all the varied forms of wild life simply multiplied at will as always happens when not checked by any powerful enemy like the automatic firearms of the human race. Eagles once again stood on the top of every mountain fastness; ducks and geese by the hundreds of millions once again swam in the inland lakes and waterways, while the prairie chicken roamed over the deserted harvest fields of past centuries. In every way large areas of land resembled the America that was before the westward rush of the Englishman, before and following the Revolution. Daniel Boone would have felt at home in Kentucky, Crockett have recognized Tennessee and Texas.

The menace to civilization came from the ocean. It was particularly terrible because it existed for so long before it was recognized. It came from the ocean, but by the back door, and thus for a long time its real source was unknown. It was not till the researches of Long, the biologist, that the real and primary home of the menace was determined.

Part of the credit for the actual discovery of this terror should be given to the Tube Exploring Club of New York City. It was on the occasion of their twenty-seventh annual exploring expedition. This club was the only one that was permitted to make exploration of the ancient underground communication channels of the city. The death of several amateurs had closed this form of sport to all except the most experienced tube explorers, and a city ordinance required that even these be roped together to prevent straying from the main party and consequent disaster.

Long, the biologist, Smithers of Chicago, and Peterkin, head of the Universal Air Transportation Company, were among the thirty who made this particular trip. As several of the party were guests, it was decided that nothing spectacular be attempted but that a simple trip through the old tube from Thirty-Second Street over to Harlem, at the abandoned D. L. and W. Station, be attempted. There at a convenient place, the party was to be met by airplanes and the rest of the day devoted to a sightseeing tour of the city.

The party had hardly gone halfway down to the lower platform when it was realized that a decided change had taken place in the tube since the last exploration. Instead of a few inches of moisture, there was now a sullen, black, long stretch of water some feet deep. It was easy to tell what had happened. The tube under the river had broken and the water had risen in it to a level corresponding to that of the river.

"I am very sorry that this has happened," said the President of the club. "I am especially sorry because we have these guests, some of whom have come some distance and have never seen one of our tunnels. Has any member a suggestion?"

"I certainly have," at once answered one of the men. "Among my treasures from antiquity is a boat. It is the kind that used to be called a rowboat. Our family has kept it in excellent repair, just as we have treasured our guns though no one in the family has hunted for over a hundred years. I will go and get that boat and bring it down. It will hold about six persons. We will go down the tube as far as we can and see how things are. Of course, that does not provide for the rest of the club, but it will be a fine experience for our guests—first time in a tube and no doubt the first time in a boat."

"A wonderful idea. Please hurry and put it into execution. I will go in the boat with you, Madison, and I think it no more than proper to ask our first club president, James Smith, to join us. That will make three club members and three guests. Gentlemen of the Club, we will have to cancel all of our plans except the ones for the annual banquet. I will ask you all to wait here and help pass the time for our guests till Madison returns with the boat. I feel the keen interest of a boy. I know what a boat is, but like millions of my fellow New Yorkers, I have never been in one. How are you going to get it here, Madison?"

"Easy. I will take some of our members with me. We can carry it from our family museum to the movable sidewalk on Fifth Avenue and have it here in no time. You just tell some of your funny stories and before they stop laughing we will be back."

Some hours later amid the cheers of the club the six men carefully sat down in the boat. Smithers of Chicago and the biologist, Long, being older than the others, were asked to sit in the ends of the boat while the other four of the party were each given an oar and an elaborate lecture on its use. Smithers, in the front, handled a powerful hand lamp, operated like all illuminating apparatus, by converted atomic energy. Long, at the back, also, had one of these lamps but it was thought best for him not to use it except on some special occasion. A few of the club promised to stay at the landing and await the return of the boat.

Exactly one hour and fifty-five minutes later, the boat reappeared. The president of the club was paddling with one broken oar and Long, the guest, was doing his best with another one, the handle of which was gone. Both men were breathless and thoroughly exhausted from their unusual exertion. It was some minutes before they could even tell a part of the story in disconnected words. Smithers, Peterkin, James Smith, and Madison were dead. They were unable to tell how they had escaped. The city officials must be told to barricade the openings of the tube at once.

That night the club held their banquet as arranged for by the program committee. But as guests, they had the Mayor of New

York and the Commissioner of Public Safety. The club president, his nerves shattered by the unusual and harrowing experiences of the day, simply introduced Mr. Long, who was unusually suited, as a biologist of long standing, to describe what had happened.

"We had gone some miles in the boat, at least it seemed that far," began Mr. Long, "when Mr. Smithers at the front of the boat gave a cry of astonishment. I feel that there was some fear in that cry and I am not attacking the bravery of a dead man when I say that, because I know that we were all afraid. You will recall that we had no weapons save the oars and we started to use them the best we could. Some of the men fought, and as I recall it, Mr. Young, the club president, and I tried to reverse the direction of the boat. We finally started backwards amid scenes of the greatest confusion. I fortunately had a light and by means of this we made our way. We did not dare to look back, but now and then a dying scream told us that another of our group had been taken from the boat. When we finally reached our starting point, all were gone save Mr. Young and myself."

The startled guests looked at each other as Mr. Long came to a pause. But the Mayor of New York City broke the silence.

"What did you find in the tunnel, Mr. Long? Or what do you think you found?"

"I can hardly answer that," replied the biologist. "It was some kind of animal with a mouth at least fifteen feet wide when fully opened. We only saw it from the front, so I can give no idea as to how long it was or whether it had feet. All we saw and all we fought was the head and mouth. I feel sure that it swallowed our four companions. Why it permitted us to escape is hard for me to imagine. Certainly it did not stop because of fear."

"Only one of them?" asked the Mayor.

"Only one that we saw."

"Nothing to be afraid of, then," said the head of the city. "We will close all the exits of that tube, cement our barricades, and let the thing starve to death or go back to the ocean."

The Winged Snakes

JUST then a batch of radiograms were handed to the Mayor. Excusing himself, he read them slowly, one at a time. Then he reread them. Finally he put them in his pocket and faced the club members.

"Gentlemen," he said gravely, "the death of these four men in the tube was but one of the great threats that has faced our nation today. The radiograms I have received are from many of the great cities of the nation. Apparently, there has been a tremendous influx of peculiar animals, not only on the coastal cities, but inland. Every city is on the defensive. It is believed that already the population of New Orleans, Memphis, San Francisco, Pittsburgh, and Denver are wiped out. St. Louis reports the death of many thousands of her citizens. In Chicago the people are fleeing from the lakefront. I feel that we are fortunate in having only one of these animals threatening us. It seems that in the other cities these killers have appeared by the thousand. They could not all come from the ocean. That does not explain Denver and Pittsburgh. I feel that the only thing to do is to appoint an investigating board and when that group of men makes their report, we will be better able to know how to handle this menace. Mr. Long, will you head this board? I will give you as members some of the most brilliant minds in the city. Can you give me, in a few words, your plan for conducting such an investigation?"

"This would be an honor that I do not want and certainly do not deserve," replied the biologist. "I personally feel that we are threatened by an unknown form of life, but simply because it is unknown, I do not feel that it is necessarily new. I am willing to admit that the simultaneous appearance of a killer in inland cities like Denver and coast cities like San Francisco appears as though there were more than one form of this menace, but you must remember for a fact that many years have passed since we have had any intelligent, idea of what was happening in our rural districts. Over twenty-five years ago a few adventuresome souls and I started to walk from New York to Philadelphia and we had hardly gone ten miles before we were forced to retreat, fighting every inch of the way before a number of wolves. I feel that these killers came from the ocean primarily, and the reason I feel this way is that the animal I saw this morning is like nothing I have ever seen on land. At the same time, I do not feel that it is a new form of life, developed by nature in the last few hundred years. It has probably been coexistent with humanity for many centuries but for some reason has never ventured within the domains of the human race before. The only place where it could have hid itself is in the ocean. During the last hundred years, our harbors have been deserted and our ships no longer roam over the seas. These animals have become bold. They have gone up the great rivers; they have landed on our deserted coasts. Perhaps they have been living in our forests and swamps for over a hundred years without our realizing it. How could we know about it? When we soar over a forest, a thousand feet, five thousand feet above it, what can we know about the life existing in that forest or the animals that are hid in that swamp? On land these large animals had no opposition. I say large because the one we saw this morning had a mouth spread from jaw to jaw of over fifteen feet—so the rest of it must have been large—and there is no way of telling whether this was a young one or fully grown. In our deserted rural districts, these killers had no opposition. Food must have been abundant. We know there are large herds of wild cattle. They multiplied without human or animal hindrance and finally the time came when, restless and urged on, perhaps by some common psychic force, they decided to see what the rest of the country was like and the only part of the country they did not rule was the part covered by the cities.

"I think that nothing can be done about it till we know more about them. These killers present a thousand questions and we cannot fight them successfully till we know more about them and their habits. To do that we will have to go where they are. The attack on the cities must have been sudden, otherwise the people could have escaped into the air. It must have been made in large numbers, hundreds of thousands in each city, for otherwise many from each city could have escaped while a few of the killers were working. Panic must have been a vital part of the failure of these people to defend themselves. It is peculiar that entire cities were wiped out when the people, or at least some of them, could have gone into the air. Mr. Mayor, is there no information on this point in your radiograms? Surely these killers did not go into the air after their victims."

"The messages are very confusing," replied the Mayor. "They were no doubt sent in great haste as warnings. There is not a word in any of them about the use of planes as a means of escape. This one from Denver is typical of all of them. Suppose I read it to you, gentlemen!

TO THE MAYOR OF NEW YORK; CITIZENS OF DENVER BEING DESTROYED BY THOUSANDS OF KILLING REPTILES. ESCAPE IMPOSSIBLE IN ANYWAY. REQUEST ALL NATIONAL HELP. PREPARE TO DEFEND ALL CITIES FROM SIMILAR ATTACKS. SIGNED; MAYOR OF DENVER.

"EVIDENTLY," the Mayor of New York concluded, "escape by plane was impossible. Therefore these killers are able to fly. I think, Mr. Long, that you should consider this in making your investigations. If you go by air, you run the same danger that has already overtaken millions of our countrymen. Does it not seem to be best to wait here and prepare in every way for the defense of the city?"

"I have never waited for anything in life except death," the biologist replied, "and even that I have prepared for. I think that the best thing to do would be to go to some smaller city that is being attacked and be an eyewitness of the entire situation. Up to the present time, we are completely in ignorance of what we have to fight. If we do not know what we have to deal with, how can we go ahead with our plans? You let me have one of the swiftest planes you have in the city and one or two of your best pilots. Then we are going out West, perhaps a long ways out West and perhaps only a few miles. As soon as we gain the desired information, we will return and start to defend the city."

"The fastest plane here is a two-man racer, but it is certainly speedy," the Mayor assured Long. "I think that it is as fast as any plane on earth. The pilot who won the last international race with it is still in the city. He is a fearless man and I think will consider it an honor to go with you. Suppose we make arrangements for you to start early in the morning and then perhaps you will be able to meet with the officials of the city tomorrow night. How would that suit you?"

"Fine. In the meantime, I would advise that you prepare the citizens of New York with every possible form of fighting weapons, and tell them that they may have to fight for their lives. You get that aviator and his machine ready and arrange for a start at daybreak tomorrow. May I suggest that you form a board of experts in every scientific field and have them meet with the city officials tomorrow evening. I will be back by that time or I will be dead."

At midnight, Long joined Jerry Johnkins, perhaps the finest ace among world fliers. A hasty plan was made and then the biologist went to bed for a few hours of much needed sleep. At four, he was awakened and a few minutes later the fastest plane in the world was speeding westward.

Conversation was perfectly possible in the glass-enclosed cabin, and once started, the biologist had many questions to ask. How fast could they go?—How slow—how high, and how low? Was it dangerous to go too near the ground? Could they land on a field and then start without leaving the plane? Finally Jerry Johnkins had to say what was on his mind.

"You don't know much about flying, do you, Mr. Long?"

"Not much. I have a plane that is about fifty years behind the times, and I never use it till the absolute necessity arises. Great Scots! I bet you would laugh to hear the way my children jeer at me for being so old-fashioned, but do you know, I would rather walk than anything else. However, I really had to know about this plane and what you and it could do. Do you think you could go faster than a bird?"

"There is no bird I cannot pass."

"Faster than a snake with wings?"

"There's no such animal, but if there was, I could beat him with one engine stopped."

By this time, they were far past the old and deserted city of Harrisburg. They had crossed the mountains over which Forbes and Washington had cut a road for the conquest of Fort Pitt in the

French and Indian War. They were nearing the beginning of the Ohio River where the city of Pittsburgh had made such a desperate struggle for over a hundred years to keep alive. At Long's request, they were flying slowly about three hundred feet from the ground.

Suddenly Johnkins exclaimed, "My body and soul, Mr. Long! Look at that thing running after the man."

"We were flying about three hundred feet from the ground and very slowly," said Mr. Long that evening to a gathering of over fifty of the most learned scientists of New York City, in company with a few of the city officials. "We were flying very slowly because I felt that we would see something interesting soon, and then suddenly Mr. Johnkins, the pilot, exclaimed, 'My soul and body!'— No. He said, 'My body and soul, Mr. Long! Look at that thing running after the man.'

"It was a fine place to observe. The man was running down one of the old country roads, and behind him was running one of the killers. The man and the killer were going in the same direction as the plane, so we saw the whole performance. In less than a hundred yards, the thing caught the man and simply swallowed him. That is all. He didn't bite or chew him. He just opened his mouth and swallowed him. Then he looked up at the plane and I said to Mr. Johnkins, 'Better go up, and fast, too.' The killer came after us and we knew then that this one, at least, could fly. We went up and up and lost it at thirteen thousand feet. I decided then that we ought to go on to Pittsburgh but that we would have to go rather carefully.

"We saw Pittsburgh. There were probably a thousand of the killers there and I think that the only reason we were able to escape was the fact that the killers were not hungry. We did not see a living being, although there were a few planes hurrying eastward. Then we decided to go on to Cleveland. That was just like Pittsburgh, only worse. The loss in human life must have been terrible. There were thousands of the killers there and they were still eating the poor people. We were only saved by our great speed. The average plane has no trouble at all to keep ahead for a few miles but from our altitude we saw plane after plane destroyed in the air by the flying killers. Several times we were chased, but Johnkins was too clever for them. They can fly but they seem to be more at home on the ground. On our way back to New York, we crossed Lake Erie and there are literally millions crawling out of the water along the lake shore."

DURING the description so far, the Mayor of New York had held a glass of ginger ale in his hand. Now he raised it to his lips, but much of it was spilled on the cloth. Trying to control himself he asked, "What are these killers, Mr. Long?"

"Perhaps it would be easiest to call it a snake, some kind of water snake, though personally I prefer to use the word dragon. However, suppose we use the word snake. They are very large. Large snakes have been described before, but we thought the men who wrote those tales were liars. Pliny says that a snake one hundred and twenty feet long was destroyed by the Roman Army in the River Begrada during the Punic War. Malory tells of a snake so large that it drank a well dry. In June, 1673, Joliet and Marquette saw two dragon forms painted on a bluff overlooking the Mississippi River at what is now Alton, Illinois. They gave a very complete description of these paintings. The army of Alexander saw a dragon in India that had a head as large as a shield. Charles Gould believed that these dragons existed in China, and in his account of them he gave them the ability to fly and devour men alive. Olaus Magnus saw a sea snake and said it was two hundred feet long and twenty feet in circumference. Hans Egede, a missionary to Greenland, saw a similar monster that was very large. Pontoppidin claims that one he saw was at least six hundred feet long and as large around as two hogsheads.

"Is all this tiresome to you, gentlemen? They are just a few of the facts that I hurriedly collected in the Public Library this evening before I joined you. My memorandum shows that large sea snakes were seen in 1819, 1822, 1837, and in 1875 the sailors on the bark *Paulin* saw ones wallowing a small whale. The Norsemen believed that these snakes spawned on the floor of the North Sea.

"I feel that after the experiences of the past forty-eight hours, we will have to apologize to these scientists of past ages. They really saw these large reptiles, even as I saw them today. Civilization has abandoned the world to live in cities. Perhaps conditions during the last few hundred years were especially favorable for their production in large numbers. At least, they were not only undisturbed by man, but they lost their fear of him. Then they became restless and began to migrate in millions. Perhaps they were hungry and had exhausted their normal food supply. Now as to what they are.

"Those we saw were all very much alike except in size. They varied from fifty to three hundred feet in length, scaled, like a snake, but with wings, a definite body, and a tail. Under the body there were a number of pairs of legs. The neck was long and the head enormous. Several we saw plainly had distinct lumps in their necks. I judge these were human bodies they had swallowed like a snake swallows a toad. So we have a reptile that can walk or run on the ground, that can swim in the water and fly in the air. Johnkins thought that they could make two hundred miles an hour in the air, but he was sure that high altitude was too much for them. He also said that they seemed to be clumsy in turning. I feel that we will have to give full credit to the reports that have come to New York over the radio. No doubt at all that over twenty-five million people have been killed since the invasion of these killers started, and where it will stop is hard to say."

The men of New York looked at each other. At last the Commissioner of Public Safety spoke.

"But surely a reptile of fifty feet, or even three hundred feet can be killed," he said.

"Certainly," was the calm reply, "I can imagine a dozen ways in which they could be killed, one at a time. For example, a large explosive bullet planted in their brain would tear their heads to pieces, but it would have to be a large bullet, several pounds in weight, fired from a gun. The artilleryman would have to be a clever shot. They could be poisoned by food or poison gases could be dropped on them. But you must remember that there are literally millions of them. Killing them one at a time would do no good whatsoever. Perhaps an army of infantrymen with machine guns could stop their advance, though I am not sure but that their hides would stop the average bullet. Armored tanks carrying one-pound guns might help, but lots of the snakes we saw today could almost swallow a tank. I feel that something new will have to be discovered, some novel means of warfare now unthought-of of, otherwise it is only a question of time before the United States will be a deserted land."

The Mayor turned to the dean of the newspaper reporters. "What is the latest news, Mr. Hereford?"

"Just plain, unadulterated hell everywhere," was the startling reply. "They are having a time of it over in Europe. London has been attacked. Ireland is a deserted and desolate island. Every city of North America is being attacked except three, Boston, New York, and Philadelphia. We had one of the killers in the tube, but it must have been a small one. The other two cities are absolutely free of the menace."

"Then," said the mayor, "it is for us to invent some means to save these three cities. Mankind cannot live in the air at high altitudes. They can escape from these flying snakes by going up, but the time would always have to come when they would have to return to earth. They cannot live under water. The only place where man can live continually is on the earth and for three hundred years we have been city dwellers. I fear that we must take the defensive rather than the offensive. Perhaps we will have a little breathing spell to prepare. Those killers, millions of them, may have had their hunger satisfied. They may return to the ocean till they become hungry again. In the meantime we must prepare for a second invasion and when that attack comes, we must be in such a position that we cannot be harmed. That is our problem. I will ask you scientists to solve it. Please secure contact with the wisest men in Boston and Philadelphia and see what can be done for the future safety of the three cities. Mr. Long, we cannot pay you and your fearless aviator for the work you have done, but we do want you to continue to advise us and I want you to know that you have won the thanks of a great city."

For the next week, isolated aviators arrived in one of the three surviving cities of the United States. All told the same tale of a terrible and almost complete destruction of life by large numbers of gigantic reptiles. In a few places, the United States Army and the State Militia had endeavored to protect the cities, but this only delayed the destruction and in no instance was the resistance of any good. In fact, it only seemed to infuriate the snakes. The general opinion was that human life was no longer existent north of the

Panama Canal save in the three cities that were so peculiarly spared. One man said that the land was picked dry as a bone. Others described with varying degrees of accuracy the destruction of their communities and families.

Cities of Glass

THE three cities waited a day, a week, two weeks and then sent out scouting parties. Not one of the killers could be seen. They had either withdrawn to the coyer of swamp and forest or to their deep-sea homes. For the time being, the menace had become simply a foreboding sense of final disaster at the time of the second attack.

The civilization of the world was not destroyed as much as it was decimated. Reports from other continents seemed to indicate that the loss of life there was far more terrible than in the United States. There was practically no one left in all the world save in the three cities of the United States. These were unharmed, but London, Paris, Constantinople, even the four hundred million people in China were simply nonexistent. Scientists of a mathematical trend tried to calculate the number of killers necessary to eat these hundreds of millions of people in the short space of a few days, but all such calculations were guesswork. All that could be definitely said was that mankind, having reached a certain degree of intellectual development, disappeared—not completely, however, for there were probably twenty-five million men, women, and children in the three saved cities of the United States, that had once boasted of a population of nearly two hundred million.

The city of Washington being desolated, it was thought best to form a new republic to be called the United Cities. This was to be for mutual defense against a future menacing gesture from the killers. There was, at first, little need for law, and the prostrating neurasthenia was so complete that for some months, the only manufacturing was of the necessities. There was no commerce. The large freight planes rested idly in their airdromes. Even amusements dwindled for lack of support. Financial standards were twisted and warped. When millions of people die in a day and the living millions face the same danger, people think of other things than to be entertained. Religious reformers stood on every street corner preaching and warning the people to repent of their sins. The advocates of birth control now had a logical reason for their doctrine. Why give birth to dear children who would only serve as dragons' food?

The first year of the new order of life passed without a single sensible plan being brought forward for the future protection of the three cities. When the final plan was first proposed, it was so peculiar and fantastic that at first the inventor was met with silent ridicule. Later he was hailed as the savior of humanity, man's greatest friend, but for weeks and even months he was looked upon as almost insane. However, Adam Geibel did not mind that. He was so busy, so completely enthused and preoccupied with his dream of making the city of his birth safe for all time that he was not even aware of the scorn which most of his fellow men were casting on him.

He went to the specially created Department of Inventions and was unable to secure an interview with any of the departmental chiefs. He tried for two weeks to secure an interview with an intelligent member of the Mayor's Cabinet. At last, in despair, he recalled the fact that a Mr. Long, a biologist, had taken an important part in the affairs of the three cities in the first days of the menace. Perhaps he would give some consideration to a worthwhile plan to save the city?

Mr. Long was such a great man that he was not hard to see. In fact, he was so great that he did not even realize it. Adam Geibel felt at home in his company within a very few minutes, and at the end of fifteen minutes was talking freely about all of his plans for the protection of the Three Cities. The biologist was at first polite then interested, and at last enthusiastic. He expressed his indignation at the delay caused by the stupidity and lack of interest of the department heads.

"I tell you what we will do, Mr. Geibel," he finally said. "You and I will go to see the Mayor of New York this afternoon and we will ask him to go with us at once to see the President of the United Cities. I think your plan is the first worthwhile idea that has been proposed for the safety of the world in case these killers ever come again. You let me do the talking."

In a half-hour, they were in the Mayor's office. Another hour saw four men, the President of the United Cities, the Mayor of New York, the celebrated biologist, and the unknown inventor, in conference. Mr. Long apologized for the urgency of his demands for an interview.

"I know about these killers," he said. "I have actually seen men eaten alive. I saw them by the millions crawling out of the waters of Lake Erie. I believe they will come again. Ever since those terrible days, I have preached preparedness. Now we finally have a worthwhile plan and I want that plan given careful consideration. It seems to me to be entirely practical."

"How much will it cost?" asked President Morrow.

"That is not the question," declared Long indignantly, unabashed by the thought that he was talking to the President of nearly the entire human race. "The question of cost cannot be taken into consideration in any way. No matter what it will cost, it will be necessary to save the human race. What will money be worth to you or me when we are being propelled down the throats of three-hundred-foot-snakes, to be finally killed in their gastric juices? What is money anyway? What can it buy if it cannot secure and insure the perpetuation of the human race? Already the existence of the *genus homo* is threatened by race suicide. Do you realize that the continued threat of extermination has lowered the birthrate till now it is only ten per cent of the death rate? I feel that the Three Cities should devote their entire strength, wealth, and manpower to making these cities safe. Adam Geibel has a solution that really solves the problem. That is my answer to your question of the cost."

"I apologize," said the President. "You are more than right. What is your plan, Mr. Geibel?"

"In its simplest explanation, it can be given in a few words. I would have a commission determine the size needed for each future city and then I would cover each one with glass. In other words, the Three Cities would have glass roofs. This glass would be so thick that not even a three hundred foot monster could crush it. It would be so strong that the total weight of millions of these reptiles could not break it. We would make it of quartz glass so that no life-giving rays of the sun would be excluded. The city would be a great observatory. Practically no artificial heat would be necessary. Fresh air would be pumped into the city through air tubes too small and too finely guarded to permit a snake of that size to enter them. In summer time, refrigerative machines can lower the temperature. At the top of the glass dome, special openings can be made to permit the passage of airplanes, but these openings can in a few moments be tightly closed. I even believe that glass tubes of the required strength can be built between the three cities so that if the air ever becomes dangerous, communication can be maintained between us and our allies. That is my plan. The building of this roof of glass is a problem for the engineers. I am not capable of doing anything except suggest the plan as a whole; the details would have to be cared for by a special construction board."

At this point, Mr. Long spoke.

"I want to say something before either of you two gentlemen make any comments. I believe that the idea is entirely practical. In fact, I feel that it is the only rational plan that has been presented so far. The menace of these killers may become a real one next year or a hundred years from now, but when it does come, it will have to be faced successfully or the human race will be exterminated. The plan suggested by Mr. Geibel has the beauty of permanency. Put these glass roofs over the three cities and they will still be there a thousand years from now. I would strongly advise that you take this plan and put it into execution as soon as possible."

The President of the United Cities and the Mayor of New York looked at each other thoughtfully. At last the President spoke.

"We will do it. I will have a bill passed at once making available every resource and all the manpower of the nation. I know that I can count on help from every source just as soon as it becomes known that you, Mr. Long, recommend the plan."

"That is kind of you to put it that way. President Morrow," the biologist said, "but due credit must be given Mr. Geibel."

"We will give him all the credit we can," the executive agreed. "He will head our construction board."

BEFORE work could be started, it was necessary to estimate the future size of each of the three cities and build a roof covering only enough of the old cities to comfortably provide for this population. In the centers of all the cities, there were sufficient tall buildings to provide for supports though many buildings had to be both lowered and raised. Finally, everything was in readiness to start building the frames. A circular foundation of cement was laid and on this, the glass walls slowly rose. Machinery was invented to pour the molten glass into the frames like so much concrete and allow it to harden in its final resting place. The population of the cities now worked as they had never worked before because there was lots of work to be done that could not be performed by machinery. The labor law passed placed every male between the ages of eighteen and sixty at work of some kind. The younger and older males were given four-hour days. Even the women were put to work in the offices and as suppliers of food in the commissary department.

Finally, after several years of labor, unceasing and exhausting, the glass domes were completed. The cities were connected with tunnels equipped with twelve-foot glass walls. At the top of each dome was an outlet for airplanes so constructed that it could be hermetically sealed at a few minutes' notice. Ventilation was provided by a single opening defended with terrible steel barbs pointing outward which were considered a perfect protection against any invader. Besides, the opening was too small to admit the body of a three hundred foot animal. Through this opening, the air was drawn in by turbines operated by the same atomic energy that had been so successfully used in all power machinery. A final tour of inspection headed by the officials of the United Cities and the Board of Construction was made and the work pronounced perfect.

The four years of effort had done serious damage to the population. Many of the adults had died and the birth rate continued to fall. When the cities of glass were finally completed, there were a scant million people in New York, a third of a million in Boston and about a half million in Philadelphia. The three cities had been domed to provide for a total future population of twenty-four million.

The work having been completed, there was a terrific letdown in the interest of the human race. During those four years they had kept feverishly at work driven on by the thought that at any moment the attack might come from the killers and find them unprepared. Now that they were safe life seemed more dull and less endurable. There was room for all to live, and everyone could secure the government ration and yearly clothes for a minimum of labor. The nightly entertainments were provided free of cost by the government. If life in one city became dull, it was easy to go to one of the other two, but life there was just as dull and uniformly standardized. It was the boast of the United Cities that at last a stage of civilization had been reached where every citizen had all the necessities of life and many of the luxuries. There were still rich people, but there were no poor ones. Pauperism was an impossibility. A family could not exist in poverty even if they wished to.

There was no incentive to toil. In fact, there was little necessity to do so. An hour's work a day supervising the work of complicated machinery enabled the worker to provide himself and family with everything they desired. Muscles became small and flabby. Minds became inert and dull. Life was safe but uninteresting. Everywhere there was security, nowhere danger.

On this soil arose a danger that was more horrible in its threat to civilization than the reptile killers had ever been. For the snakes at the worst simply destroyed, life but these human reptiles demoralized without destroying. The three cities produced a generation of perverts, men and women who grew to maturity so eager for thrills that the breaking of the Ten Commandments ceased to interest and efforts were made to invent new commandments for no other purpose than at once breaking them. The growth of this part of the population was rapid. Within two years after the completion of the glass cities there were so many instances of law violation of the most serious kinds that the thoughtful members of society became alarmed. In the emergency, President Morrow called on Mr. Long for advice.

"But I am not a criminologist," insisted the biologist.

"But you know more about all forms of life than anyone else, and we want your help."

"I have only one suggestion to make and that is so gigantic in its scope that I fear you will not accept it."

"Go ahead. Speak everything that is on your mind."

The biologist sighed.

"It seems to me that I am rather tangled up with this matter since that unfortunate day when four men were killed in the Hudson Tube. What a change has taken place in the world since then! And what changes will take place in the next ten years? Well, as you were talking to me about this sudden flare in crime records, the thought occurred to me that there were two classes of people living in the United Cities—just as there always have been two kinds of people. There are good people and bad people. Perhaps the bad people are bad because they are sick, but really that makes but little difference. The killers did their deadly work because they were hungry, but nonetheless, they killed. These criminals may be constitutional perverts, but nevertheless they are a very definite danger to what is left of humanity. I think that unless something is done, they will make us a race of savages. So here is my plan.

"Make a list of every law violator known. Then slowly bring all the people in Boston over to New York and Philadelphia. Leave the city of Boston, the machinery, the houses, everything just as it is now. In the tunnel between New York and Boston construct a number of revolving doors so constructed that persons can go through them to Boston but can never return to New York. Mobilize your entire legal machinery and on a certain date arrest every pervert, law violator, and menace to the community and force them to enter the tube. Tell them that in Boston there is food, liberty, and license. They will have to manufacture their own food, their own clothes, and they can make what government and laws they wish to. If they do not want to live in a glass city, they can return to the wilderness. Then in the future, when anyone breaks a law of any kind, simply send him or her to Boston. In New York and Philadelphia the good people will live, and in Boston the bad ones. It is an ideal arrangement, and there is not the element of cruelty in it that the former method of life imprisonment had.

"There is another factor that is of value in my plan. Like breeds like. By this method we will free the better part of humanity of the danger of continually breeding criminals. No doubt the Bostonians will degenerate but the remaining part of humanity will become more worthwhile. How about such a plan? Is it impracticable?"

"It sounds all right to me," replied President Morrow. "In fact, I was thinking of something like that myself, only I considered simply sending these criminals into the wilderness. Your plan is far more humane. I like it and I am going to put it into execution at once as soon as I can confer with my Cabinet. It will have to be done secretly, otherwise it will be a difficult task. We will begin by building the revolving doors; then we will take all but the criminals out of Boston by plane, and on a certain date send as many criminals as we can gather together and force them to enter the one-way tunnel."

The plan was placed into force within a month. So silently was it put into action, so secretly had the plans been kept, that before any united defense could be made by the criminal perverts, over two hundred thousand of them were segregated in Boston. At once the crime incident lessened in New York and Philadelphia and while, during the next year, over five thousand more law offenders were segregated, still the beginning of the new year showed a population in the two glass cities that was almost one hundred per cent good citizens and this, not because of any terror of the law, but because of innate desire to keep the Golden Rule.

In that year of segregation life had not been pleasant for the criminals. It was one thing to prey on defenseless citizens and it was another to injure hardened criminals. The murder rate rose; life became the cheapest commodity in Boston. A succession of super criminals rose to power as temporary kings, only to meet death by the assassin's blade or poison given the same evening as a favorite's kiss. There was no law in Boston save that of might. Work was only done as a necessity. Within the year all of the feeble-minded and epileptics had become virtual slaves, treated, housed, and fed as though they were so many animals, forced by their labor to support the colonists who were mentally superior adults.

The death rate was high. Murder, neglect of hygiene, insufficient food, all contributed to a rapid reduction of the population. There were practically no children born and those that were born alive were frequently killed by their criminal parents. There was no security of life or property.

And ever in the minds of all the Boston criminals was a deep resentment that they had been handled in such a manner by the rest of humanity. The psychopath always feels that he is being badly treated, and more than ever, these isolated defectives felt that they had been dealt with unjustly. They spent their spare time planning revenge, the ones of lower intelligence dreaming of rape and murder and the super mentalities planning revenge of a horrible and subtle nature, hitherto undreamed of in the criminal sadistic records of the human race.

The Criminal City

THREE years after the successful isolation of these degenerates, two men were in control of the city of Boston. Thaddeus Garland, known among his gang as the Beautiful Spider, and Hannible Cocke, whose favorite nickname was the Brainless Wonder. These men had risen to unchallenged control of the prison city sheerly through their intellectual supremacy and their cold brutality. They lived for three reasons: the ultimate destruction of New York and Philadelphia, the final overthrow of each other so that one could reign supreme, and the accomplishment of self-pleasure in every way that had for thirty thousand years been a matter of repugnance and detestation to the better nature of mankind. On the surface they were friends, held together by ties of affection and mutual interest; below the surface they hated each other. They had ruled Boston for three months, thereby establishing a record.

"We will never be satisfied," said Garland one summer's afternoon to his royal partner, Cocke, "until we settle once and for all the real ownership of this city. You know as well as I do that this idea of having two rulers is all buncombe and bosh. Hell! There is only room enough here for one head and if the fool women keep on killing the occasional baby that happens now and then to be born, there will not be anything to be head of soon, anyway. I think we ought to settle the matter. Throw the dice or cut cards or go up in the air and shoot at each other till one drops to the ground dead. We would do it, too, if we could only be satisfied with the death of those other cities first. It is a funny thing, this hate business. Here we are dreaming of killing each other but we hate those people in the other two glass cities so much more than we hate each other that we just go on living and working together as though we were business partners, simply because we have not sufficient intellect to figure out how to kill them. Men call you the Brainless Wonder because you look as though you bad no brains in that pinhead of yours and yet I know that you are capable. They call me the Beautiful Spider because I have the head of a Greek God fastened on to a body of such monstrous deformities that a spider would blush to have a body like it. And yet, in spite of the shapes our parents gave us, we are kings of Boston for a day. Different from the old days in this town. Why, I read that they used to take first class books and refuse to let the Bostonians buy them. Think of that! And now we hire authors to pander to the depravities of our citizens. Ha, ha! That sounds like the battle cry of a jackass."

The Brainless Wonder rubbed his receding forehead and then twisted his beaked nose with a gentle, loving gesture. Looking at Garland he whined, "Ah! Let's do something. How would it be to drop a lot of explosives down their airplane opening?"

"Yes, and a fat chance you would have of getting near there in a plane. Don't you know that every plane that goes out has a wireless code word and when they want to return to the city the pilots have to send down that word before the air gates a reopened? You could drop all the explosives in the world on that glass dome and it would still be a glass dome."

"Do you know how they open and shut the air gates?"

"Certainly. Just like we do ours. Simple mechanism. Just a couple of buttons. Press the blue one and open goes the gate. Press the red one and it closes."

"That is the way it used to be. You don't know that it is that way now, do you?"

"Sure. Did I ever tell you about Lizzie, the Golden Girl?"

"I know about the dame, but she is dead now."

"No, she ain't. She lives in Philadelphia. I hear from her every now and then."

"Not in Philadelphia?"

"Yes, I placed her there. She is a sure enough good girl now. I wanted to know the weakness of the other cities and so I thought we might use some of the cats for spies, and Lizzie, she was sore at being sent here and she rather jumped at the chance of going back. She is in Philadelphia and what's more, she is married to one of the men that keeps the air gate watch."

The Brainless Wonder looked more cross-eyed than ever.

"That is just one more reason for killing you, and I am going to do it someday. You knew that the Golden Girl was my girl, and you told me she was dead. Sure she run away from me when I tried to make her live with me, but that was no reason for you meddling with the matter. Hell! I am going to Philadelphia and get her, and when I place my last kiss on her dead face, I am going to come back for you, and your face will be less beautiful and kissable when I am done with you."

The Beautiful Spider sighed.

"This sort of thing is just the one reason why we are still living here without doing a thing to those curs in the other glass cities. If we could only work together, we could do something. Ain't there enough dames here to suit you? Mollie Black told me the other day that every time she thought of living with you she quivered. There is a nice girl, and you would appreciate each other. Course she has killed five, but she might spare you.

"Well, I am going. You can take a chance with Mollie."

"If you go now, you won't ever comeback."

"Oh! You need not worry about that." And at that, the Brainless Wonder walked out of the room. Fifteen minutes later he was in his airplane going through the air gate of Boston. In less than an hour he was flying over the glass city of Philadelphia. He found the air gate of that city tightly closed and he saw something else that gave him room for plenty of deep thinking.

ON THE GLASS DOME, sprawled out in careless attitudes, thoroughly enjoying themselves in the reflected sunshine, lay thousands of the winged snakes. The Brainless Wonder had never actually seen any of them at the time of the last threat, but he, like all the rest of the citizens of the Three Cities, had been well instructed in the details of the killers. When he saw these snakes with wings, feet, tails, enormous heads, stretching and yawning and scratching themselves in the sun, he knew that they could be nothing else. They had found their food but between it and them was a twelve-foot glass dome. So they just made themselves comfortable and waited there. They were used to waiting.

As the criminal watched them, a brilliant thought came to him. Perhaps, by apiece of strategic flying, he might be able to destroy the city and at the same time satisfy his desire for revenge on the Golden Girl. It involved a feat of remarkable flying, but the ability to handle a plane was one of the accomplishments of the Brainless Wonder. He spiraled twelve thousand feet into the ether and then hovered over the air gate of the city. From that vantage point he radioed to the watchers of the gate.

"Am going to drop into the city. Unless you open the gate for me I will be killed by these killers. You can open the gate and close it in lots of time. Watch out for me. I am dropping in three minutes."

Twelve thousand feet below the watchers were in a quandary. Who was this man in the plane above the gate? Should they let him fall to be a helpless prey of the devourers, or should they save him? Hastily they telephoned to the Mayor of the city. He could not be reached. The Head of Councils could not be found. Minutes were passing. There was no one to assume the responsibility. From far above, the message came.

"I am dropping in fifteen seconds."

The watchman of the air gate muttered,

"It would not be right to let a human being die if he can be saved," and he pressed the blue button. The gate opened.

The Brainless Wonder let his plane drop. A special landing attachment made dropping perpendicularly a perfectly safe performance. He dropped rapidly at first, but when within a thousand feet of the gate, he lessened his speed and started his siren whistle. At once, hundreds of the indolent snakes aroused, alarmed at the new noise. As the plane rushed down toward the air gate, they rushed by the thousands towards the plane.

The Brainless Wonder arrived safely on the landing platform. The closing gates crushed the head of the first snake who had arrived at the opening. The criminal jumped out of his plane and ran toward the office of the watcher of the gate. That official ran forward to welcome and congratulate him on his escape. The man from Boston killed him with a dagger and ran into the office. He again pressed the blue button, and the heavy gates opened. Instantly a living stream of hideous reptiles poured through the opening. They came by tens, by hundreds, and later by tens of thousands. Their cries of hungry rage called their comrades to the feast. Escape for the people of Philadelphia was impossible. There was only the one air opening. There was a tunnel to New York, but in a few minutes that was hopelessly blocked by the suffocating bodies of those who had rushed there in their helpless and hopeless panic.

Finally all of the killers were inside the city. They were all roaming through the streets, reaching into the rooms and climbing up the houses after their victims. Through the opened air gate, the summer sun streamed. Far above, a lark sang. From the opened mouth of the air gate rose the combined clamor of hopelessness and hell. Suddenly a single plane shot up through the sky.

A half hour later, a single plane landed in New York. A woman stepped out of the glass cabin and staggered towards the office of the watcher of the gate.

"I want to see the Mayor at once," she whispered, "and you better tell him it is important."

And then she collapsed. When she roused from her unconsciousness, a trained nurse was taking care of her under the directions of a physician. She was in a hospital and the Mayor was waiting for her message.

"My name is Catherine Gower," she began, "but in Boston they called me Lizzie, the Golden Girl. No use telling you why I was sent to Boston; you wouldn't believe me anyway, if I told you I didn't do it. Boston was a mess when I got there. Two men, perhaps you know of them, the Beautiful Spider and the Brainless Wonder, think they are kings there. This one man, the Brainless

Wonder, wanted me for one of his women and I guess that my stomach was too delicate, for I just could not even bear to look at him, so I went to the Spider and he said that he would help me if I would go to Philadelphia and be one of his spies. Well, anything to get out of that hell city and away from the Brainless Wonder, so I went and the first thing I knew, I was in love with one of the watchers of the gate.

"He was a good man, and we were going to be married soon. I decided to double-cross that Boston gang and go straight. This morning I was sewing in his office; it was his eight hours on duty. Things were dangerous; I guess you know that for a week the glass dome of Philadelphia has been covered with the killing snakes. We received a radio that there was a man in a plane twelve thousand feet above the gate and he wanted to drop into escape the killers. My lover could not reach anyone in authority. Something had to be done, so we opened the gate and down came the man. He was the Brainless Wonder, but we didn't know that till we had the gate shut. My man ran to congratulate him on his escape from the killers and he was killed by the Boston King. Then this fellow ran and opened the gate and in swarmed the snakes. That was the end of Philadelphia. Of course it was easy to see what the thing meant, when it was too late. He made a grab at me and I kissed him and pulled him into the office and turned out the lights. The killers streamed past us. My God! I thought they would never stop. I wanted to warn you New Yorkers, not against the snakes, but against the killers of Boston, so I proposed to the Brainless Wonder that we use the emergency plane and get back to Boston. He had lost a little of his nerve; the roar of the snakes and the cries of the people was a horrible mixture. So we started out, and after we got up in the air, I killed him—with the same dagger he had used on my lover, and then I sailed back and threw him down the hole of the air gate so one of the snakes could eat him. Of course that was the end of him.

"But those people in Boston are not going to rest till they kill the New Yorkers. You good people do not realize the hate those fools have for you. They never will forgive you for shutting them up by themselves—they are going to get you. There is a girl here; she has a red birthmark on the back of her neck and that is why she wears her hair long. She is a spy. The Beautiful Spider sent her here the same time he sent me to Philadelphia. You better find her and send her through the one-way tunnel."

And with that the Golden Girl became unconscious again.

As far as Philadelphia was concerned, there was nothing to be done. Without loss of time, the tunnel between the doomed city and New York was tightly cemented. So long as the air gate of New York was closed, there was nothing to fear from the killers. But the Boston snakes were a different proposition.

In that city were thousands of criminals. One of these, to satisfy his lust for revenge, had deliberately wiped out one of the three cities of refuge even at the cost of his own life. In Boston there were many men as desperate. In what way would they strike at New York? And how could the Metropolis defend itself?

THERE were just two places in the entire world now where human life was possible. One was New York, a rather decent place now for men and women to live, a crimeless city where the people were good because they had been bred good and wanted to be good; the other was the city of Boston, enforced city of refuge for the criminal, the pervert, the psychopathic personalities. It was a modernistic representation of the old idea of heaven and hell, light and darkness, good and evil, day and night.

Each city had the same equipment, the same manufactories for the necessities of life, the same protection for human life against the beasts of the wilderness. There were equal opportunities for enjoyment, pleasure, and amusements. The only difference was that one city was filled with good people and the other with bad people. All the good folks wanted was to be left alone; all the bad wanted was to destroy the good.

The Mayor of New York realized this. He could think of nothing else during the next few days. This alone was in his mind as he attended the memorial services held in memory of the dead of Philadelphia. The secret dread of a similar occurrence in New York City held him in insomnia's persistent chains. The more he thought, the more hopeless he felt. At last he determined to carefully review the history of these last eventful years in the story of the human race. Not being an eminent student, he called in a historian, a student of modem history, one who had a keen grasp on the swift rushing events of the world. He asked this man to begin with the first days of the killers in America and outline the eventful years since then. As the man talked, the Mayor listened with closed eyes. Finally the lecture came to an end with the services held in honor of the dead of Philadelphia. Thanking the historian, he dismissed him and sat alone, thinking to himself.

"In every crisis known to mankind," he mused, "since that first day in the tube there has been one outstanding figure and that is Long, the biologist. He has taken the lead and forced through to a successful ending every important step. I wonder how old he is now? I wonder whether he is mentally keen enough to face one more problem for the welfare of his beloved people? At least it will be worthwhile to talk to him about it."

And so he sent for Long.

In a few hours the man arrived. He did not look as old as his seventy years proclaimed him to be.

"I am glad you sent for me, Mr. Mayor," he exclaimed, "for I wanted an interview with you. Briefly, there are some friends of mine, twenty-five men and an equal number of women, who have been thinking over some facts in social life and we, the fifty-one of us, want permission to leave the city. We feel that we would be happier outside."

"But—why, it's impossible! How about the killers? What is the idea?"

"Simply this. We feel a lack of interest here. We feel that if the human race remains bottled up in this city of glass, that eventually it will die of weariness. Every day is the same. The former struggle that made life a gamble for our ancestors, also made life endurable. It was the uncertainty that added the vital charm; it was the struggle that made existence worthwhile. We are all well educated; we have studied conditions in the wilderness around the cities. We want to go out there and conquer the wilderness like our ancestors did many generations ago. For a while we will live in caves. We will wage a war of extermination against these killers like our ancestors did against the cave bear and the saber-tooth tiger. Eventually we will win, for man the supreme animal must survive. The odds against us will be large, but that will make the struggle all the sweeter. May we go?" The Mayor saw his chance.

"On one condition. That you rid us of the Boston menace."

"I thought of that. The fifty-one of us can no more live in the new world with the criminals than we can with the three hundred foot snakes. For the sake of our women and the unborn children, it will be necessary to exterminate them. I have a plan. I promise you that there will be no more Boston menace."

"You can go on that condition."

"Good."

The biologist smiled.

"You are anxious to rid the world of them, and so am I. By the way, I was wrong when I said that there were fifty-one of us. There are really fifty-two. Miss Gower is going with me as my bride."

"Miss Gower is going with you?"

"Yes, the Girl with the Golden Hair. I always was partial to that type, and when I met her and heard her story, I said to myself, 'Here is the woman that will best help me carve out a home for myself in the wilderness. And fortunately for me, she said she would. I told her that she was throwing herself away on an old man, but she said that I was just the kind of husband she wanted."

The mayor laughed.

"Always heard that every man had his weakness."

"Well, she's my weakness now. We will prepare things and start for Boston soon." A few days later a fleet of airships thoroughly equipped for every emergency sailed out through the air gate of New York City. In this fleet were the self-appointed exiles. It was fortunate that they left when they did, for only a few hours later, the killers came north from their feast in Philadelphia and started to wait for something to happen, on the glass dome of the metropolis.

THREE MILES from Boston the fleet cautiously settled to the ground. The place had not been selected in a haphazard manner. The objective had been the openings of the ventilating system of the city of Boston. There certain merchandise was unloaded, and Long addressed the colonists.

"When the cities of glass were first thought of," he said, "it was realized that some arrangement had to be made to supply the inhabitants with fresh air. Consequently each city had an air tube constructed, through which fresh air could be constantly pumped into the city and at the same time the tube was so built that no wild animal could enter the city. Here we have a tube twenty feet in diameter. Once it reaches the city, it is divided and subdivided in such a way that eventually afresh air tube enters every room of every house. The fresh air flows into the room like the water. The air is sucked into the tube with terrific force. We stand a thousand feet away from the main opening and yet we can feel the draft. What I propose is simply this. I have a large supply of poisonous fluids which, when liberated from their steel containers, will become gases. These gases are far more terrible than those used in the former wars of the world. As soon as these reach the inside of the city of Boston, the people will die. I am not sure that they deserve to be killed but the fact remains that it is necessary to kill them to survive ourselves. In our freight ships we have a hundred of these steel cylinders. I carefully figured out the dilution that will take place when this gas spreads through Boston and I feel that we have enough to kill ten million persons and there are only about two hundred thousand there now. I want you to help me carry these cylinders close to the mouth of the tunnel and then turn the cocks. There will be no danger as far as we are concerned, because the draft will protect us."

The exiles at once started to carry out his orders. Not a moment was to be lost as the killers might appear at any time. At last the work was completed and the men and women started to return to their airships. A dull thud shook the earth and a few minutes later a one-passenger plane came soaring through the air. The pilot landed near the fleet of ships and, leaving his plane, walked over to the little group of New Yorkers.

"Well, this is a surprise," he exclaimed. "I never thought that I would find so many strangers so near Boston. Welcome to our city. Hello, Lizzie, what are you doing here with these highbrows? Sunday school picnic?"

"That is the Beautiful Spider, Paul," explained Mrs. Long to her husband. "Perhaps you better break the news to him."

The Spider heard her.

"Perhaps you better hear my news first. I have real news to tell you. We have been working on the problem for some time, me and my friends. We planted a mess of high explosives on one side of the foundation of the glass dome of New York and when I found that the killers were congregating there, I sailed over and lit the fuse. Had a narrow escape, too, but I went up in the air higher than the winged boys could follow me and made my getaway. Well, the stuff blew a hole in the dome big enough to send a zeppelin through and you had ought to see those hungry killers swarm in. I bet by this time there are mighty few New Yorkers alive. So now that that little job is done and the Brainless Wonder's dead, as I understand he is, I guess it will be fine to be in Boston as a real king. Want to go back there with me, Lizzie? My body does look like hell, but I have a beautiful face."

"I want to tell you something, Mr. Garland," interrupted Paul Long quietly. "First the lady you are speaking to happens to be my wife. When you speak of her or to her, please remember that. Now in regard to your being king of Boston. I guess you are. At least no one else wants the honor, for all of the Bostonians are dead. We have just gassed them through this ventilation tube. I am sorry that you were not there to die with them. I am also sorry that our friends in New York are all dead. All human beings have to die when they cease to defend themselves. All life is a struggle and the only way to win a war is to attack. The error I made when I advised the Cities of Glass was that I forgot this matter of attack and recommended a simple defensive. The zest disappeared from life. We forgot to fight and now, except for the few of us here, the human race is wiped out. We came into the wilderness deliberately so that we could fight; many of us have been preparing to destroy wild animals; we know that we have to do this or have them destroy us—and so—"

And without further preamble, the biologist raised an automatic revolver and killed the Beautiful Spider. The monstrosity fell and the leader of the exiles walked over to the dead body.

"Right between the eyes," he cried proudly. "Not so bad for an old man." He turned to the colonists of a new world and a new life.

ONE-WAY TUNNEL

"And now, my friends, let us begin our adventure. Our plans are made and the future will determine the wisdom of them. But at least we will be happy, because from now on, we will have something to live for and will have to fight tooth and toenail for the right to keep on living."

His wife came near him and caught his hand.

"You are not such an old man," she cried. "You have the secret of perpetual youth. How have you accomplished it?"

"By the constant overcoming of new difficulties," he replied.

Some minutes later, the survivors of what were once the Lords of the Earth sailed slowly into the western skies. They were more than Lords now; they were Gods and Goddesses of Destiny.

THE END

The Timeless Man

BY FRANK BELKNAP LONG

He never knew what mystery of time and space had set aside his death, entered him once more on the roster of the living...but it hardly mattered, for in either era he had the same mission to perform. Holden, you see, was—

"MAN, YOU must be insane! To paint *now*—"

The clicking of the Geiger counters almost drowned out the voice. Holden did not turn. He was spreading pigments on a canvas which stood half in shadows, half in flickering light, a strange kind of exaltation swelling within him.

Roger Holden did not want to die. To the artist life is almost unendurably sweet, and Holden was no stranger to fear. But when he painted, his work absorbed him to the exclusion of all else.

It had always embarrassed him, however, to paint in another's presence. Suddenly he found himself resenting Langley's presence, without ceasing to feel grateful to him.

He swung about with a gesture of reproach. "You promised me a few days' grace," he said. "If you didn't want me to paint, why did you invite me to bring my easel and brushes along?"

"You had to have something to occupy your mind." Langley laughed harshly. "Any game would do. We could have sat here playing chess. But when Death does the checkmating chess isn't a very amusing game."

"This isn't a game," Holden said impatiently. "Or a gesture of bravado, either. You're amazed because I can still paint—is that it?"

Langley was a powerful giant, dark haired and dark eyed, with a nervous strength in his fingers that made it easy for him to break things. He twisted his own wrist as he returned Holden's stare, as though snapping it would have been less intolerable to him than trying to frame an answer.

"Not amazed exactly," he said slowly. "Under stress, human nature is unpredictable. But somehow—I expected logical behavior from you at five to twelve."

"But my behavior *is* logical," Holden said. "You know the old saying— Life is short but art is long, or, if you prefer, eternal. It may be a thumping platitude, but I happen to believe it."

"But no one will see your painting," Langley protested. "No human eye will ever look on it again. When your brain dies it will become a meaningless jumble of pigments!"

"It will still be eternal," Holden insisted. "You're confusing duration with eternity. Eternity is timelessness—it's the antithesis of duration. If I paint a masterpiece I'm creating something that will live forever—in the one deathless moment of its creation."

Langley shook his head, a tortured skepticism in his gaze. "That's sophistry, Roger."

Holden turned slowly, as though he were balancing an invisible burden of sorrow on his shoulders, and picked up his palette. He began to paint again.

"Lord Dunsany once wrote a little fantasy to summarize the futility of all human effort," Langley pursued. "He compared humanity to a man falling from a high building, plunging to certain destruction and yet reaching out with a piece of chalk to scrawl something imperishable on the face of the building." Langley's lips twisted in a sardonic smile. "He didn't succeed."

"He tried," Holden retorted. "The effort wasn't futile. It was the man's glory—the one thing that set him apart from the brutes."

Holden seemed oblivious to the clicking of the Geiger's, only half-attentive to his conversation with Langley. His eyes shone as he bent toward the canvas, as though his vision of beauty had kindled flame in his brain that nothing on earth could quench. No—not even the terrible spreading radiations which were even now a part of him, a seal of destruction on his flesh and his bones.

Holden's work consumed him as it had consumed Rembrandt, Keats, Mendelssohn, Tchaikovsky. He remembered how Proust, gasping for breath, had staggered to his desk on the day of his death, to finish his last and greatest novel.

Holden told himself fiercely that he must summon a like courage—must paint until the pain in his arms became unbearable, until the brush dropped from his leaping fingers.

If only his memories were less bewildering in their richness! There were so many of them and they clamored so insistently for expression.

A boy alone with his thoughts, staring across a shadowed brook at a leaping trout. A toy fire engine, rusting in a woodshed choked with dust. Night on a lake in the mountains, a swaying rowboat and the chirp of crickets.

High school. Football in the russet autumn, with wood smoke rising into the clear sky. The slowly dawning worlds of art and the natural sciences and the deathless song of youth in the early novels of H. G. Wells.

College. Chess and mathematics—and someone arguing about a smelly briar pipe. Was it better to scrape out the dottle or let the bowl alone?

The girl next door—and the one at the other side of town. The girl he'd met at the sophomore prom, walking in a cornfield with the sun in her hair. He'd stopped and kissed her, not quite meaning to.

People who grew old deliberately were of another breed. He'd wanted to stay twenty-two forever, for his love of life was a pure flame. Well...he was thirty-four now, and it was the world that had grown old. So old that the death it harbored was reaching out for him.

The beginning of World War II...a hill in Italy...the red dawn over Salerno...

He'd known Langley a long time. A soundman, Langley, an able physicist, but—literal! Couldn't see a sunset for the trees, and—the spreading dust.

Hiroshima. The End of World War II.

Humanity had known that another war would destroy the dreams of men along with their bodies. But how could men with warring impulses tame that wild steed, electric with the power of exploding suns?

On the little square television screen in Langley's laboratory, one warning, over and over, like a motif from *Todtentanz*. "The guided missiles are still descending! Stay indoors! Take shelter underground!"

He'd clicked off the screen because he couldn't endure watching despairing fear become a certainty in the eyes of men like himself.

He had to get a timeless perspective to paint at all.

Was that selfish—inhuman even? He didn't think so. Only the dream was eternal. The rest was sound and fury signifying—the end of pain.

Holden was still painting when the roar of the counters became a dirge.

THE BODY of the alien gleamed like an iridescent spider web in the waning sunlight. Pictures formed in its mind as it gazed down at the shattered laboratory, the radiation riddled skeletons, and the painting that had become a problem and a challenge.

When in motion the alien resembled a gigantic scorpion, but when it settled itself in repose it became a weaving blob of light, wrapped in a pulsing aura of thought.

The alien was accompanied by its mate and others of its kind. The spaceship which had brought the aliens from their home planet in the Sixth Galaxy to the third planet of an unexplored solar system close to the core of space carried instruments of science which could be used for purposes of research or defense.

But the aliens had quickly discovered that only research would be needed here, for the planet had been ravaged by the energy locked up within one of the smaller units of matter.

It seemed unlikely that any of the inhabitants could have survived so terrible a scourge.

Had the inhabitants released the energy themselves?

The problem was to reconstruct an inhabitant, and explore the planet's history through the medium of a living mind.

Could an inhabitant be reconstructed from a visual impression reproduced in pigments—obviously made by the inhabitant?

The alien thought so.

No two living creatures thought alike, and their thought patterns were implicit in their handiwork, their creations in stone and metal, even in gaudy colors on a fabric so flimsy that it could have been destroyed in the alien's claw as easily as a film of mist.

Once the thought pattern had been reconstructed, restoring the physical body would present no problem at all. The spinning of a matter-rebuilding web would take care of that. For were not all physical bodies' reflections of a multidimensional thought-pattern in the Eternal Now?

The inhabitant could be brought back to life as surely as though he had never died.

"His skeleton is still intact!" a companion voice said. "We could build on that!"

Flourishing its massive fore-claws, the alien turned to look at its scientist mate.

"We could—but why bother? We'll build a complete new body. The key pattern is there, implicit in his handiwork. The web will fill in the gaps."

The pulsing deepened about the alien's head. "Fortunately the catastrophe which destroyed the inhabitant's body has preserved his handiwork. The radiation shave not only energized the pigments—they have altered the physical structure of the fabric itself!"

"It is powerful—that creation!" came the pulsing agreement. "I'm beginning to feel it too—the entire shining fabric of his thoughts. He was a big-brained biped who reveled in the impressions of his senses. He was consumed by the beauty of his world, and he put all of himself into his handiwork!"

"Yes...there is tragedy there too. Beauty and compassion and grief. A mist on the hills as the day draws to a close...a flaming redness lighting up the dawn. Laughter and gay mockery...and a sadness like a great sea, ebbing, flowing. If ever a living form lived and suffered and triumphed over his pain—"

"Have you noticed? He had a complex, subtle brain, but his vision was as limpid as a pool of still water, depth beyond depth. We must see to it that he lives again!"

"But we may have to leave at any moment," the other reminded. "The terrible, destroying fires have burned themselves out, but even a faint residue could injure us genetically. If we find that the radiations are still dangerous—"

"The web will complete the restoration. It will take time, of course. We may have to leave before it is done. But we'll know that he has returned to live out his life to complete fulfillment."

"As a replica of himself..."

"He won't know that. He'll simply return with all of his memories intact. I'd...like that. Wouldn't you? Just knowing, I mean."

"Yes."

For a moment the two aliens remained silent, their thoughts pulsing in close inner harmony. Then they were in motion again.

Approaching the canvas, they busied themselves with their exacting task, twitching and weaving about until a thin, gleaming transparency floated from them over the ravaged soil.

The transparency wavered and changed shape, becoming conical and then spherical. Like a great, rainbow hued water bubble it settled to rest directly in front of the canvas, its base flattening as the aliens continued to knead it with their minds.

Deep cradled were the first faint stirrings of life; fluted and fragile, like a sighing cocoon caught in a gust of luminous wind. A twisting and a swaying and a hungry reaching out for a nourishing flame that was both breath and substance.

Breath and more life...and ever more life...until there came into view in the depths of the web the outlines of a human shape.

THE BURST of flame was incredible—a white and dazzling flare crossing Holden's returning vision, burning into his brain.

He was lying flat on his back, staring straight up at the sky. He could see the red disk of the sun, sinking into clouds that seemed to be writhing in the glow of some great fire from the depths of space.

Were the clouds explosions, shaking the earth? Something in Holden's mind rejected that. The clouds were mushroom-shaped, but they floated high above the earth and seemed to trail off from along, cylindrical shape which was dwindling skyward directly overhead.

The light seemed to fuse with the clouds, to blend with them, as the receding cylinder plunged deeper and deeper into the sky.

The cylinder was gone.

Holden sat up. For an instant his mind seemed to seesaw back and forth across black gulfs of emptiness. Then his faculties steadied and the curving surface above him resolved itself into a glowing web, veined and rainbow colored.

He thought for a moment before moving again. There was no yardstick he could apply to a thing so incredible. Had the laboratory collapsed? Was he staring up through a curving, heat-fused pane of glass wedged in the debris, but open to the sky? It seemed unlikely, for he could see the entire wide sweep of the horizon, stretching away on a level with his drawn up knees.

Holden was suddenly aware of a stirring in the gleaming convexity which arched above him. A swirling and a bubbling, as though the sunlight had turned it molten.

He opened his eyes wide. The surface above him was melting, whipping away and evaporating as he stared—like a cobweb vanishing in a blast of heat.

Memory had returned now in a full, rushing flood. He remembered the agony in his limbs, the brush dropping from his stiffening fingers. He remembered Langley dragging himself along the floor, smiling a little despite his torment.

He was free now to get up, to walk in any direction. But he did not get up. With a hoarse cry he dragged himself forward until he was stopped by a vision of horror—stark, mind numbing.

The two skeletons seemed to grin up at him in the reddening sunlight. He was swaying on his knees directly above the fleshless eye sockets of one, and by simply stretching out his hand he could have touched the long bones of the other.

After the first flush of realization died away, Holden found himself staring at a single bright object. A small object, trivial in itself.

A gold ring, oddly lumpish now, welded into a mass of radioactive isotope, but still recognizable. The ring was on the second finger of a skeletal hand.

As Holden stared down at it, the blood drained from his face, leaving it ashen.

Slowly, like a man in the grip of an overmastering compulsion, Holden stared at his own firm fleshed hand.

The ring he wore wasn't lumpish. But the two were identical...and identical...and identical...

It seemed to Holden that his mind had become a vast, echoing vault. A whispering gallery, filled with shadows that plucked and tore at his sanity.

No man was meant to endure this and live.

FIRST DAY. He was deathly calm now—as calm as the distant ruined cities, smoldering into dust. As calm as the night of stars which arched above him, and the waste which stretched around him.

Fortunately hunger had not touched him yet; only the goading reality of his rebirth. He had returned to a world that had died, had been reborn in Time in some strange and unfathomable way. Not as an infant in a recurring cycle of eternity, but as a grown man with all of his faculties intact.

Far to the east the outlines of a vast ruin rose against the sky, but some instinct warned him to avoid the cities.

Here in the open countryside there was no detectable radiation, but when he knelt to drink at the edge of sluggish streams which mirrored his haggard features he could not repress a shudder. How could he be sure that the water wasn't contaminated? How could he be sure...of anything?

Second day. Hunger was a goad now. No animal cry broke the stillness, but there were a few berries, growing on dwarfed, pallid shrubs which hugged the ravaged soil like little white ghosts.

Were the berries tiny carriers of death? Was there a hidden, grinning skull at the heart of each berry, waiting to be laid bare?

In sudden desperation he plucked one and crushed it in his palm. The juice was sweet-scented. Summoning courage, he picked a handful of berries and devoured them greedily, like a famished wayfarer in a parched and intolerable wilderness.

Third day. Life! Animal life! In the air, in burrows opening on a bleak seawall. Something huge and lobster-like moved on a shining beach, dragging itself sluggishly over the sand. He saw a gull, far out, skimming the waves. In deep rock pools sea anemones unfolded their flowerlike fronds, and the badly grown cucumber bodies of sea gherkins pulsed with the pulsing tides.

Had all life retreated to the sea?

Turning shakily, he moved inland again.

In a valley of shadows he saw a humming bird. A flash of brilliance, the incredible whirring of a tiny, airborne mite a yard from his face. He saw it clearly for an instant as it settled to rest on one of the dwarf shrubs.

A wedge of turned up earth gave the mole away. Using his hands as a trowel, Holden widened the excavation, and caught the little beast as it scurried into the sunlight.

It was a hammer-headed mole, as blind as a bat. He hated killing it, but he knew that his life would be forfeit if he did not eat.

That night, replenished, he sank to rest beneath the only tree he'd seen in a two-day search. A scrub oak, filled with little animal whisperings. There was more life up there. Tomorrow he'd set a few snares!

FOURTH DAY. The cave rose bleakly at the edge of a rock-strewn waste, but Holden's thoughts were the opposite of bleak as he approached it with a brace of brightly plumed wildfowl dangling from his waist.

It was a little wonderful that he could have brought two birds down with a slingshot. Wonderful, too, that there should be a cave so close to the scene of his triumph.

If he could get a fire started—he'd be dining on roasted quail!

Holden straightened his shoulders. The old visions were coming back, surging back now like a singing flame. A man who loved life as he did could never stay wretched.

True, loneliness could leave a torturing ache. But there had been joyful hermits before in the world.

A girl walking in a cornfield, with the sun in her hair. He'd stopped and kissed her, not quite meaning to…

Well…he'd have to get over that, he told himself fiercely. But now the flame was dwindling again, sweeping from him in gusts of chill mockery.

With an angry shrug he quickened his stride and entered the cave.

They stood in flickering firelight—five men and three women and a girl with wide dark eyes who didn't seem quite a woman yet.

Not quite eighteen, Holden thought. Then—startlement exploded in his brain! A dazzling burst of startlement and a high leaping wonder that held him rooted to the earth.

Living men and women, solid as the animals he'd trapped—uncouthly clad in the skins of animals, but not uncouth in their primitive human dignity and bronze limbed strength; standing about a rude fire like a stone age museum group, with straggly hair on their shoulders, leaping shadows at their backs!

The new barbarians—the ones he'd scoffed at, refused to believe in. The survivors, sinking back into barbarism, living by their wits, by sheer animal cunning, as the terrible spreading dust lost its power to cripple and kill.

No, no—he was imagining this!

But if he was imagining it why were they all about him now?

Why were they exploring the strength of his arms with iron fingers and making strange signs in the air before his face, as though he'd brought something evil into the cave with him?

Suddenly Holden knew that the cave dwellers were no illusion, for their angrily muttered words made sense.

He was a stranger, an outsider. Did he come as an enemy or a friend? If he came as a friend did he come as one wishing to throw in his lot with a tribe of proved courage—a great and fearless tribe with many talents?

If so—what could he do? What was he *good* at? Was he a mighty hunter, a trapper of beasts? The birds he carried—how had he caught them? He carried no weapons, so perhaps he was not a hunter. Was he then a fire maker? A healer?

Holden retreated a step before the press of gleaming bodies and the faces he had ceased to fear now, though some were still etched with a sharp hostility and others with dread. He smiled and made a deprecatory gesture.

But his voice, when it rang out in the shadows, was vibrant with pride. "I am an artist!" he said.

THE CAVE wall was high and smooth.

A flickering stone lamp stood at Holden's feet and his palette was a crude one, fashioned of birch bark. Crude too were the pigments which covered it—the distilled juice of berries and red and yellow ocher drawn from the earth.

But the vision in Holden's mind was as bright as ever. He was putting all of himself into his work, bringing an imperishable dream to fulfillment again. Shadows flickered on the walls of the cave and danced on his bare, bronzed shoulders and the animal skin which hung in loose folds from his lithe torso.

Holden knew as he painted that he was creating something that would live forever in one deathless moment.

For Roger Holden was living at the top of his bent, shutting out Time as he struggled to surpass himself.

THE END

If you've enjoyed this book, you will not want to miss these terrific titles...

ARMCHAIR LOST WORLD-LOST RACE CLASSICS, $12.95 each

B-48 **THE DRUMS OF TAPAJOS, Illustrated Edition**
by S. P. Meek

B-49 **THE TEMPLE OF FIRE, Illustrated Edition**
by Fred Ashley

B-50 **THE FACE IN THE ABYSS, and other Fantastic Tales, Illus. Ed.**
by A. Merritt

B-51 **INLAND DEEP, Illustrated Edition**
by Richard Tooker

B-52 **THE SILVER GOD OF THE ORANG HUTAN, Illustrated Edition**
by David Douglas

B-53 **THE KING OF THE DEAD**
by Frank Aubrey

B-54 **THE BOATS OF THE GLEN CARRIG, Illustrated Edition**
by William Hope Hodgson

B-55 **THE SECRET OF THE EARTH**
by Charles Willing Beale

B-56 **THE WORLD OF THE GIANT ANTS, Illustrated Edition**
by A. Hyatt Verrill

B-57 **PHALANXES OF ATLANS, Illustrated Edition**
by F. Van Wyck Mason

ARMCHAIR CLASSICS OF SCIENCE FICTION SERIES, $12.95 each

C-80 **OPERATION: OUTER SPACE**
by Murray Leinster

C-81 **THE FIRE PEOPLE, Special Illustrated Edition**
by Ray Cummings

C-82 **THE BLACK STAR PASSES, Special Illustrated Edition**
by John W. Campbell

ARMCHAIR SCI-FI & HORROR GEMS SERIES, $12.95 each

G-29 **SCIENCE FICTION GEMS, Vol. Fifteen**
Milton Lesser and others

G-30 **HORROR GEMS, Vol. Fifteen**
Henry Kuttner and others

If you've enjoyed this book, you will not want to miss these terrific titles...

ARMCHAIR SCI-FI & HORROR DOUBLE NOVELS, $12.95 each

D-221   **UNDER VENUSIAN FLAGS** by Nelson S. Bond
          BLOOD ON MY JETS by Algis Budrys

D-222   **CITIES IN THE AIR** by Edmond Hamilton
          THE WAR OF THE PLANETS by Harl Vincent

D-223   **MISTRESS OF MACHINE-AGE MADNESS** by Jack Williamson
          THE IMPOSSIBLES by Randall Garrett & Laurence M. Janifer

D-224   **WALL OF FIRE** by Charles Eric Maine
          TOO MANY WORLDS by Gerald Vance

D-225   **THE VEILED WOMAN** by Mickey Spillane
          PELLUCIDAR by Edgar Rice Burroughs

D-226   **LOOT OF THE VAMPIRE** by Thorp McClusky
          THE MAN WHO MADE MANIACS! by Jim Harmon

D-227   **COLOSSUS** by S. J. Byrne
          ISLE OF DOOM by Robert Moore Williams

D-228   **RETURN OF CREEGAR** by David Wright O'Brien
          EIGHT KEYS TO EDEN by Mark Clifton

D-229   **THE TIMELESS MAN** by Roger Arcot
          ENEMY OF THE QUA by Dwight V. Swain

D-230   **THE MAN THE TECH-MEN MADE** by Fox B. Holden
          A WORLD HE NEVER MADE by Edwin Benson

ARMCHAIR SCIENCE FICTION CLASSICS, $12.95 each

C-77   **THESE ARE MY CHILDREN**
         by Rog Phillips

C-78   **STRANGER SUNS**
         by George Zebrowski

C-79   **THE SECOND DELUGE, The Ultimate Illustrated Edition**
         by Garrett P. Serviss

ARMCHAIR SCI-FI & HORROR GEMS SERIES, $12.95 each

G-27   **SCIENCE FICTION GEMS, Vol. Fourteen**
         Robert Moore Williams and others

G-28   **HORROR GEMS, Vol. Fourteen**
         Manly Banister and others